The Good Listener

The Good Listener

Pamela Hansford Johnson

M

SBN 333 18124 7

First published 1975 by
MACMILLAN LONDON LIMITED
London and Basingstoke
Associated companies in New York Dublin
Melbourne Johannesburg and Delhi

Printed in Great Britain by
WESTERN PRINTING SERVICES LTD
Bristol

To three young men:

Martin Taylor
Philip Mansel
Robbie Lloyd George

I

It was the second day of term, in Toby's third year at Cambridge. The weather was mild and sunny, and the young men were able to sit along the Backs enjoying the October warmth. There were three of them in a group, Toby Roberts, Bob Cuthbertson and Adrian Stedman. Toby was perhaps the most conspicuous; he was double-jointed and sat with his legs crossed beneath him, like a practitioner of Yoga. He could even do a parlour-trick, performed on rare occasions, which was to twist his feet behind his neck, producing a risible egg-like appearance. He was tall, freckled, his features contriving to be both blunt and delicate, and the shine of the day struck reddish sparks from his hair. He was twenty, Bob six months older. Adrian, almost two years Toby's senior, was reading Theology and hoped to be ordained into a High Anglican order. Of this Toby disapproved, but he did not say so. He was not accustomed to saying much.

Bob, bullet-headed, of Scotch parentage but born and raised in Sheffield, where his father was foreman in a steel works, was reading Physics. He had hopes for himself, and not much feeling for the sensibility of others. So he said to Toby: 'You're keen on Maisie, aren't you?'

Toby smiled. 'I don't know her very well. But she's attractive. I saw a bit of her last term.' He reflected that he knew all about Bob, Bob nothing about himself.

Toby was reading History, and what his future would hold he did not now know. He did not expect a First Class Honours degree, and so might have to resign himself to teaching. He doubted whether he had the innate literary gift for publication.

'What are all those books?' Adrian asked him.

Toby silently spread out Michelet, Carlyle, Mathièz. 'You see.'

Along the Cam the punts were still sliding. Over the bridge the stone spheres gleamed in the pure light and behind it the college was stately. Such stateliness Toby and Bob had never known before they had come there.

Adrian, austere, picked up each volume with a frown. He also was tall, but his Italianate face was sharp and ascetic. He was the son of a suffragan bishop, now dead. He was also, Toby thought, less ecumenical, a man to appeal to rather perverse girls, and he didn't like the idea that Adrian was more or less committed to a life of celibacy. Pretty silly, so young.

'I've never read Carlyle,' Adrian said. 'What's he like?'

Toby paused. 'Oh, you should. Rather like a film spectacular in glorious Technicolor. But not strong on history. Mathièz is good, but then, he knew more.'

'Take in a flick tonight?' Bob asked. He had made no attempt to modify his accent, a blend of Scotch and North Country. Professor Higgins would have had no difficulties with him. He would have had great difficulties with soft-spoken Toby.

'Can't. I have to get down to things.'

'You, Adrian?'

'Some time. Not this evening. Same reason as Toby's.'

Bob looked disappointed.

'You're bright enough,' Toby said, 'not to have to slog like us lesser mortals.' He himself was not, in fact, going to work, but to take Maisie out for a meal. Not a grand one: he could not afford it. But she was a contented sort of girl.

'Oh, well, back to the grind.' Bob rose and walked away, his stocky shape casting a short stocky shadow.

'Speaking of Maisie,' Adrian said, causing Toby to jump inwardly as if at a wonderful exhibition of extra-sensory perception, 'my mother knows hers quite well. Apparently she keeps open house for artists and writers and so forth. She must have a good bit of money. Has Maisie told you about her?'

'Only that she lives in Suffolk. Maisie isn't specially communicative.' (Toby knew that the thought had crossed Adrian's mind: 'That, coming from you!')

However, Adrian said, 'I wonder where we'll all be five years from now.' He often switched from one subject to the other, without any apparent break. This lack of concentration tended to make his work hard for him, serious about it as he was. He answered his own question. 'I expect to have a decent curacy, with some prospects.'

'Spike, certainly,' Toby teased him.

'What you call spike, yes. The ritual has meaning for me.' Adrian could not resist a holy overtone to this.

'Father Stedman.'

'I hope so, eventually. You're not a believer, are you, Toby?'

'Perhaps. Perhaps not. I've never been too sure about it.' The thought of Maisie's home was seeding in his mind. Did Mrs Ferrars keep what used to be called a *salon*? He would love to see one.

'I wish you would think about it,' Adrian said earnestly, 'it really works.' He hesitated. 'Prayer really works.'

Toby nodded amiable agreement. He had never tried it since infancy.

'And you? What do you expect in five years' time?'

'Nineteen fifty-five. I shall be twenty-five, which makes a neat calculation within my limited range. I haven't the slightest idea.'

'You'll marry, I suppose.'

'And you won't. It seems a pity. For the women, I mean.'

Adrian blushed like a girl. 'I don't know about that. I suppose what you never have you never miss.'

Toby made no reply. Whom could he expect to meet if he were ever invited to the house in Suffolk? He had a somewhat exaggerated faith in the advantages of meeting people. How should he get her to ask him? He pondered. He could ask her to his own home. But what would she think of it? He felt a rush of defensiveness for his parents. They were dear to him, and he was grateful for the sacrifices they had made. But – he could not help it – every time he returned to SE1 he felt like Fanny Price paying a family visit after a long spell at Mansfield Park. In any case, he would step carefully; he was not in love with Maisie yet, though he suspected that she had begun to be fond of him. He wondered just how much unfamiliarity she could weather.

A leaf fell, and he displayed it in the palm of his hand. It was brilliant as beaten copper.

'Pretty,' he said.

She met him in a small café in Regent Street. She had bicycled from Girton. Her face was sunny. She looked, as Toby had imagined before, rather like the young Frieda Lawrence: triangular face, bright eyes with a downward turn at the corner, turned-up nose, broad, curling mouth. Her hair curled too, nearly gold, but he thought of it as wholly so.

'I wish this were Claridges,' he said to her.

'It's Claridges for me.' She sat down opposite him, waiting for him to speak. When he did so, he only asked her how the work was going. She was reading English, and had all the popular *idées reçues*, which was strange in a girl so otherwise independent.

'So-so. Isn't George Eliot wonderful?'

He said he had always found her a bit ponderous and that *Middlemarch* was maddening. The Casaubons, the Lydgates, yes: and then you were always being switched on to somebody else, which was an intrusion.

She was disappointed. 'I can't believe you really mean that.'

He wondered whether she had ever disliked a writer she had been told to like, or whether she had ever appreciated somebody beyond the pale so firmly set down for her and others.

'If you like her, I will like her. Dickens?' he asked.

'Dickens is only an *entertainer*.' She was scornful, and quite sure of herself.

Toby smiled, and asked her what she would like to eat.

She answered promptly, 'Plaice and chips.' After a pause – 'You see, that was never part of my childhood experience. That's why I like it so much.'

'I like things,' he said rather cautiously, 'because they were a part of mine. I like steak and kidney pudding.' With this, he knew, he must have told her more about himself than ever before. He wondered how she would react.

But she simply nodded. She liked to eat things which had been no part of her youth. She was, as he had remarked to Adrian, not very communicative about herself, but she had a lively flow of chatter, and her curling smile charmed him. She ate heartily, sprinkling her fish with vinegar as to that particular manner born: but he knew she had not been.

'That's a pretty dress,' he said. It was made of a soft, muted tartan wool. Had it cost a lot? He knew little about clothes.

'It's almost too warm for an Indian summer. My mother will be sorry she's missing this weather, but she's on holiday trying to escape from what she thought would be the cold.'

'On holiday?' Toby asked, permitting himself a question.

'She's in Jamaica.'

He reflected that his own mother had never been abroad at all.

'She's rather tired. She has people in all through the summer, and it sometimes gets too much for her. How's your work going?'

He told her, while she nodded encouragement. 'You're going to do *well*,' she said emphatically, as if she had inside information.

He was self-depreciating. No, he was not a flier. He hoped to take a respectable degree, but no more than that. 'Now, you'll do brilliantly,' he teased her, 'so long as you remember to give all the right answers.'

For a moment she looked huffy, then gave a bright smile. 'I have got a mind of my own, you know.'

'It's a lovely mind.' It was the first intimate thing he had ever said to her. 'I like it.'

Pleased, she looked away from him. 'Not particularly. I just happen to have a good memory.'

The neon lights of the café were garish; from the kitchens came the hum of a refrigerator. Undergraduates, with their friends or their girls, came and went. He thought she looked at home there, in fact would have looked at home anywhere.

Maisie talked about theatres, gramophone records and films. Had he seen *La Ronde*? It was terrific fun, and haunting. Then she stopped abruptly. 'Please let me pay my share. I've been eating like a horse.'

'Oh no, you don't,' he replied, 'I'm old-fashioned in my ways.'

He was living on a grant – he had made his way from a grammar school – and on the small allowance his father was able to give him. He made do perfectly well with this and had always judged his expenditure with care.

She did not press him, but looked at her watch. 'We've been eating for hours and I've done all the talking.'

'Nice talk.'

'But it's late. I shall have to be going.'

'If you'll walk back to college with me, I'll get my bike and ride back with you. We're not so cabined, cribbed and confined as you unfortunate girls.'

He pushed her bicycle for her down the street, up Petty Cury where the lights still shone on the glossy new publications in Heffer's windows, through the Market Square, which, like all market squares, had an air of excitement, a promise of delightful things to come, and into the magnificence of King's Parade. There was a full

11

moon. King's College Chapel gleamed in the drenching light. 'Someone once said it looked like a sow upside down,' Toby said, 'but to me it's wonderful.' The Senate House, in its black and whiteness, seemed larger than by day. The passage behind it was for the moment deserted.

Propping up her bicycle on the kerb, he bent to kiss her. It was for the first time. 'I meant that,' he said. Maisie gave a nervous giggle, then fell silent.

He did not quite know how she had taken it. His kiss had been too brief and too sudden for her to return the pressure: but he had been slightly disconcerted by the giggle, which seemed out of key with her personality – she might have been a housemaid, he thought, though of housemaids he had no experience. As they rode together down the Huntingdon Road towards Girton he said, 'It was good tonight. Will you come out with me again? Saturday?'

But she said she was booked. Her mother would be coming home and she wanted to see her.

He did not try to kiss her again outside the gates of her college. It was then that he decided that he would go home for the week-end himself.

2

He was back on Friday by the mid-afternoon, giving himself time to go to the London Library. His parents had scraped together, on his nineteenth birthday, a life subscription for him, and he was very grateful. He collected half a dozen books, then went on to the district where he lived.

The day was dark and rainy, and the street lamps were doubled in the wet pavements. The greengrocers' shops were particularly pleasing, showering their wealth of orange, lemon and bright green into the streets, drowned fruits of the night. There were still a few naphtha flares – relics of the past – to be seen above the stalls.

He went first to see his father. The shop window was full of lurid sweets, magazines and – a concession to prestige – paperbacks, which nobody bought. They had achieved the velvety patina and dignity of dust. There were no customers; but, at the tinkle of the bell, his father came out from the inner room, a place for stockpiling and for relaxation.

Mr Roberts was a tall stout man, with hazel eyes that were like his son's and features that were blunt without the delicacy. 'Well, here you are.'

'Mummy got my letter?'

'Yes. And she's laid on the fatted calf.' Mr Roberts glanced at the fly-blown clock, said that in five minutes he could close. 'How are you, boy?' he said affectionately.

Toby, who had a different idiom from that which he used to his friends, said that he was as fit as a flea and working like a beaver. 'But,' he added, 'it's early days still to see whether I can keep it up.'

'You will, old man. Your mum and me haven't the slightest doubt of it.'

This confidence Toby felt slightly unnerving. He did work – yes – but ought they to expect so much of him? He did not wish to let them down.

'More books?' said Mr Roberts.

'Half a dozen. They weigh a ton.'

'If I had my time again' – this was wistful – 'it would have been books, books and more books. But they weren't things you could live on, not in those days.'

They came to the small terraced house in the mean, respectable street. It was distinguished from the others only by the exercise of his mother's taste: the curtains on both floors were identical, cretonnes with a bold pattern of pomegranates, which had caused some of the neighbours to raise their eyebrows.

At the gate, flanked by sodden privets which caught the light from a street lamp, Toby fractionally paused. It was always so on his returns. *He was dreading the smell.* Not that it was the smell of dirt: Mrs Roberts was spotless in all her ways. No, it would be compounded of past meals, the reek of which was slow to disperse in the narrow passages, of carbolic soap (she still believed in this), of turpentine and, more mysteriously, of age: the house had been built about 1912. Of fug. He wondered why the houses, some far older, of one or two of his friends had not that aged smell, and put it down to their superior spaciousness. Mingled with this customary, and passing, repulsion was pleasure at the thought of seeing his mother. They were close. And he admired her for her stubborn artistic and intellectual efforts.

Hearing her husband's key in the lock, Mrs Roberts came out to greet them, a little sparrow of a woman with small eyes of uncommon brilliance. She gave Toby a great hug and kissed him heartily on both cheeks: it would have seemed like a Russian embrace, if she had ever seen a Russian.

'Well, look who's here! We never thought we'd see you again so soon.'

'I had to come up. How are you, Mummy? By the smell of turps, you've been on artistic pursuits.'

'Hark at him,' said his father.

She was not quite a Sunday painter, for she painted every day. She put her plasterboards in the spare bedroom, propped against a chair-back. Had she been a little better, she might have deserved comparison with Grandma Moses; but the 'little' must be, Toby thought, light-years away.

'Can't complain. I've just done a flower-piece, imaginary flowers.' She held him from her. 'Let me look at you.'

14

'You looked at me only last week. I haven't grown since.'

She asked him if he were hungry; she had quite a spread awaiting him, everything he liked. They went into the kitchen, which had been extended during a brief period of the Robertses' prosperity, and was the biggest room in the house. The checked tablecloth had a continental air: Mrs Roberts had seen to that. It was adorned by a small bunch of yellow chrysanthemums, arranged with Japanese skill.

'Yes, I'm hungry as a hunter. By the way, did that mean the huntsman or the horse?'

'Get away with you,' said his father, 'you're so sharp you'll cut yourself.'

There were, indeed, all the things that Toby liked. He had once tasted *pâté de foie gras* at the house of a rich friend, and he liked that too; but did not know when he was ever to taste it again. Sausage rolls, home made, brown and sweating from the oven; potato crisps: a pork pie, also home made (Mrs Roberts was a dab hand at that): tinned salmon, which Toby preferred to fresh and always would: pears stewed with a cinnamon stick: an iced orange cake: a gigantic, steaming pot of tea. He felt his mouth water. He thought, come what may, this will always be the kind of food I shall care for most, and he wondered what the future would bring to him. Had he ever eaten pheasant? No, but he suspected that he might like that.

'Well,' said Mrs Roberts, 'tell us about Cambridge.'

Toby said carefully, 'After a week, there's not much to tell. Much new, I mean.'

'Is it looking beautiful?' she asked him, lingering on the word, as though beauty had not been much a part of her life. In his first year, he had tended to be unforthcoming, but she still asked the question.

He considered this. 'I suppose so. Sometimes it hits one. But I'm working too hard to notice things much.'

'I hope you're getting some fun too.'

'Oh yes, in moderation.' He had by now started on the meal, his gastric juices stimulated. In Cambridge he ate more poorly than they knew, and they would be shocked if they had known. 'Smashing.'

Mrs Roberts watched him eat with a kind of sacrificial passion. She knew, as her husband did not, that eventually he would leave them. He spoke an approximation of their language: but his voice was already like – she couldn't resist the cliché – a gentleman's. 'Are you going back tonight?'

'No, if you can put up with me. I've got to digest all this, and I don't feel like running for trains.'

When he felt the meal was properly digested, three cups of tea and six cigarettes later, he asked his mother if he might help with the washing-up. She refused; she was conditioned to feel that this was not man's work, and in this her husband gladly encouraged her.

'It can wait. But I'll show you my painting, if you like.'

They went upstairs. It was a bold composition, against an indigo background, of white and yellow flowers in a terracotta jug. The jug was the least good thing about it, having no solidity and casting no shadow: but Toby liked it enough to ask her if he might have it for his room in college. She blushed. This was the height of praise.

'I'll have it framed for you.'

'No, don't do that. I know a good place where I can get it done.'

He was tender towards her. She was so little and so light; and he knew he had inherited something of her gingery hair, which was done in a bun – old-fashioned or artistic, it all depended upon how you looked at it. He knew that he had delighted her, and he felt the stirring of an emotion like that of his childhood, when he had pleased her by some kind or clever action and her face had become refulgent. The smell of the house seemed to have gone, except for the pervading turpentine, as though all the windows had been thrown open: but her chest was inclined to weakness, and she was cautious about draughts.

He wished he could always be a child for her sake, but he realised for how little longer he could be. Did most sons feel that their parents, however kind, however loving, did not realise at all what those sons were like?

'Do you see what I've been reading?' She held up to him pridefully an old paperback edition of *Anna Karenina*, second-hand. 'He knows so much about people it frightens you,' she said thoughtfully, picking her words.

'And who may you be?' He was making fun of her in the way in which she delighted. 'Anna?'

She gave him a push. 'Fancy me in black velvet with mignonette in my hair.'

'No, you can't be Anna. It's a great shame, but Anna was definitely stout. Tolstoy said so.'

'There are some things I like to forget,' said his mother, 'and that's one of them. It spoils the picture. Are you really going to hang my picture up?'

'For all to see. I'll call for it next time I come. For the moment, I'm lumbered with books.'

They went back to the kitchen. The parlour, as in so many similar houses, was traditionally kept for not very intimate callers, such as the insurance agent.

His father was dozing before the small fire, replete. Mrs Roberts began clearing the table. 'I can at least do my share of that,' Toby said, following her into the scullery. She did not resist. He guessed that she had still much to say to him.

The first thing was this. 'Do you feed yourself properly?' It was another of her inevitable questions.

'I look well, don't I?'

'Do you eat in the college?'

'Mostly. The food's not bad, but of course rationing's still tight.'

'I suppose if you had a bit more money you could go out to cafés sometimes. I wish we could give it you.'

He smiled, and shook his head.

'You must meet some well-off people there.' She began her affectionate and solicitous prying, which he did not resent at all; he was not obliged always to return direct answers.

'Some. But a good many are on grants, like me.'

'Some come from big houses?'

'Again, some. But not many. My friend Bob's dad's a foreman in Sheffield.'

'I expect you must meet some girls.' She was too absorbed in her questioning to notice that he was drying the dishes, which was something that normally she never allowed.

'Matchmaking, Mum?'

She said of course she wasn't, tossing her head. She was just interested. He wondered, with an inward grin, for he knew she was far from unsophisticated, whether she was insuring against his possible homosexuality. Well, there was no need for that. Suddenly, weighing up the evening, he made up his mind.

'I may bring one home to tea one of these days.'

She looked excited. 'Who?'

'Maisie Ferrars. I'll let you know well in advance.'

'I hope she isn't one of the posh ones. I'd like to be able to live up to her.' She was not looking at him now, but furiously scrubbing the stains of tannin from a teacup.

'You'll live up to anyone, Mummy,' he said. Once he had called her Mum, but couldn't often bring himself to do so now.

'Well, people may think you're better off than you are.'

'Stiff-necked,' Toby said, 'that's you. No, she's just very nice. But don't go thinking this is serious. I don't even know whether she'll come.'

She was radiant again. This was the first time since his schooldays that he had suggested bringing anyone home.

'You've made the house look very nice,' he said, and he meant it. Her plain blue stair-carpet, her white walls, did set her apart from the neighbours and he knew she had had to pay a certain price for this. Only one patterned fabric to each room. Hand-hooked rugs. Her husband hardly noticed these things, but Toby did. He reflected how different her life would have been if she had been born in other circumstances. Her artistic gift manifested itself in many ways, except in her dress: that was pretty drab. For one thing, she had little money for clothes. For another, she cared about what her hands could do, but little about herself personally.

When they returned to the kitchen, Mr Roberts had woken up. 'We'll have a little nip to celebrate,' he said, 'we always like to when you come home.'

'I'd better not come too often, then,' said Toby, as his father produced a half-bottle of whisky, 'or I'll bankrupt you.'

Mr Roberts fetched out a jug of water and two glasses. Mrs Roberts did not drink; it was the sole relic of her Methodist upbringing. She simply said she did not like the smell of the stuff. The men sat before the fireplace, cosily sipping.

Cosy, Toby thought. That was the word. It did not seem to him that, in whatever circumstances the future might hold for him, he would ever be so cosy again. I am as I am. But I am not so sure that I shall show it. However, enfolded by the warmth of his family, by the whisky, the fire, he was content. He was unsure whether he would always be so, but did that matter? He had lived for the pleasures of the moment, whatever they had been.

In the second bedroom, his own, he slept like a log. He had just time to notice, before his eyes closed, that the sheets smelled of lavender. So like his mother, that final touch.

3

They were sitting over coffee in Toby's room in college. It was late at night. Handsome Adrian, by request, was expounding, 'The strength of sin is the law,' in a manner neither Bob nor Toby understood. When he had run out of exposition he added, 'Of course, it's not easy.'

'It's buggering well not,' said Bob, who did not offend. 'Anyway, that's all past history.'

'Don't say that to me,' Toby put in, 'all my history's past. That's the trouble.'

'Why?' Adrian asked.

'Because you don't know who's telling the truth, except that you have to give the credit to the most recent practitioners. They have all the documentation.'

'I like Saint Paul,' Adrian mused, 'few people do.'

'Well, I don't like him,' said Bob, 'he seems to me rough on the birds. And what should we do without them?' He switched the conversation to politics. The Chinese had just occupied Tibet.

'I'm afraid,' said Adrian with a pastoral smile, 'that that must be pretty awful.'

'Oh, I don't know. They can scarcely be in a worse muck-up than they are. Buttered tea!'

Adrian demurred. 'I can't agree with you. Some people have neither tea nor butter.'

'A disciplined country is what all those lamas need.'

'I'm not as convinced as you are about the virtues of discipline.'

They went on arguing, and Toby grew impatient. He wanted to know about Mrs Ferrars' *salon*, but no opportunity for enquiry at once presented itself. He had been out several times with Maisie, had progressed no further than a good-night kiss; he fancied she was not the kind of girl likely to sleep with him. But a week or so ago, he thought he had caught a look of naked love. Was he ready for this? He had no idea.

But then Adrian brought out his trump card. He would not have done so had he not been badgered about Tibet. 'I went to Haddesdon last week-end.'

'Where's Haddesdon?' Bob asked.

'Why you?' asked Toby, somewhat giving himself away.

Adrian looked surprised. 'I told you, my mother knows Maisie's.'

'What's it like?'

'Nice place. She keeps open house for literary lions.'

'What's she like?' Bob asked.

Adrian considered this. 'A personality.' He was not good at descriptions of any kind.

'Oh,' Bob sounded uninterested. He was not allured by personalities: he liked people to be ordinary.

Meanwhile, Toby was thinking about his friends. Bob was ordinary in himself but, by some chance, mathematically gifted: he would make a good physicist. Adrian was not ordinary. He was by nature a good man: Toby had never heard him utter an edged or spiteful word, which for most people was rare. He was also profoundly pious, an embarrassing trait; but he meant well. Toby thought again of the waste Adrian proposed to lay to his life. He did not believe that he was low-sexed: simply that he had a kind of monomania which might steer him over the rocks. He wondered what rocks he was likely to strike. Father Stedman, slim in his cassock, the adored of hungry women.

'Who did you meet there?'

'Well, Edward Crane's a regular.'

The name dropped wonder into their souls, even to Bob's. Edward Crane was perhaps the most successful playwright of his day; at one time he had had three plays running in the West End simultaneously. They were commercial plays, but they had depth and intellect. The fashion had not yet begun to run against him: Toby, thinking of some theatre clubs, believed that it soon might, and that if it did he himself would be sorry. He remembered with pleasure a play about John Nicholson and the Indian Mutiny. What was it called? Something a bit flashy, for the whole tone of it. *The Bible and the Sword*? – something like that.

'Who else comes?' he asked.

Adrian mentioned a very young homosexual novelist, a highly successful poet who really managed to sell his work, a woman painter of growing repute. 'But, of course, I've only been the once.' He added, 'High thinking, but also high living.'

Toby speculated as to how this could be managed. His own mother was a genius with few materials, but most people were feeling the pinch. An egg was becoming something of a treat. There were no eggs in the horrible scramble offered for breakfast in Hall.

He yawned. 'I'm sorry, but I'll have to say good-night now though it won't mean much sleep for me. I've got to finish a bloody essay on Calonne, which is bloody dull.'

Adrian tried to conceal a look of affront, but did not quite succeed. He was always being ejected from somebody's rooms, since he was a notorious stayer. Time meant nothing to him.

When he had gone Toby worked, as he had said he would. It was three o'clock before he got to bed. In the morning he read his essay to his Director of Studies, a young don of great brilliance, who simply said, 'Don't you think that sounds a little tired?' This man was called Noel Hartford, and he had all the honours that could be bestowed upon him by the age of twenty-seven.

'Very tired,' Toby admitted. 'I was. I'll do better next time.'

After lunch he went into the town and there, through the window of Bowes & Bowes, he saw Maisie who, surprisingly, was sampling the racks of detective novels. He saw her before she saw him, and prepared an opening. 'Hullo, pet.' He let the casual endearment drop, as if it had been involuntary.

She turned to face him. She would have liked to pretend that her interest was in more serious works, but it was too late.

'Caught in the act,' said Toby. 'I thought those were specifically forbidden.'

She paused. He thought she was looking extremely pretty. Then she said defiantly, 'They're disapproved of. But I must have some relaxation, mustn't I? *And I love them.*'

'Don't be unnecessarily emphatic. So do I.'

With a slight bounce she selected a John Dickson Carr and went off with it to the cash desk. He followed her.

'Time for coffee and a bun?'

She hesitated fractionally. 'Thank you. I haven't got to be back till dinner-time and I'm well up with my essays.'

'We could take in a flick, just about.'

22

Here she was positive. 'I'd like that. But not if you won't let me pay for my own ticket.'

He demurred.

'Then no flick,' she said.

He could not budge her from this, though he did not like it. He also disliked the fact that she owned a motor car, though she used her bicycle in Cambridge. All he owned was a driving-licence: he had taken his test as a method of touching wood for the day when some miracle might bring him a car of his own.

It was November, and the weather was chilly. She was wearing a suit of some bright but heavy tweed, which seemed to him a little too bulky for her slight figure. Over the coffee they debated as to which film they should see, decided on *Rashomon*. Toby, whose Calonne had been returned to him for extensive revision, knew he should not be sparing the time: but he wanted to be in the light-sifted dark with Maisie.

In the cinema he could just see the fine edge of her features. He watched her, she watched the screen. Half an hour had passed before he put his arm around her shoulders. She made no move away, but still she did not look at him; yet he could feel the tremor of her body. The smell of her hair, freshly washed, and of her tweeds, was pleasant to him. They were seated in the back row; he had seen to that. Soon he put a hand under her chin and turned her gently towards him. He kissed her. The eagerness of her response communicated to him something of her excitement. 'Darling,' he said. Now she did draw apart from him, but let him keep her hand in his.

He thought, she is rather sweet. He no longer saw the ferocious Japanese faces. Haddesdon. What was it like? However he imagined it, it would be different. Everything one imagined was. Tudor. Half-timbering. Her mother, handsome and bony, in hostess draperies. The guests. At least he did not have to imagine Edward Crane or the novelist, whose faces were familiar to him from the Sunday papers.

When they came out into the drizzle of early evening she seemed flustered. 'I'm terribly late. I'd better get a taxi back. I came in on the bus, so I'm not encumbered.'

They walked across the Market Square to the rank, where he kissed her briefly again. 'God bless you eternally,' he said.

Taxis. She could afford them. He watched the tail-lamp till it was out of sight round the corner of the street.

Then it came to him. He must work, not only that evening but steadily. Make something of himself; it was not too late. He would ask Hartford what, if he put his back into things, his chances might be. He would resist the impulse to boredom, where certain elements in his course were concerned. If I were like Bob . . . but he was not. Yet, he had got to work if only for his parents' sake, and if working brought extra bonuses, so much the better.

He walked back to his college, unmindful of the damp, a little more than half in love. It was a curious sensation: he had never felt it before, though he had had several girls over short periods of time. This seemed to be different – not altogether so, but yes, to a degree. Haddesdon. A car. Nothing venture, nothing win.

In the morning he telephoned her, asking her to visit his home. 'It isn't grand,' he said, 'but it has its comforts. My mother would like to see you.'

He had hardly expected her to assent so easily. But she replied, 'It can't be for a fortnight. I can't get away till then.'

(Why couldn't she?)

'Saturday fortnight? You could come to tea, and then we might go out somewhere.'

He knew she had relations living in London, an aunt and a married sister, so that the problem of overnight accommodation did not arise.

'All right.'

He told her they would work out the further details. 'Good-bye, pet.'

'And to you.'

It was a week before he wrote to his mother. It was a difficult letter to compose.

'I told you I might bring a girl home. Tea on Saturday? Have some paintings ready to show her. One thing. She has an appetite like a fly.' (Not true) 'So not high tea, much as I love it. About 4.30? Perhaps some sandwiches – she likes cucumber, and you cut them marvellously – and a cake. There won't be any need for anything else, so we shan't eat you out of house and home.'

He imagined his father's outrage at offering such a mockery of a meal – as he would have thought it – but knew his mother would understand. In her young years she had been a servant in a rich London house. He threw her a sop. '*Not* the parlour, unless you really must. The kitchen's much nicer. Maisie won't think less of us for it. She's really very nice and simple. It's just that I'm taking her out afterwards, so she won't want a heavy meal.' Had he overdone it? He thought not – quite. He added, 'Make things nice, but don't bother to make a fuss. She's quite unfussy.

'You'll be glad to hear that I'm slogging away. Hartford thinks I shall get a moderately decent degree if I stick at it.'

(Her knowledge of the gradation of degrees was small: she only wanted him to get one, to be able to write letters after his name.)

'"Foot, foot, foot, foot slogging over Africa,"' he went on, knowing she would take the reference. She had always loved, defiantly, even in the days of his unpopularity, Rudyard Kipling. She knew many poems by heart. 'So don't mind if I come home dirty and travel-worn, with sand in my hair. Let me know if all this is O.K.

'Fondest love to you and Dad.'

He knew she would be hurt by his rejection of high tea: there was nothing she loved so much, in her love for him, than putting on a splendid meal after her own fashion. She would know by his letter that Maisie was of superior class and so be stiff, a little on her guard. He did not like the idea, since he liked her best unguarded, but did not see what else he could do. To hurt was endemic in children of loving parents, even in loving children: he would try to hurt as little as possible.

Whatever she had said about her tastes, he could not face Maisie with high tea. Yet whom am I kidding? Perhaps nobody at all. He nearly tore his letter up, then went resolutely out and posted it.

He was sufficiently realistic and far-sighted to know that if one day he married and had children of his own, similar hurts might come to him. Chickens always did come home to roost, he thought, every one of them. How I know that I don't know, but I do.

His mother's answer, dignified, but with no more chill on it than a very slight frost on the garden laurels, came by return of post.

'We shall both be pleased to meet your friend. Of course she can have the kind of things she likes, but it seems mean to me and to your father. I expect she's used to such things. You won't mind brown bread and butter as well. But not the kitchen, please. I will make the parlour nice and get the chill off it. I know it sometimes seems clammy but I'll have a fire in it two days running.

'I'm glad you are hard at your books. I know there's nothing you can't do if you try. I am doing something new, the street outside, with children going to school. I will show it to your friend if you think she won't laugh at me.'

Better than he had expected. Remorse wriggled in him. But he was taking a risk, wasn't he? For a moment he burned with resentment at Maisie, thinking she might indeed despise his parents. But she was not like that. She was so whole and so sweet. Haddesdon: a mackerel to be caught by a sprat.

When Maisie was shown into the parlour, her response was a cry of spontaneous admiration. 'What a pretty room!'

It was. White walls flushed with pink (Mrs Roberts had painted them herself), a dark blue carpet with a close pattern of roses. Curtains lined with pink sateen. A dark green suite, three chairs and a sofa. Two of Mrs Roberts' flower paintings on the walls.

'I'm glad you approve,' she said. It was not quite the right remark, but Maisie met it.

'How could anyone not approve?'

The room was warm. The promise of two days' fires had been met. But there was no sign of tea.

'Dora's a good hand with decorations,' Mr Roberts said spaciously, 'she ropes me in.'

'Are those your paintings?' Maisie asked.

Toby's mother nodded. '"Poor things but mine own,"' she added a little gravely, from some vestigial memory of words remembered. 'I'll show you my latest afterwards, if you like.'

Maisie said she would love to see it.

Mrs Roberts disappeared into the kitchen.

'Well, well,' her husband said, 'and what are you studying?' She told him.

'I'd have thought you knew English already,' he said, with a brief hilarious laugh.

'It's more complicated than you think,' said Toby.

Maisie seemed completely relaxed. Toby thought she would have been so anywhere. They all chatted amicably till his mother brought in two brand-new objects: a tea-trolley and a cake-stand, the latter piled high. Mr Roberts looked startled.

Maisie made a fool of Toby by eating robustly: half a dozen or more sandwiches, white bread and brown, with home-made jam, both kinds of cake. He saw a faint glint of amusement in his mother's eyes.

She asked Mr Roberts whether he worked near his home; she was always direct, and gave no impression of curiosity for its own sake.

'I've got a newsagent's shop,' he answered, looking surprised that she had not already been told. 'Papers, sweets, cigarettes and all that.'

'If I'd got your shop,' said Maisie, 'I'd spend all day reading the papers and eating the sweets and smoking the cigarettes. I've always thought it sounded so nice.'

'Go broke if you did.' She seemed to have finished eating. 'You do smoke?' He offered her a packet of Player's.

'More than I should. Thank you.'

'I like a girl to be sociable and have one with me.'

'Be careful, Maisie,' said his wife, 'you'll get something wrong with you in the long run.'

She gave her curling smile. 'I suppose we all do.'

'Yes, but better later than sooner. That's what I say.'

Mrs Roberts took them up to show them the new picture: and as they looked at it, wiped her hand automatically on her dress. She was not nervous of Toby's opinion, but instinctively of Maisie's. It was the painting of a crocodile of schoolchildren in bright green blazers, crossing a grey street beneath a gathering of clouds gravid with rain. It was vaguely reminiscent of Lowry, but it had something purely her own, something she had worked automatically to achieve. Toby praised it and congratulated her almost at once. Maisie was slower. Then she turned and said, 'It's really lovely! How clever you are! Where did you learn?'

'Never had a lesson in my life. I know it's crude. The figures aren't good.'

'May I see some of your other things?'

Mrs Roberts brought out half a dozen paintings and stood back while they were inspecting them. She looked dark with suspicion. Maisie continued to admire, but turned back always to the street scene. Toby sensed something knowledgeable in the way she peered at it.

'You know about pictures,' he said.

She looked at him frankly. 'A bit. We've got some at home. My mother collects them.'

'Rembrandts and Turners?' Mrs Roberts suggested, her nervousness giving the effect of something like a sneer.

'No, not quite that,' Maisie answered seriously, 'but some nice ones. We both go to sales. Why don't you show these?'

'Show them? You mean, an exhibition?' Mrs Roberts was dumbfounded. 'I wouldn't know how to begin. Nor would Toby.' Quickly she stacked the paintings and stood them with their faces to the wall. 'You're only pulling my leg.' But Toby could see the idea had seeded.

It struck him that for the first time since he had returned to the house, the first time in his memory, he had smelled only the turpentine, and that faintly. His mother must have been airing the place for hours.

They left her shortly after that: they were going up west to the New Theatre, to see *Henry IV*. His parents said good-night to Maisie and expressed the hope that she would come again.

'Please ask me,' she replied.

Toby knew it had been a success, that she would make anything a success.

When they were parting that night, she in a cab for Chelsea where her sister was living, she said, 'Thank you. I did enjoy it. And I liked your parents.'

'They liked you.'

'Oh, I do hope so! It is weak of me, I know, but I can't bear not to be liked.'

'Come on, come on,' said the driver, a surly man.

As she got into the taxi, she called back to Toby, 'You must come to us at Haddesdon.'

4

To his chagrin, he learned that this event would be unlikely to take place before the spring. Amanda Ferrars, it seemed, opened her house only to relations and to a very few old friends during the winter months. She postponed her more mass invitations until the mild weather came; she loved to entertain in the garden, whenever the climate made it possible. 'Which isn't,' Maisie said, 'as often as she would like.'

Meanwhile, Toby was becoming more and more fond of her. She had that rare thing, sweetness. She had behaved beautifully in his house, if she could ever be said to 'behave'; behaving was a conscious action, and she was perfectly natural in all things. He thought about her a great deal, took her out whenever he could afford it. He had to consider his prospects, he knew, and he carried out his intention to ask Hartford what they were likely to be.

'Well,' Hartford replied judiciously, stretching out his long thin legs to the fire and intimating that Toby might help himself to sherry, 'if you go on as you've been going in the last few weeks and keep it up next year, I should say moderate to bright.' Not being a tutorial but a consultation, this was a special occasion. He liked Toby, though he knew little about him: something of his background, of course, but little else. He sensed that he was ambitious; but how far his ambitions would take him, or even where he wanted them to take him, he could not guess.

'If you can stop being bored with the bits you don't like—'

'See Calonne.' Toby could presume to cheek him, for only a few years divided them.

'—precisely, and stop getting too involved in the romantic aspects, you'll do well. The French Revolution wasn't purely a matter of Dickens and *ça ira*.'

'Do you ever get bored, Dr Hartford?'

'Frequently. But it's a self-indulgence, like over-drinking or over-sleeping. There's a certain charm in fighting it, believe me. It's a great pleasure to get a difficult piece into proportion. Even the top novelists get somewhat bored with their characters on occasion, and have to fight that. Not Tolstoy, the great exception to every rule and the most daunting. Do pour yourself a sherry, will you? I don't want to get up. Just as you are on occasion intellectually lazy, I am always physically so.'

Hartford was a bachelor who lived in the college, but they had all heard that he would marry soon, that he was buying a house in Chaucer Road. 'What do you want to do, Toby?'

'I don't know yet. Do many people?'

'The fliers do, or most of them. Some of them are just prepared to go on flying, regardless where their wings will take them.'

'I'm not a flier. But I do know that I have to earn a living. You'd written a book when you were only a little more than my age.'

'Precocious and premature. Still, I admit that it helped.' Met by an eager, waiting gaze, Hartford was hypnotised into being side-tracked into a discussion of his early experience. It was agreeable to talk to Toby. He was such a good listener.

'I couldn't match up to you,' Toby said at last.

'Why not, if not just yet? You have quite an amiable prose style. Look, I'm expecting a pupil soon. You go ahead as you are going, and if there's anything I can do for you I'll do it.'

From this peaceful and consoling scene, Toby went to a very different one. He had arranged to pick up Bob Cuthbertson forty-five minutes before Hall and go down with him. He found Bob slope-shouldered, boiling-eyed, his clenched fists hanging down between his knees.

'What's up with you?'

'I've got a girl in pod.'

Toby made the obvious remark. Was he sure?

'Sure it's true or sure it's mine?'

'Both.'

'Absolutely.'

Toby sat down. 'Tell me about it. That is, if you want to.'

It was a commonplace story. She worked behind a draper's counter in the town and Bob had picked her up while buying handkerchiefs. Her name was Rita Champion. She was nineteen, and he had been the first with her. To make things worse, he added, her father was a policeman – at which information Toby had to suppress a grin.

'So what will you do?'

'What can I do? She's eight weeks gone. She's tried everything, jumping downstairs, gin and hot baths, pills – it's hopeless.'

'She wants you to marry her,' Toby said. It was a statement not a question.

'If only she could get rid of it! How can I marry her? I'd have to leave here and get a job. That's the only way.'

'You can't. You've got your Finals next year, and after that you'll have real earning power.'

Bob looked as if he might be on the verge of tears. Toby brought beer from the cupboard and gave it to him.

'You don't know anyone, do you, Tobe?'

'Not in my line. I might ask cautiously around.'

But where? His circle of friends was not given to raffishness.

'A back-street abortion,' Bob said bitterly, 'all muck and dirt and danger.'

'Think of the alternative,' Toby said.

At that moment Adrian came in. He was aghast when he saw Bob's face. 'What's the matter? Am I butting into something?'

'Oh, don't mind us, Father Stedman,' said Bob, his bitterness increasing, 'we could do with some spiritual guidance.'

'I'm not fitted to guide anyone yet,' Adrian said simply. 'But may I hear about it?'

Bob seemed incapable of further speech, so it was Toby who told the story.

Whether or not he were fitted to guide anyone, Adrian proceeded to do so. 'You'll have to marry her, of course.'

'Oh, don't talk out of the back of your shovel hat,' Bob said, regaining the use of his tongue. 'We've got to get rid of it some-how.'

'That,' said Adrian, 'would be murder.'

'You needn't use big words. It's not even a *thing* yet.'

'In my mind it is, from the moment it's conceived. It has been diagnosed?'

'There's a test with rabbits. She's had that.'

'Abortion's illegal. But even if it weren't—'

'Stuff it. How can I marry?'

'Even as a matter of form—'

'But who'd keep the kid?'

'It would be your child.'

'I know,' Bob said surprisingly, 'I've thought of that. But it doesn't alter matters.'

'Suppose you did "get rid of it", as you put it? You'd be getting rid of a human soul. How do you know what it might turn out to be?'

'A mongol, I dare say.'

'Or an – Einstein,' Adrian said carefully, remembering Bob's own skills.

'Come off that.'

'None of us has the right to take life.'

'Still life.'

'No. Far from it.'

After a pause Toby said, 'We'd better get down to Hall.'

'I don't want anything to eat,' Bob said.

'Well, I can't afford to miss my dinner. But I'll do some thinking.'

He left him to Adrian's spiritual counsel, speculating, as he did so, just how long Bob would be able to stand it.

He was sorry about his predicament. It was a sufficiently commonplace one, but that made it no better. He knew that Bob was by nature honourable: believed he would have to do as he had contemplated even to the wrecking of his Cambridge career. He supposed he could get a teaching job on his showing in Part I, but it would be a come-down from his potential. What was the girl like? He fancied something flashy, skimpy, with dyed hair. As he sat down at the long table, the lights sparkling down on plate and glass, the portraits of Masters and of the famous dead shiny on the walls, he saw Adrian come in, downcast, but the latter did not come to sit beside him.

Toby made up his mind. After dinner he went back to Bob's rooms and found him sitting in much the same position as before, except that his arms, apelike, were dangling almost to touch the floor.

'I've been thinking to some purpose,' Toby said. 'You must see Markham.' (That was Bob's tutor.)

'What could he do?'

'He's a wise old bird. That's what he's there for.'

Bob tended to trust Toby's judgment. Most people did, though he did not always give justification for such trust. 'If you really think so.'

'Are you fond of Rita?'

'I suppose I am. She's as dishy as most, though she hasn't a brain in her head.'

'She may have brains of her own kind,' said Toby. 'Though not many girls have the type of yours. – Yes, I do think so. I think you should see him.'

Bob got up with a stumble and poured himself more beer. He forgot to offer any to Toby who, however, helped himself. 'I'll go tomorrow.'

'No time like the present. It's only nine-fifteen. Why not find out if he can see you?'

'Goddamn, I'm not ready!'

'As I said, no time like the present.'

Bob went out of the room. When he returned he said, 'He'll see us now.'

'Us? I'd only be a passenger.'

'I need some support. He may blow my bleeding head off.'

'Markham? He's barely capable of a mild puff.'

'All the same. If you can stick it.'

So they went along to the rooms of Bob's tutor, a small, fat, bald man, who greeted them with warmth and caution.

'You know Toby Roberts,' said Bob.

'Of course I know him, though our paths don't tend to cross much. Sit down, both of you. What's the trouble?'

He was told. Markham sighed into his considerable flesh; the sigh held a world of experience.

'So what do you mean to do?'

'Barring some slip-up' – Bob meant a miscarriage – 'I'd better marry her. That will mean the end of my career here.'

Markham poured himself a glass of port from the bottle at his right hand, but did not offer it. That was not the usual custom in those days. He took a long while to reply, he had never seen any reason to hurry his own thoughts. At last he said, 'Well, let's take this piece by piece. You have your university grant and your college grant. Is there any hope of more help from your parents?'

'No,' Bob said, grinning ever so slightly. 'There are seven of us. And four of them are younger than I am.'

33

'Any contributions likely from the young woman's family?'

'Search me.'

'I may be able to help you out a bit. Not much, but I dare say I could raise something.'

'I couldn't let you—'

'You've got to accept what help you can get. You can't chuck everything up now. Nobody's going to let you, certainly I'm not. Next year you may have something healthier to offer her. But you must not – I repeat, must not – throw up the whole thing. It would be lunacy. Look, you go away now and I'll see you again tomorrow. Don't let him make a fool of himself, Roberts, and tell him the world hasn't come to an end.'

The young men walked through the two courts back to their rooms, which were on the same staircase. The trees were glittering under an emergent starlight. The night was sucking the scent from the trees.

'Does he mean it?' Bob asked. 'If he could tide me over, I'd be able to pay him back eventually.'

'He'd want that. He's not being Santa Claus.'

'Tell you a funny thing. Old Adrian went off mad with me to-night, but he'd got something through. Not the mumbo-jumbo stuff but the realities. That kid would be mine. Mine. In about five months he'll not only be alive but kicking. It's something to think about. Anyway, I've made up my mind – though I'm still praying to be saved in the last reel. I shall sleep better tonight.'

In the town next day, after the shops had closed, Toby met Bob and his girl. She was not as he had pictured her; she might have been an undergraduate. Small, gently rounded, an inch or so shorter even than Maisie, she wore a plain grey coat, a coloured scarf. She had a dark, sharp-featured, delicate face, and her straight hair was turned under at the ends into the page-boy bob still fashionable.

'Rita, this is Toby.' For some reason, Bob always got his introductions the right way round. 'Toby, Rita.'

'Nice to know you,' she said, in her quiet, genteel voice.

'Well, we mustn't stop. We're going to a show at the Arts.'

They talked only for a further minute or two.

'Bye-bye,' she said, with a little lift of the hand.

Toby watched them as they walked on.

34

Well, he thought, might have been far, far worse. But if this had happened to him? He shivered. The future lay so brightly unexplored. To be tied down while still in his twenties would be quite intolerable, unless he were quite sure as to whom he could endure to be tied to. It was quite unlike the shrewd, cautious Bob to have acted with such silliness. What could have happened? He must have taken no precautions. Perhaps he had relied on her for that and she had let him down. Or perhaps he had been carried away on an impulse (far more likely), believing that things never went wrong the first time. Or hadn't it been a single time? Toby had no reason for thinking so. He supposed Bob would wait for a while, in hope, before offering her marriage: but if nothing happened, then he would do so. He was hyper-responsible. Toby had been home with him once to meet the horde of his family, and he had seen that.

Bob and Rita were married at a registry office just before the beginning of the Christmas vacation, when there were decorated trees and collecting boxes outside the churches, cotton-wool snow all over the shop windows and, even at eleven-thirty in the morning, carollers wailing *Silent Night, Holy Night*, a mawkish Teutonic tune that Toby detested.

In Cambridge, the crowds swarmed over the pavements, bearing baskets full of presents, swags of brilliant wrapping paper bursting out like cornucopias. Toby was not fond of the Christmas scene: it was so repetitive, so precisely the same each year that it seemed to occur every six weeks. He knew his own parents were building up the repetitive celebration, and spending far more than they should. He wished they would let him off the pudding, which invariably gave him indigestion. In the windows of most of the terraced houses in his neighbourhood there would be a small tree with brittle glass balls, tinsel and candles, and all the rest of it.

No one could have called the wedding gay. Toby was there with Maisie (they were now regarded as an attached couple), the policeman, big and lowering, with his nervous, twittering wife, Bob's mother, bullet-headed like himself, obviously torn between sentiment and anger, Markham, who had made various financial arrangements and had contributed a hundred pounds out of his own pocket, trying to make things go with a swing. Bob's father had been unable to leave his work, or so he said. Only Rita looked really

35

self-possessed, in a small hat made of white cloth flowers and wearing white flowers on her lapel. The ceremony, as always in registry offices, seemed distressingly perfunctory.

After it, they went to an edgy lunch at the Dorothy Café (unlicensed). The only person who seemed really cheerful – though attempts were made by Toby, Maisie and Markham to be so – was Bob himself. No sooner had he put the ring on Rita's finger than his whole demeanour changed. He was proud to be married. He was proud to think that he was to become a father. Rita looked neither grave nor gay, but took her part in the conversation and left it at that.

Bob was not to go down for the vacation. He was to spend it with the Champions, and afterwards to occupy with Rita a sizeable back bedroom which would do for them both till something else could be arranged. Toby felt it all to be inexpressibly dreary. Yet Bob, decision taken, seemed positively happy. Rita, Toby thought, had, despite Bob's comment on her brains, the makings of a clever girl: however far her husband might climb, she might not be a drag upon him. Whether he liked her or not he did not know, but he felt some respect for her.

'May as well go to the pub,' Mr Champion said heavily, when the meal was done and the bill paid, 'must have a bit of proper celebration.'

It was near opening time. They went to the Red Lion, where he downed several pints of beer in succession. All the women, Maisie included, drank gin and tonic, and Mrs Champion was at once affected by it.

'It's not often one sees one's little girl married,' she said. It was the first maudlin word uttered by any of them.

'I hope you won't see me married too often,' said Rita, making a joke.

'You'll catch it if you do,' Bob rejoined, 'I can tell you that.'

Whenever I get married, Toby thought, it won't be like this.

'That's a pretty hat, Rita,' said Maisie, wanting to please.

'I got it from Joshua Taylor's. Do you like it?'

Maisie said warmly, 'I like everything about you,' and then the girl flushed richly, unused to such compliments, so direct.

Still, on the whole it was a painful business and she and Toby were glad to break away.

He said, 'Adrian would not have approved of this, even with the circumstances being what they were.'

'In white?'

'I think he might have drawn a line there. He's something of a purist, is Adrian.'

'I'm afraid it was pretty bleak,' Maisie said.

'When you or I get married,' said Toby (he had been careful not to use the word 'and'), 'I hope it will be a bit more lively.'

But he was not lively himself. The thought of the foetus had been weighing upon him, as it had not upon Bob.

Maisie, however, felt the fever that any wedding is likely to arouse in a woman. Besides, she had had an unaccustomed amount of gin. When he said good-bye, she clung to him. 'I think I love you.'

Toby was not taken aback. 'God bless you and keep you eternally, pet,' he said diplomatically. But in love, only a direct response is acceptable: and he knew it.

5

Maisie astonished Toby by writing to him during the vacation. They never as a rule wrote to each other, perhaps because he did not to her. She wanted to come to his home again: she had tentatively been feeling her way towards plans for his mother. She had spent Christmas at Haddesdon, she said, but had then returned to visit friends near Cambridge, where she had certain things to clear up. 'May I come? I'll bring the car, so if I might borrow half a dozen pictures to take back, it would be helpful.'

'Whatever does she mean?' said Mrs Roberts, looking excited. 'I can't wait to hear.'

'She said it was all in the air for the moment. When can she come? Any day will do.'

'I think it had better be a week-day,' said his mother thoughtfully, 'if it's what I think it is, it would only work your father up.'

Toby asked whether anything could work him up. Mrs Roberts replied that he did not know him as she did. 'Ask her for next Tuesday, then. To a midday meal. And this time, she'll get a square one. I can tell just how much that girl eats.'

Maisie arrived in a Volkswagen, causing a stir of envy in Toby's heart. She came into the house as if she had been a frequent visitor, her cheeks flushed from the January air. 'I hope I'm not being a nuisance.'

Mrs Roberts assured her that she was not. This time the meal was laid in the kitchen, for which Mrs Roberts apologised.

'I think it's lovely in here. I love kitchens. I usually breakfast in ours, because I get up too late for my mother's liking.'

'Early to bed, early to rise,' Mrs Roberts said mechanically. Her mind was plainly on what Maisie had to tell.

But Maisie told nothing until they had eaten, and were drinking tea. Toby had told his mother that coffee would be better, but she said that she had to draw a line somewhere. She was not good at making it. He knew she was good at making anything, and guessed that this was a small demonstration of independence.

Then Maisie said, 'Mrs Roberts, I've been doing some spade-work on your behalf. Just tell me if I'm butting in where I shouldn't be.'

She had been making enquiries at a gallery over a shop in the Market Square which held small exhibitions from time to time, mostly of local work. Certain of the work was sold, sometimes, but more often not. The owner was of independent means and this was his hobby. He had been interested in what Maisie (whom he obviously knew well and respected) had to tell him. He would like to see some paintings and consider the matter. He could, of course, make no promises.

'You'd need to show at least a dozen,' Maisie said to Toby's mother, 'but if I could take six back with me now it would be a fair sample. Have you done much since I last saw you?' Toby was amused by her sudden air of authority. This was pleasure for her, but it was also business, and he guessed at once that she was no poor hand at that. She had previously shown Mrs Roberts guest-like deference, but now that had for the moment disappeared.

'You've got my head in a whirl and I can't think straight. Yes, I've done several pictures. Two more street scenes and one in the park. Not painted in the park, of course. I just kept it in my mind.'

'May I see them?'

'Nothing will come of it, will it?' Mrs Roberts said rather plaintively.

'I don't know,' Maisie replied, 'I'm simply casting around.'

So she was taken up to see the paintings, Mrs Roberts much flustered. She had, indeed, done a great deal of work, varying in quantity but all the pictures attractive in their own way. Maisie inspected them, frowned, smiled: professional. She did so for a long time. At last she stood up.

'If it comes off, you'll have to put a price on these.'

'You mean I'd be paid for them?' Mrs Roberts said, dumb-founded.

'Of course, if they sold, and even so, the gallery would take fifteen per cent.'

'I shouldn't have the foggiest idea what to ask!'

'At a guess, I should think ten pounds for the smaller ones to thirty pounds for the street scenes. You don't want to put them at too low a price. A price in itself can be impressive.'

'Thirty pounds!'

'Well, we'll see what Mr Driffield says.' Maisie gave her sudden sweet smile. 'We may not bring it off at all, and if so I may have led you up the garden path. But it's worth a try, isn't it? And you won't hold it against me if it doesn't?'

'Hold it against you! I don't know how to thank you for what you've done already.'

Toby had never really guessed the extent of his mother's ambitions, or perhaps they had not existed until Maisie had awakened them. He knew she had gone to this trouble partly because she believed in the paintings, but more so because she longed to please himself. Towards his mother she was becoming openly affectionate, at one point touching her arm in her enthusiasm. Mrs Roberts involuntarily drew away, not because she did not like Maisie – she liked her very much – but because she was not used to demonstrativeness outside her own family. Then she realised the nature of her movement and for a second brought herself to lay a hand on Maisie's.

Maisie said it was time for her to go. Darkness came early and she did not much care for driving in the dusk. Toby carried down the dozen paintings she had chosen, and stowed them in the back of the car.

When he went back into the house, he found his mother sitting with folded hands and a look of utter stupefaction. 'Don't hope for too much,' he said, 'just keep your fingers crossed.'

'To think this should even have been thought about, for *me*!'

'You deserve something for yourself.'

He went up to his bedroom to work, but it was hard to concentrate. He foresaw his mother having her strange little period of noteworthiness, and hoped that whatever publicity there might be – it couldn't be much, perhaps the odd note in a local paper – it wouldn't fall on him. He was a very private person.

When he returned to Cambridge, he found Maisie waiting for him at the station. He always took the same train. She was so excited that at first she could hardly catch her breath. 'We're getting our show! Driffield's quite keen on your mother's work, in so far as he's keen on anything. He wants a dozen at least, preferably more.'

'That's wonderful,' Toby said. 'You are wonderful.'

'It can't be till the first week in March, though. But anyway, there's a good deal to be done. We'll open in style, too; I'll see about that. Wine and cheese, what press we can rake up.'

Toby wondered who was going to pay for this, and he suspected her. Had she subsidised it to any extent? He simply did not know how these things worked. 'This calls for a celebration,' he said, 'don't you think so?' He mentioned a small Italian restaurant, rather beyond his means, but he could go slow on other things.

They had a carafe of Chianti between them. She told him all Driffield had said: he thought Mrs Roberts was a primitive painter of a very interesting kind. He had wanted to know about her, how she had started to paint and how late. He had thought they might make a sale or two. (So the man had been subsidised, Toby thought, with much uneasiness. He did not like taking money, however obliquely, from Maisie: it put him under an obligation, and obligations were things from which he attempted to shy away.)

'My mother will come,' she said, 'and I dare say Edward will, and you must gather all your clans. Oh, I am looking forward to it all! By the bye, Mother's "season" hasn't properly started yet, but I think you'd better come to Haddesdon pretty soon. There won't be many people there for you to meet, but Mother matters most.'

His heart leaped, and for the moment he forgot his dubieties. 'I'd like to do that.'

When he had seen her back to her college, and had said goodnight with special tenderness, he returned to his room and opened the window. The winter night was exceptionally mild, and he did not get much air at home. When he had done his work – he was by now working very hard – he went to bed and lay on his back, looking out on the leaves flickering in a strong blue moonlight. He let the thought fly for the first time: would he wish to marry Maisie? (If that were ever possible.) Certainly he had met no one else whom he liked better. He did not feel too young to think about such things, though he knew he was young to adventure upon them. It made him ill at ease to think of her in the rôle – which he was sure she was playing – of Lady Bountiful: yet was too realistic to shrug off the idea that, in the foreseeable future, he might need a degree of bounty. He thought it best not to tackle her head-on about her probable part in his mother's show. If he did so, and she admitted what he increasingly believed to be true, he might have to stop the whole thing; and he could not bear to contemplate the disappointment that would be caused, both to his mother and to Maisie herself.

Better keep quiet and see what happened. She could think him innocent. And there was Haddesdon ahead.

It would be cold by dawn. He rose and closed the window, returned to bed and sleep.

6

He was invited to lunch on a Saturday in February. Maisie was going to Suffolk the night before, but said that if he took the train to Sudbury she would pick him up there.

The day was bright and sharp, with a sprinkling of hoar-frost like half-hearted Christmas decorations. When he rose, he was exercised as to what he should wear. It was a country house: what would be appropriate? But all he had was a pair of flannel trousers, two pairs of blue jeans, and two woollen sweaters hardened by much washing. He had been considering these during the watches of the night, which were not common watches with him. Indeed, he was not given to trivial anxieties.

He considered his wardrobe with disfavour. The yellow sweater was not quite clean, the green one too shabby. It would have to be his formal blue suit, kept for examinations and the more conventional social occasions. As he shaved, he imaged Haddesdon once more. The Tudor chimneys, the wide green lawn sloping towards the roadway. Rose-brick was filling his mind. He even went so far as to imagine peacocks on the lawn, but knew that few people kept these birds: the noise they made was a nuisance, and there had been a rumpus about a college which had kept some in Cambridge.

The countryside was sweet as the train moved through it. The early frost had gone, and the fields were spangled with dew. He passed through Haverhill, Stoke-by-Clare, Clare itself, Cavendish. Nearly there. He felt unusually nervous. He was not bothered about his social manners: he had learned too much for that. But he was bothered by the thought of Mrs Ferrars, queenly in her floating draperies, and by the thought of the people he might meet. He hardly thought of Maisie at all.

Sudbury. Maisie was waiting with the car. She was wearing an oddly out-of-date-seeming beret, like a tam-o'-shanter, which increased her resemblance to Frieda Lawrence. As usual, she looked euphoric and welcoming.

'It's only three miles,' she said. 'Are you hungry? I am.'

At last they swept through abrupt gates into a circular drive, and came in sight of the house.

Not Tudor. A modern house, large, in white stone, which caught the light of the morning. It was elegant, but in no style that Toby recognised – indeed, he knew little of architectural styles. It was a long, two-storied house, flanked by curved stone walls which gave the impression of wings. A mahogany door between twin pilasters, and above it a graceful fanlight. He had just time to take all this in. He realised quite suddenly that he was longing for a drink.

The door was opened by someone whom he presumed to be a housekeeper, wearing a white overall. 'Here we are, Sukie,' Maisie greeted her. 'This is Mr Roberts. Where's Mother?'

The question did not have to be answered.

Sweeping out upon them came a large woman in tweeds, dark, with swarthy skin and large features, a great bun of black hair hitched behind her head.

'Toby!' she cried. 'You're very welcome. Did you have a good journey?'

'Very. But it's not a long one from Cambridge, is it?'

'It seems to me to crawl. Come right in, and Maisie will show you where to wash your hands. Then we'll all have sherry and be happy. You are happy, aren't you? I mean, a happy type? I always know, somehow.'

He wondered how he was going to cope with her. He believed she might have an idea that she was clairvoyant. She was as unlike a mother for Maisie as anything he could possibly have imagined. How had her husband looked? He hoped there was a portrait about, even a photograph. He could gain only the slightest impression of the interior of the house, except that the rooms were lofty and bright. Whiteness everywhere, and bright paintings on the walls.

He enjoyed his brief spell in the bathroom. Fitted carpets: shower curtains: towels of inconceivable softness and soap that smelled wonderfully. He could cheerfully have spent half an hour there.

He was shown into the drawing-room by the housekeeper, who had been waiting at the foot of the stairs for him. Only Maisie and her mother were there.

'Now, Toby,' said Mrs Ferrars, 'I know all about you from Maisie, and about your mamma. So there's no need for social skirmishing, is there?' She went to the side table which was set out for drinks, and prepared to pour them herself. 'You prefer sherry?'

Toby did not; he would have liked a pint of beer, but did not feel this the moment to ask for it, though he supposed it could have been provided in this house. So he assented.

While Mrs Ferrars was supplying them all, he had time to look around him. A spacious room, two splendid windows giving on to a large tree-shaded garden: it might have gone on to the limits of sight, although, recognising his own inflated imagination, he guessed that it did not. A superb painting on the wall, which could well be a Constable.

'*All* about you,' Mrs Ferrars said, returning with a glass. Though she did not know. 'Why don't you write a book about Saint-Just?' she shot at him. 'You must publish some time. An interesting man. "No freedom for the enemies of freedom." And I don't think there has been much written about him, though, of course, there are gross *lacunae* in my knowledge.'

'I need a bit more experience first,' he replied, 'I'm only a beginner.'

'Never too late to begin. Do *you* like Saint-Just?'

'He interests me. But I'm not sure that one could exactly like him.'

She nodded her head, three times, solemnly. 'Well said. No snap judgments, eh?'

'I'm not qualified to form any.' Toby was beginning to think she was an ass, while not being ungrateful for asses of her sort.

'But you must! You must! You can always modify them later. One must make a beginning. Ah, here's Edward!' she cried, as the large grey man came into the room. 'Edward! Should Toby Roberts write a book about Saint-Just? Edward, Toby.' This served as an introduction.

Crane kissed her and kissed Maisie. Then he shook hands with Toby. 'Do you want to?' he asked him. 'I don't see why not. There can be nothing against it.'

He had a pleasant unassuming manner, but his eyes behind the thick glasses were sharp.

'Sherry, Edward?'

'You know I never drink sherry, Amanda. I've grown out of it.

45

Scotch, please.' He sat down heavily at Toby's side. 'Do you really like sherry?'

Toby hardly knew what to answer, as he was half-way through his glass. He made a non-committal noise. Then he said shyly, and part of the shyness was genuine, 'I admire your plays, sir. I never miss one if I can help it.'

'Thank you. I don't know that people are going to admire them for long, though. They have a beginning, middle and end and call for a proscenium arch.' He turned to Maisie.

'How are you keeping?'

'Working moderately hard,' she replied, 'but nothing like so hard as Toby.'

'Don't overdo it,' said Crane. 'Moderation in all things.'

'I'm afraid my course calls for more than moderation.'

Crane surveyed him. 'I was a don once. Did you know that? On the day before examinations, I always sent my young men on the river. What they didn't know before they couldn't make up in a day. And looking up things at the last moment always means forgetting something one has learned before.'

'I suppose they always went,' said Toby.

'Some of them did. But some sat all day and half the night on last-minute swotting, with the result that they were dead tired next day and riddled with nerves. By the way, I've been told about your mother's painting. I'd like to come to the opening.'

'She'd be very pleased, and so should I. Both of us are over-whelmed.'

'Oh come, I have not enough to overwhelm anyone, except per-haps sheer physical weight.'

Amanda laughed. 'Don't make yourself sound like Mycroft Holmes, Edward. You can't weigh more than twelve stone.'

'Yes, but I'm small-boned. Any news of Claire?'

'She's been in Florence. We'll see her in the spring.'

A maid announced luncheon.

They went into an oval dining-room. This, too, was a lovely room, an oval table in the middle of it, with white linen, shining plate and glass. Toby noticed that there were three glasses by each place.

'We're a small party today,' said Mrs Ferrars, 'but you shall come to more representative gatherings, Toby. And by the way, lunch is

46

always chosen to suit Edward's tastes when he's here for it, so I hope yours coincide.'

Whitebait. *Crêpes de volaille*. A *soufflé Grand Marnier*. Hock and claret. Port to follow, which they took with coffee at the table. Toby was much impressed. He was surprised to see that Mrs Ferrars smoked between courses. He had always believed that lovers of wine did not.

During the course of the meal, she dominated the conversation. What did Toby think of —— and —— and ——? These were the writers most lately in fashion. He said he was afraid he wasn't well up in recent novels; he had his nose too hard to the grindstone.

'But you must make time! It is absolutely essential to *keep up*, isn't it, Edward?'

'I don't know,' he said slowly. 'Seeing the stuff all three of them write, I think it's sometimes better to keep down.'

'Wicked Edward,' she replied, unruffled. 'I don't believe you've read a word they've written. Anyway, I shall have them all here in May. What *have* you been reading?'

'Dostoievsky, more or less as usual.'

'Do you know,' she said, her eyes bulging, 'he terrifies me? I adore him, but he makes me like a child afraid of the dark.'

'Well,' said Maisie, 'I expect that's what he wanted you to feel. Otherwise he wouldn't have gone to such lengths.'

'Are you still reading Proust every year regularly, Edward?' Mrs Ferrars asked.

'Most years, but not when I'm writing myself. He's too infectious.'

'Isn't Dostoievsky?' asked Toby, on the shy note.

'Not for my kind of thing. Some writers are like measles. If I were a novelist I wouldn't dare to read James Joyce, though I'm afraid far too many of them do.'

'Jane Austen isn't infectious,' said Maisie, 'she is too perfect to be so.'

'I'm glad you don't refer to her as Miss Austen, at least. People who do that because they rate her so highly, in fact above all others, don't refer to Mr Shakespeare.'

'Edward, you are naughty,' said Amanda Ferrars, rather mechanically.

They returned to the drawing-room. The weather had darkened

and with it, apparently, Amanda's mood: Toby noted it, and concluded that she was subject to these sudden changes. The great cedar on the lawn lost colour in the springing wind.

Crane sat beside him, trying to draw him out: but Toby seldom came out. He was courteous, indeed, but not to be drawn.

'This is becoming a dull party,' Amanda observed. 'Edward, say something witty.'

He turned to her. 'Oh, but I'm not a wit. Or only in the seventeenth-century sense, which nobody recognises.' He seemed to defer to her, but not to suffer her. After all, he was the most distinguished of her lions and did not roar at will, if indeed he ever roared.

'Mother,' said Maisie, 'do you want Edward to jump through hoops? Because he is quite the wrong type for it.'

'What are you hoping for?' Crane asked Toby.

'A decent degree. No more.'

'Shall you write?'

'I suppose I shall have a crack at it.'

'You realise what it means? Sitting on your backside at regular hours? No waiting for inspiration, because it never turns up. Trollope knew that and said so, but they only despised him for it.'

'Toby has been keeping very regular hours,' said Maisie, who wanted all to be to his credit.

'Saint-Just isn't a bad idea, at that,' said Crane, 'all Amanda's ideas have something in them.'

Toby was suddenly filled with gratitude that this man should take so much trouble with him. 'If you say so,' he replied, 'I'll try. But not just yet.'

'Now don't tell me I don't start people off,' said Amanda, recovering her spirits.

'I was saying just the reverse,' Crane put in.

'I hope to start Toby's mamma off. But of course I haven't seen anything of hers yet.'

'She'll be terrified when you do,' said Toby, and Crane gave him a glance.

'Why?' asked Amanda, pleased. 'Am I so terrifying?'

Toby gave a contrived wriggle. 'To some people, I suppose—' and Crane glanced at him again.

'Not terrifying to you, surely!' Amanda appeared to loom.

'I hope you won't think that,' Toby replied, 'you've been so kind.

48

And I never know whether it's proper for people to say so, but I had such a marvellous lunch.'

'So you and Toby have much in common, Edward!' Amanda exclaimed. 'No, it's quite proper. I don't know why one thinks out a meal if people aren't going to enjoy it. Toby, I approve of you.'

He could not help but feel pleasure at this, though he did not want her to approve too much, being as yet not altogether committed to Maisie. He was by now fully aware of her wealth, or her mother's: he would have called it riches. Yet he still had a world to win. He thanked her, said he should be going.

'You can't,' Maisie said, 'there isn't a train till five. Let's play *bouts-rimés*.'

It was the first he had known of her passion for parlour games. Luckily, he thought he could hold his own at them.

'I'm no great hand at that,' said Crane.

Toby found himself with the following, supplied by Crane:

> '———— knife,
> ———— hammer,
> ———— clamour,
> ———— life.'

He wrote rapidly:

> 'When I took up the knife,
> When I applied the hammer,
> Calf gave a dreadful clamour—
> It's with me all my life.'

He passed his paper, which was acclaimed.

'A slaughter-house,' said Crane, 'very neat. I thought I might have had you foxed.'

'He's an asset!' Amanda glowed.

They played this game till tea-time, Toby flagging somewhat. Nevertheless, he felt he had done well. He was, in fact, settling to Haddesdon. He could keep this kind of thing up, if need be. When they had had tea – a substantial one – and he rose to leave, Crane spoke to him. 'You'll go a fair way.'

'Thank you, sir.'

'I appreciate the old-world courtesy, but I'm Edward here.'

'Thank you, Mr Crane,' said Toby, 'I don't feel I'm ready for the other name yet.' This, he could not help feeling, was charmingly deferential.

'I hope you soon will be.'

The enchanted afternoon was at an end. He made his thanks and farewells.

'We'll see you,' said Crane.

Toby felt he had been a success. Maisie drove him to the station, where he kissed her more lingeringly than was his wont. 'It was wonderful. I like your mother.'

'I like yours.'

'And I like Edward Crane. He looked as I thought he would be, but he wasn't in himself. He was much nicer than that.'

The train came in, the slow train to Cambridge making its way past the river and the beautiful villages. He waved to Maisie till she was out of sight.

7

During the next fortnight Maisie appeared to take over Toby's mother. Letters passed between them. Maisie made two visits to SE1, both of them in Toby's absence (the latter was genuinely working hard) and on the second triumphantly brought back five more paintings, three on canvas, two on plasterboard, which she delivered straight to the gallery, telling Toby that he must get round there as soon as he could and see them. 'Then we must get them framed as quickly as they can be done. Phillips are very good people, and quite cheap.'

All this made Toby very uneasy. He did not wish her to enter intimately into his mother's life before he had decided that she should do so. Also, he was worried about the framing. He knew perfectly well that this was something his mother had hardly thought about, and that Maisie herself was likely to have it done. This he was determined not to permit. He had some savings – to be precise, fifty pounds thirteen shillings and fourpence – and he meant to use them. He told her this at once, and in no uncertain terms. His certainty made her rather uncertain.

'But Toby, it won't cost all that much. We want something very simple in the way of frames, fairly narrow white ones, or unpainted wood. Wait till you see.'

He went with her to the gallery, and was in fact astonished by what he saw. So, apparently, was the owner, who said to him at once, 'A remarkable woman, your mother.'

There were two park scenes, one other street scene, two flower pieces: but with these latter she had learned to be cunning. She knew she could not paint vases or bowls properly, so had merely suggested them, throwing the emphasis on the flowers themselves. The effect was a little bizarre, but satisfactory. Mrs Roberts was a hard worker: no painting took her more than two days, some of them only one. She had promised Maisie three more within a week, making a total of fourteen. The park scenes had now acquired a curious evanescence: first you saw them, Toby thought, then you didn't. He began to wonder how she would enjoy being billed as a Primitive, a term she probably did not know, because it was getting to be a misnomer. The thought of the show had enormously spurred both her talent, her originality and her ambition. He wondered what his father would have thought of it all.

'I'll pick these up tomorrow,' Maisie said to Driffield, 'and take them to the framers. We won't want anything showy. It would simply detract.'

He agreed, respectfully.

When they were outside in the street again, Toby marched Maisie into a café, though she said she had little time.

'I don't suppose you have. You're spending so much with my mother. Don't think I'm not grateful, but if you go on like this you're going to flunk your Finals.'

Maisie remarked that he sounded surprisingly stern, and she raised her eyebrows at him.

He returned to the matter of the frames. 'Look, I'm a rank amateur at all this. But I mean to put up fifty pounds, if that's enough, and there had better be no argument, pet.'

'It won't cost nearly as much as that,' Maisie said, seeming resigned. 'But if you must, you must.' She looked submissive, which she often did when she was not. 'I'll let them send you the bill.'

He wondered what negotiations she might have with the framers behind his back but, concluding that she would never let him know what went on there, felt that he might accept his luck. Anyway, he would be doing most of the paying.

She said that her mother would be down almost at once to see the paintings. 'She can be of great use, but I warn you, if they don't take her fancy, she won't be.' She grinned. 'You see, I can be stern too, when I like.'

'Stern darling,' said Toby.

Meanwhile, he had a letter from Mrs Roberts.

'Your Maisie is a very nice girl,' she wrote, 'and very kind. I am afraid to impose on her. Your father says I might. In fact, I don't think he much likes the whole idea. He thinks I may be disappointed and that it may set me above myself. Also there is the money business. How much is this framing going to cost? I can't believe the man who runs the gallery is going to do it himself.'

No, Toby thought, neither is he going to provide the cheese and wine party, nor have the private view invitations printed, nor whatever is wanted for publicity. But he wished he were not so ignorant of the whole business. He wrote to his mother, reassuring her about the framing: he had a bit put by: he would see to it.

She replied, somewhat indignantly, that she too had a bit put by, and could see to that herself. He answered temperately that he could put up the money for a part of it, and if she wished, she could do the rest. He had not the faintest idea what it would ('all', he had begun to say, but scratched this out) cost.

On the Friday of the following week Amanda descended, by appointment, at the gallery. Toby and Maisie were there to greet her at the door, and he noticed that she had come in her chauffeur-driven car. She was wearing a bright red, fur-collared suit, with a debauched-looking hat to match. 'Well, *mes enfants,*' she said, 'lead you on.'

Driffield, to whom she was not entirely a stranger, received her as if she were the Queen Mother.

Reverently he brought out canvas after canvas and, to Toby's dismay, she scowled at them all. Then she asked Driffield to align them against the wall, and she squatted to see them. Her bulging eyes were bright. 'Yes,' she said, and then, 'yes, and yes, talent here, though of a rather peculiar order.' She suddenly turned to Toby. 'Imagine you're not here. I can't bring personalities into these things.' There was a note of compunction in her voice, which dismayed him further. She seemed to study the paintings for an interminable time.

At last she said to Driffield, in a little-girl voice, 'You may put a red star here and here. It will give us a start.'

She had, in fact, bought a street scene and one park scene, each priced at thirty pounds. Driffield beamed. Then she returned to her inspection. 'And,' she said, 'this flower piece. Mind you,' she added to Maisie, 'I'm not paying for it. Edward is. It will go nicely in his flat, and his pictures are not what they ought to be. I am making him very slowly replace them.'

'Mrs Ferrars—' Toby began, feeling rather dizzy.

She was on him like a flash. 'Do you think I'd do this if your mother's stuff wasn't good? I'm not a philanthropist. If I loved you better than all the world beside,' she added, with odd sentimentality, 'I would never buy a thing I didn't want, not if I hurt your deepest feelings. I just could *not* do it.' There was in her tone a degree of vainglory, but also of absolute sincerity. She would never buy a bad painting, unless the painter were in the ultimate wretchedness of want: and then, nothing would induce her to hang it.

She rose to her feet with a groan. 'Stiff,' she said.

Driffield, elated, suggested that they should all join him for a drink.

'Nothing I should like better,' she said, 'but I can't keep my driver waiting.' She patted Maisie on the shoulder. 'If you two think there's anything to celebrate, go and do so.'

'There's a lot to celebrate,' Toby said, 'and we're grateful to you, but I do think Maisie ought to go back and do some work. She's been doing so much for us here.'

'Us? Oh, you and your mother. I want to meet her. But I shall do so at the private view. Mr Driffield, it is going to be nice, isn't it? Just let me know if there is anything more I can do.'

She swept away, and for a split second Toby hated her. She was taking him over, taking his mother over, understanding nothing. Then he had a wave of reverse feeling and was remorseful.

'You're fretting,' Maisie said, when she had gone, 'don't be. Mother never does a thing she's likely to be sorry for. And we're going to have a party!'

Next day Toby received something unusual: a letter from his father.

Dear Son,

I am a bit bothered about your Mum. She has got into such a state about the Show that I wonder whether she is not in for a fall. She is working her eyes out. I can't judge how good she is, but I wonder whether your Maisie knows what she's doing. Mum will have to mix with a lot of posh people and she's not used to it, only when she was in service which is not the same thing. She doesn't tell me much, but I believe there will be some expense. I'd like to know how much. Somebody has to think about things. I like your Maisie, I think she's a good girl, but she doesn't know what she's meddling with. How good is your Mum at this painting? You'd know, I expect. Perhaps I'm worrying for nothing, but it's on my mind.

Your loving
Dad

54

To this Toby wrote a cautious reply, adding that there would be no expense, which was perhaps incautious, but he could think of nothing else to say. He said that people who ought to know did think his mother was good, and that all in all, he thought she ought to have her chance. 'Do come to the show yourself, if you can get off.' (Well, they would all know more about him, Toby, soon.) 'Maisie doesn't seem to meddle. She knows what she's about, and she wouldn't expose Mummy to disappointment if she thought there was a chance of it. Seventy pounds' worth have been sold already.'

When he had posted this, he went round to tea with Bob, whom he had not seen, except in passing, for a couple of weeks, and he did not know how he was getting on. Bob was keeping his room in college and working hard at the lab: in the evenings he went back to Rita.

Toby found her there, and Adrian too. It was too early for her pregnancy to be obvious, though he thought there was a swelling of her breasts, a slight thickening about the neck. She looked pretty and wifely, presiding over Bob's cracked cups and chipped brown teapot.

'Well,' she said, 'you're a stranger!'

'So are you. How are you?'

She went into some detail. She was quite without shyness. Toby revised his previous estimate of her possible cleverness, and mentally substituted the word 'smart'. Adrian looked embarrassed, as he always did at the mention, however oblique, of sexual matters: Toby guessed he was afraid of, but not divorced from them.

She began to talk frankly about their financial circumstances. 'But,' she said, 'if Bob's Finals go all right—'

'They will,' Adrian put in.

'Things ought to be easier. He'll be able to get a job.'

'I hope,' said Adrian, 'that he'll get a Fellowship before long. It would be on the cards.'

'Stuff that till the time comes,' Bob said, looking awkward.

He knew precisely what he expected, but was touching wood.

'That would be marvellous!' Rita cried. The idea had not occurred to her, and he had not thought fit to mention it.

'What about you, Adrian?' she asked, looking at him from under her lashes.

55

'Me? Oh, I'm through the immediate hurdles, of course. But my plans are pretty stable.'

'Bob calls you Father Stedman. Oh, dear, ought I to have said that?'

'You're simply expressing my vaulting ambitions,' Adrian replied, looking at her unsmiling.

'I'm sure you'll get everything you want. Won't he, Bob?'

Bob said he would think so.

'And you, Toby? Don't be such an oyster.' She had her own kind of impudence, the impudence of a pretty woman who is sure of herself.

'I have no such vaulting ambitions. I just hope to scrape through.'

'Fancy you being a clergyman,' she mused to Adrian. 'We shan't dare to talk to you then.'

'Clergymen are there to be talked to. Sometimes people do.'

'I'd be terrified. I'd always be sure I was being sinful, or something. My mother and father haven't been much in the way of churchgoers.'

'I'm afraid they're with the great majority,' said Adrian. 'All one can really hope for is to make a dent.'

He passed his cup, and she refilled it. 'Do you really believe it all?' she asked him curiously, her eyes upon his face. 'Don't mind me if I'm speaking out of turn.'

'Implicitly. Why else should I be doing this?'

'Bob doesn't believe in anything.'

'Stop it,' Bob said, 'if you're trying to bait Adrian, you might as well stop. It's no bloody use.'

She turned her eyes back to him. 'Bait him? Don't be a sap. I just wanted to know. You didn't think I was baiting you, Adrian, did you?'

'No. But I shouldn't mind if you were.'

She gave more tea to Toby. 'Do you believe in all this?'

'I never tell people, because I'm still not sure. I may have my certainties later in life.'

She gave a full-bodied laugh. 'Have your certainties! The way you put things.'

Yet her attention was not for him: it was for Adrian, and Toby noted it with some disquiet.

'What's this Maisie's been saying about your mother having an art show?'

'It's true enough,' Toby replied. 'I only hope to God it's a modest success.'

They talked about it for a while. Then Rita said, 'Well, this won't buy the baby a new bonnet,' with a meaningful smile. She rose and kissed Bob lightly on the top of his head, which was already showing signs of a bald spot. 'Don't be late, love. I'm making a shepherd's pie.'

'No need to be particularly early for that,' he said, his tone verging on the surly. 'It'll keep. I'll come when I can. I'm going back to the lab now.'

She left, and he followed her shortly.

Toby said to Adrian, 'You're a wise man.' (Though he did not think so.) 'What do you make of them?'

'I don't know. I suppose it's early days.'

'She likes you.'

'Girls sometimes do,' Adrian said simply and with no hint of conceit. 'And I've nothing to give them.'

'I couldn't live a celibate life,' said Toby.

'Well, I hope I can. But I suppose I could opt out, if the going went too hard.' Adrian smiled, as if he thought this unlikely. 'After all, one can't foresee everything. But in my job I shan't want distractions. I mean, when I get a job.'

'You'll be all right,' Toby said warmly, 'you'll get just what you want.'

Adrian talked into a sympathetic ear for some twenty minutes. Then they got up to go.

'I think I'll wash up the tea-things,' Adrian said, with a prim air. 'Bob will never think of it, and I hate the idea of him coming back to dirty cups.' He did as he had proposed. They went back to their own rooms.

8

As the time for the opening drew nearer, Toby's gratitude towards and resentment against Maisie grew side by side. He knew she was sensitive to his least mood, so he determined that he would have no obvious moods. Though his common sense told him that she might have an immense amount to give him, and that she was by now deeply in love with him, he could not bear the thought of being 'taken over'. Nor could he bear his mother being so treated. His class-consciousness, which tore him in two directions, made him the more defensive for her sake. Yet he had made an arrangement with Maisie to pay for the framing, and did not dare to look into whatever expenses lay beyond that. He closed his mind to them.

It was a divided mind. He realised that he would be taking a good deal from her, and that she loved to give it: but all this gave him a feeling of being trapped.

Yet she was so happy, so whole-hearted, and so was his mother. He could not bear a shadow to pass across their faces. He believed he might come to love Maisie wholly in time. Why not now? He rationalised this by the thought that he had as yet nothing to offer her. Also, he felt himself too young to make binding decisions.

The day drew near. Maisie had told him that half a dozen of her mother's friends were coming, and that she had written to a few art critics whom she knew. She had also alerted the local press.

'Look,' said Toby, 'I'd far rather the papers said nothing about me.'

'Why must people say nothing about you?' she asked him curiously. 'Why should you mind? There's nothing to be said against you.'

'I don't really know. But when I see a shell, I always feel it's my real home.'

'You should get out of that,' she said firmly, 'because you'll have to abandon shells in the long run.'

'Shall I, pet?'

'I think so.'

The private view was to be between six and eight p.m. Mrs Roberts was to come by the midday train, have lunch with Toby, be shown over the college and be early at the gallery so she could see the exhibition by herself. She would then have dinner with Toby, Maisie and Mrs Ferrars, and catch the last train home. Toby would have liked her to spend the night at a hotel, but he could not afford it and was damned if he were going to give Maisie a chance to pay. He prayed that his mother might not be too unnerved by the whole thing. His father, who certainly would have been, had decided that he could not leave the shop.

It was a bright, clear, windy day when he met her at the station. He need not have feared for her nerve. As she stepped from the train, wearing a blue coat and a small blue hat, he believed in her composure.

He kissed her. 'You look terrific. New clothes?'

'Maisie came with me to choose them,' said Mrs Roberts. 'I'm glad you like them.'

They took a taxi into the town. She looked around her as the town unfolded, and she sighed. 'You're a lucky boy to be here. If I'd had a chance to live in a place like this—'

'You couldn't have done much better if you had.'

'Seventy pounds,' she mused, 'I've earned that already.'

'And you'll sell more.'

They came into King's Parade, where he paid off the taxi. Now Mrs Roberts gasped with appreciation. The pinnacles of the chapel looked dark against the pale-blue sky – 'Cambridge blue,' she said.

They had lunch at the Copper Kettle. Unnerved she was apparently not, but she was too excited to eat much. 'To think I should be here with you at last!'

'Oh, come, I haven't been keeping you out, exactly. You could easily have come before.'

'Somehow I didn't manage to find the time. Besides . . . I thought you wouldn't want me mixing in with your friends.'

'Don't be humble,' said Toby with a grin. But he guessed that she really was not.

He took her through the courts of his college on to the Backs. The hosts of daffodils were dancing in the wind, and despite the nip in the air young men and girls were on the river. She was, for a while, speechless. At last she said, in a tone not free from envy, 'To think you should have all this!'

'One hardly notices when one's here.'

'I think I could paint it. Not the buildings, of course, but the river and the flowers, and people lying about on the grass. How can they stand the cold! But young people always can, I suppose.'

'They've got more flesh on their bones than you have,' said Toby. It occurred to him that her lack of nervousness was due to the fact that *already* she had been acknowledged as an artist. Slim acknowledgment, perhaps, but at least it had given her a place to stand. Even now, she was feeling the confidence of the creator.

The wind blew the trees white and grey. The river was laced by minuscule waves, frail as threads of cotton.

'I'm so glad to think you are here,' she said. 'You were truly pleased we could help you to it? Though of course you helped yourself, too.'

'Very pleased.' He put his hand briefly on her arm.

Next, he took her for a tour of his college and she was again dumbstruck. She had worked in a fine house, once, but that had not the fineness and majesty of an institution. She moved slowly through Hall, marvelling at the paintings, the glowing windows, the silverware on the reflecting tables. 'Must take a lot of polishing,' she said. She was speaking in a whisper, treading the floor very lightly.

'Perhaps we'll all feel spoiled when we go down,' Toby said. He was conscious of a great fondness for her, now at last she was here. He knew a twinge of conscience that he had not made her come before.

He took her to his rooms, where her housewifely instinct took over. She gave a glance of pride at the sight of her picture on the wall, then turned her attention to practical matters.

'Aren't they supposed to look after you here?'

'That was the general idea.'

'It's downright dirty. That paper basket hasn't been emptied for days! And look at the dust in the corners!'

'It does for me.'

'What makes them think they earn their money?'

Toby said he simply could not imagine, but that he was quite content. 'I suppose that's why I like to come home sometimes.' He regretted the word 'sometimes' as soon as he had spoken it, but she did not appear to notice. She comforted herself by the sight of the things she had made him take with him: a plain bright bedcover, bright cushions, a deep warm rug. 'Anyway, I suppose if you think it's all right—'

'Quite all right.'

He made tea for her: he would not let her do it. 'You're the guest today, Mum.' The old appellation slipped from him.

Bob and Adrian came in. She shook hands with them in a stately manner. Toby was amused by, and proud of her.

'This is a great day for you, Mrs Roberts,' Adrian said earnestly, 'we're all looking forward to it.'

'You'll have a good turnout,' said Bob, 'we'll all of us come for Tobe.'

At five o'clock, Toby and his mother were due at the gallery. Still she was showing no nervousness, only excitement. Driffield met them at the door.

'Mrs Roberts! This is a great pleasure. I only hope you'll be pleased with what we've managed to do. I assure you, we've done our best, but if you want anything altered there's still time.'

The stately air had not left her. She moved slowly about the exhibition, gratified by the three red stars. No, she had nothing she wished altered.

'You are an original, Mrs Roberts,' said Driffield, 'we are proud to show your work.'

Meanwhile, a trestle table was being set up, a white cloth thrown over it: bottles appeared.

'Perhaps you'd like a glass of wine now,' he suggested, 'to fortify you against the ordeal. We have several critics coming.'

'Thank you,' she said, 'but it's too early. And anyway I can't do more than I have done.' She paused for a moment beside the painting of the school crocodile, and her brows slightly furrowed. Then she moved round her show again, seemingly forgetful both of her son and Driffield. Toby noted now a faint heightening of her colour: it made her look almost pretty, and he had never thought of her like that before.

At ten minutes to six Amanda came in, coarse-featured, resplendent in the red suit, Maisie with her, and three men: one a man of about fifty, very tall and broad-chested, with light eyes and curling dark hair hardly touched with grey: one little more than a boy, saturnine, slight, with an elegant, almost serpentine head, wearing a pink bow tie: and the third, Edward Cane.

'Toby!' Amanda cried. 'Come and meet people. Idris, this is Toby Roberts. Lord Llangain. Peter Coxon. Edward you know. Now lead us to your wonderful Mamma.'

Maisie was already with Mrs Roberts, whom she kissed. This astonished Toby, for his mother was not given to any easy show of affection outside her own family.

Seeing them approach, she came gravely forward from the shelter Maisie offered and held out her hand to Amanda. 'I know how kind you've been.'

'Kind?' Amanda exclaimed, 'I've simply been getting in on the ground floor. Very good luck to you!' She introduced the men.

Mrs Roberts' composure remained undisturbed. She had probably seen a lord before, yet never at such close quarters: but she held out her hand to Llangain simply enough, and received his compliments. She was a little more disconcerted by the serpentine young man, who tended to gush at her. With Crane she was at once at ease. 'Of course I know Toby,' he said, 'and I'm glad to know you.'

'You see, dear Mr Driffield,' said Amanda, 'we've come before the hordes arrive so we can look round in comfort.'

They looked round, in the manner of persons at a private view, unspeaking but with looks of infinite arcane knowledge on their faces. Driffield pressed wine on them all, and all, barring Mrs Roberts who took a glass of tomato juice, accepted.

By twenty past six, just as Toby was dreading a fiasco, the room began to fill. Bob came with Rita, Adrian with two of his aspiring clerical friends. Several girls who were friends of Maisie's: indeed, she seemed to know everyone. Then one of the London critics, whom she greeted eagerly, and a man from the local newspaper. More friends of Amanda's. Some undergraduates, perhaps eager for the wine. And then, in a burst, as though they might all stick in the doorway, a crowd of people unidentified, at least by Toby. Soon the paintings were scarcely visible for the shoulders in front of them.

Mrs Roberts stood quietly in a corner. Edward Crane came up to her with a chair. 'As you obviously don't mean to circulate,' he said, 'I think you'd better be comfortable. After all, you're the star of this occasion.'

She smiled at him briefly before seating herself, small shoes together, hands folded in her lap. To Toby she said, 'I was glad to take the weight off my feet.'

He could see that Driffield was pleased, as he weaved his way among the guests. A red star appeared on yet another painting, then another. The room was growing hot and smoke-filled. Toby noticed that a good deal of wine was being drunk, but he took little himself. He wanted to keep a cool head.

It was hard to say who was playing host: certainly not Driffield. Either Amanda or Maisie.

At a quarter-past seven, just when some people were drifting away, an art critic whose face Toby recognised from a Sunday newspaper came in and was pounced upon by radiant Amanda. He went to the buffet, poured himself a drink, and set off on an amble round the walls. When he had completed this, he drew up another chair, sat down at Mrs Roberts' side and introduced himself.

She looked really flurried for the first time. 'I've heard your name,' she said.

'I expect a good many more people are going to have heard of you.'

'This is my son Toby.' This was more for something to say than for anything else.

The critic, a very tall man in glasses who was called Pollock, began to put her through a gentle interrogation. How had she begun? For how long had she been painting? Did she feel she had any special influences? Whom did she most admire?

Maisie, who had drawn near, looked delighted.

Mrs Roberts said she didn't really know much about art at all. She did read some art notices, but could not make out what anybody really liked.

'You shouldn't care what anybody likes,' he told her, 'just go ahead in your own way.' He was a nice man.

Llangain came up to Toby. 'Most interesting. Of course, I don't know much about it, but Mrs Ferrars can always put me on the right tracks. You've been down to Haddesdon, I believe?'

Toby said he had.

'Nice place. Did you meet Claire?'

'I don't think so.' He had only once heard the name.

'We live near Glemsford, not so far away. I really do admire your mother's work.' However, he bought nothing.

The pleasant critic rose and left. 'If we don't get a good notice there,' Maisie said excitedly, 'I shall be astonished. Of course,' she added, by way of touching wood, 'it may be crowded out by something else.'

A local photographer came to take pictures of Mrs Roberts. This flurried her again.

'Don't get up,' he said, 'I'd like you seated first. Then perhaps standing in front of one of the pictures.'

She obeyed meekly, letting him do with her as he pleased. He also took shots of some of the people remaining, of Toby talking to Amanda – he would have escaped this if he could – Maisie to Llangain. A local reporter came up, and induced Mrs Roberts to give him a somewhat monosyllabic interview.

The room was by now almost empty, and it was possible to see that two more paintings, small ones, had been sold. In all, seven out of fourteen.

'Well,' said Driffield, 'I fancy that's been a success. Congratulations, Mrs Roberts.'

With the press out of the way, she had recovered her former serenity.

Amanda bore down. 'Mrs Roberts, I think you've had about all you can take, and we don't want to hurry our dinner.' After they had made rather bemused good-byes, she swept Toby, Maisie and Mrs Roberts out to her car. 'You must see more of Peter,' she said to Toby, referring to the serpentine young man, 'he's coruscatingly brilliant. You've read his novel, of course?'

'I haven't, I'm afraid. But I will.'

'Good. In this life, one must learn to keep abreast.'

The driver took them to the University Arms, where she had booked a table. 'I think we'll go straight in, shall we?'

They passed through the cavernous lounge into the restaurant.

'You sit beside me, Mrs Roberts dear. Do you know you've had a success? Did Driffield tell you? I think this calls for champagne, doesn't it, Maisie?'

'I'm afraid I don't drink,' Mrs Roberts said timidly. Alone with them, she was forgetting her rôle of creative artist. Also she was very tired.

'Do you think, Mummy, that on this special occasion, you might allow yourself one small sip?'

'It will only make me tipsy.'

Amanda beamed, as if something clever had been said. 'It won't. You have it positively from me, and I'm never mistaken, am I, Maisie?'

'Never in this world,' Maisie replied, already intoxicated to be with Toby.

The champagne was brought, Mrs Roberts toasted; to Toby's surprise, she did drink half a glass of it. 'This is very nice!' she exclaimed.

'I expect it is, Mummy, after all that tea and cocoa.'

'Now it's a funny thing,' Amanda said, 'but I adore cocoa. I expect it's a throwback to my childhood. So few people seem to drink it nowadays, though.'

'It depends on how you make it,' said Mrs Roberts, on home ground. 'You must never let the milk boil or you get skin on it.'

The dinner was lavish. Also, to Toby's surprise (this was an evening for astonishment) his mother ate heartily. He guessed that it was out of pure relief. Besides, she had had a minimal lunch.

'Well,' said Amanda, 'we shall see the local paper tomorrow and a couple of reviews, I hope and pray, at the week-end.'

'I hope you know how grateful we are to you for all you've done,' Toby said.

'Me? I wouldn't have done anything if the cause wasn't worth it. Thank Maisie for the spade-work.'

'Thank you both,' said Mrs Roberts, 'this has been the most exciting day of my life, since—' She paused. 'Well, since Toby was born.'

Young men hate any reference to their infancy, and he flinched.

At last it was time to go. 'Are you sure you won't stay for the night?' Amanda pleaded. 'I can get you a room here and you can have a nice leisurely breakfast. I'm sure you're tired out.'

'No, thank you, but I can't. Stan – my husband – would be worrying himself stiff.'

'Telephone him!'

'We haven't got a telephone.'

'Then, bless you, you must have recovered the lost art of letter-writing,' said Amanda.

'Toby writes nice letters,' said Mrs Roberts.

They drove her to the station, and Toby saw her off on the train. He urged Maisie and her mother not to wait for him.

'Did you enjoy it all?' he said to Mrs Roberts. 'I thought it went off with a bang. And I was proud of you. Besides, you looked so nice.'

'Maisie always knows what's right,' she said.

He did not catch the bus, but walked briskly back to his college. Then he went to the library and consulted *Who's Who*.

'Llangain, Idris Daniel Falls, 4th Baron; *b.* 1898; *m.* Moira Susannah Powell; one *s.* one *d. Educ.:* Winchester and New College, Oxford.' He was a director of a merchant bank. No other occupation. No hobbies listed. '*Address:* Barden Manor, Glemsford, Suffolk. *Clubs:* Garrick, White's'

Well, it told Toby something.

9

Next day the local paper carried a handsome account of the show, but it was more of a gossip column than a review. It was not gossip about Mrs Roberts, who had apparently remained obdurate to all personal questions and had merely talked about her painting. There was a picture of her, somewhat self-consciously pointing to the largest of the canvases: and a picture of Toby, subtitled 'Artist's Undergrad Son'. It might have been worse so far as he was concerned, and he respected his mother for preserving the privacy of them both. Still, it was interesting enough to encourage visitors. He wrote straight off to her, enclosing the cutting.

Then there was the wait until the week-end. Maisie telephoned in excitement. One of the two London critics had not noticed the show at all, but Pollock had given it second place in his column. Here was high praise for the new 'Primitive'. He urged everyone who could get to Cambridge to do so.

'Isn't it marvellous, Toby?'

'Yes,' he said, 'Mummy is going to be as pleased as Punch. But there's something I want to say. Can you meet me for tea?'

Of course she could.

He had rehearsed what he was going to say, and for once he asked questions.

'You've been a blessing,' he said. 'But I have to know this. What has it all cost you?'

She blushed. 'Cost me?'

'Yes. The wine and cheese party. I can't believe Driffield paid for all that.'

'Then you're wrong,' she said triumphantly, 'or almost wrong. He paid for most of it. Mummy helped out a bit, but that was nothing. She was glad to do it.'

'I'd like to know what I owe her.'

'Mummy would have kittens if you asked her! Honestly, Toby, it was so little. She said she wanted to be in on the ground floor and that was her way of doing it. Purely selfish, darling.'

'If it was so little, how on earth does Driffield make his money?'

'He'll get his money back over this show, anyway. He's got private means, anyway.'

'And who paid for the printing of the invitations?'

'Driffield did, of course. It's customary.'

'I hope,' he said slowly, 'that you're telling me the truth.'

'I always tell the truth,' she said with mock indignation, 'it was rubbed into me from childhood.'

He knew it would be no use pursuing the matter; besides, he had not much money left. 'Thank your mother, then,' he said, 'very warmly, from me.'

Soon after that he went down for the Easter vacation.

Mrs Roberts was eager with her news. 'Wasn't it wonderful? Mr Pollock, I mean. And Mr Driffield wrote to say he'd sold all the pictures but three. It will be quite a little money coming in. And I've had people asking to see what else I've got.'

Mr Roberts still seemed bemused. 'It seems I've married a genius,' he said. 'I thought your mum was just following a hobby.'

'I'm not a genius,' said his wife, 'and nobody's said that I am. But it all gives me a reason for going on. And I'll be able to afford some canvases now; everything seems to dry out on plasterboard, though you can size it till you're silly. I did buy four canvases, just for the show.'

All this, however, looked like being a nine-days' wonder. But soon she received a letter – tentative – from a London dealer. He would like to see what she had. 'And the trouble is, I've got almost nothing left! The whole thing was so exciting it put me off my stroke.'

'That's no way to go on,' said Toby. 'She must get down to it again, mustn't she, Dad?'

He did not see Maisie during the holidays, and he received no invitation to Haddesdon. He was not too sorry; he was muddled about her in his mind. He found himself missing her, the curling smile, the way her eyes lit up as with electric batteries when something pleased her. But he threw himself into his work, and kept to his bedroom most of the day. Mrs Roberts did the usual housework routine, cooked with her usual concentration and skill, and in the afternoons and evenings went on painting.

However, he did write to Maisie, beginning his letter 'Pet', telling her about the projected visit from the dealer and about his mother's bout of work. 'She's doing some nice stuff, I think. And I am slaving away like a good boy. Miss you.'

Her reply began: 'Darling Toby.' She was glad to hear all his news and was thrilled by what he had said about his mother. The vacation would soon be over, and he would be able to tell her everything in more detail. 'I haven't bothered you or asked you down, because I knew you would be hard at it and wouldn't want to be disturbed. I shouldn't want in any way to be a drag on you. But I miss you too, and it won't be long now, will it?' He had finished his letter, 'Love'. She finished hers, 'Ever your Maisie'.

He was bothered by her reference to being 'a drag'. Had she sensed that he had been holding back? Her antennae were delicate, as he had often observed. He did not want her troubled in any way, for being troubled could only lead to a heightening of their relationship, and for this he simply was not ready. She had not directly put the least pressure upon him, except by her involvement in his mother's affairs and for that, seeing the latter's daily joy, he had to be grateful. He wanted Maisie simply to be serene; it was her serenity that made him so fond of her.

He noticed that she had written a P.S. overleaf. 'I went to see Driffield the other day. All the paintings except three have gone. I collected them and am keeping them for you, but if you want them I can easily run up with them.'

He did, of course, want them to add to his mother's stock, but since she was well ahead with her new work and since he did not want Maisie to come to London just then, he decided to say nothing.

He had returned to Cambridge by the time the dealer paid his visit. Maisie did not come to the station to meet him, but he telephoned her that evening. Her voice was eager, her tone a little too light. No, she couldn't see him for a couple of days. She had got so behindhand; she had let so much go last term, and she did not think her Director of Studies was very pleased with her. 'I don't want to disgrace Mother when the results come out.'

'You won't, pet. You're far too bright. What about Saturday? Four o'clock at The Whim?'

Two days later something very uncommon occurred. He received a telephone call from his mother, ringing from his father's shop. She was nervous about using the instrument and at first he had to tell her repeatedly to speak up. What she had to say was this: she was to have a London show, in a small arcade gallery just off Piccadilly. The dealer had been, and had praised her. 'He says it will be twenty per cent, though.'

'I don't care if it's a hundred per cent,' Toby said, 'just so the pictures are seen.'

'It's going to be in July,' Mrs Roberts said, 'so I'll have plenty of time to prepare. Oh, and Toby – I've had two letters from perfect strangers asking for pictures. Mr Driffield forwarded them.'

'You're wonderful,' he said, 'a wonderful woman. Bless you, and congratulations.'

'There was a reporter here yesterday, nosing around. I wouldn't tell him much. But he knew about your father's shop, and a bit about you.'

'Well, there's no harm in that,' Toby said, though he always felt that there was some.

When he met Maisie she had brought the paintings with her, and they took them straight back to his rooms. She rejoiced in his news. She was happy for him.

But her tone remained unnaturally light, and when he kissed her she made a brisk but not urgent response. They sat in the window for a while, looking out on to the chestnut trees in the court, which were just coming into pyramidal bloom, crimson, cream, freckled with bronze. Bob was crossing the grass with Rita, whose pregnancy was now obvious. Soon he heard their steps on the stairs, but they did not come up to him. 'Well, we had better go and have tea now, or we'll only be invaded by somebody.'

On their way downstairs they passed by Bob's door, which was slightly ajar.

A hysterical voice rose from behind it. 'You swine, I'm alone night after night after night, while you're in that damned lab! I sometimes think I'll go mad.'

'Oh, shut up, Reet' – and the door was kicked violently to.

Maisie and Toby did not speak till they were out in the court. Then she said, 'Oh, dear. Is it like that?'

'It has been, yes. She's resenting his work. I expect her condition's making her on edge. She pretends to believe that he's often not at the lab at all, that he's with other women. Which is so much drivel.'

'Better forget it,' said Maisie, 'shall we? Marriages can be horrible sometimes, I think.'

The fact that she appeared to made Toby suddenly perversely sure that marriage might be no such bad thing after all.

As they returned by King's Parade she told him shyly that Amanda was giving a party at Haddesdon to celebrate their Finals whatever the results might be, and that she hoped he would come. 'God,' said Toby, 'how shall we know there's anything to celebrate?'

'But that's just the point,' Maisie insisted. 'Mother says we may not have such a nice party when we know our fate, so we can be carefree while we don't. It's odd of her, but then she is rather odd.'

'I doubt whether I'll be able to be carefree,' said Toby.

But he was delighted by the thought of a further visit to Haddesdon.

'And this time you can stay the night,' she said. 'Would you like that?'

'Of course I should. It will be something to look forward to.'

After tea they walked in the beautiful weather under the bursting trees, along the Backs. He put his arm round her waist.

'No,' she said, 'this place is full of spies.'

'Does that matter?'

'A little, perhaps.'

He wondered, and knew he had put it to himself, vulgarly, what she was up to. She was holding back from him, though he guessed that she did not want to. What did she hope to achieve? To draw him still further on? If so, she was having some success, because he felt drawn.

They went as usual to the cinema, then to the café for eggs and chips. As usual, he bicycled back with her. She would not kiss him good-night, reiterating that the place was full of spies.

In the weeks intervening before his Finals, he saw little of Maisie. She, he believed, was straining to make up for lost time.

Meanwhile, he heard from his mother. Mrs Roberts had received an invitation to come to Haddesdon. She had refused, politely, but quite firmly, on the rather absurd excuse that she did not care to travel much these days. (Though Amanda had offered to send a car to pick her up at Mark's Tey.) Obviously she meant to draw the line somewhere. He was rather disappointed, but also a little relieved; whenever she was present he found himself compelled to keep a filial eye on her, and the fact was that he needed the use of his eyes for other things.

On the first day of the examinations, when he had recovered from the initial shock of believing that the papers must be written in some tongue never seen before, such as Thai or Aramaic, he found that there were at least three questions that he could answer adequately. He knew he was a good examinee; he actually got pleasure out of these tests even when, in the past, he had not been particularly competent at them. During the next few days he scribbled busily, going to bed early, taking long walks, making no attempt at last-minute looking-up. When at last the ordeal came to an end, he felt he must have a good chance of a 2.1.

He did not propose to go down from Cambridge till the results came out. In the meantime, there was Haddesdon.

With Maisie in the car from Sudbury, he asked her how she thought she had done. 'Oh, not too bad, I think,' she replied. 'There was a question on Lawrence, and I think I did decently there.'

'It will certainly be somebody's fault if you didn't,' he said, grinning.

In that uncertain spring, they had struck a beautiful day.

'Mother will be able to have her picnic,' said Maisie. 'And, by the way, don't you drink her sherry if you don't want it. I saw you make a horrible face last time. We've got everything else.'

They came to the house. Taking his suitcase, he followed Maisie indoors. Nobody else was about.

'They'll be in the garden already,' she said. 'I'll show you to your room, and then you come down as soon as you're ready.'

He paused at the foot of the stairs, in surprise and delight, to see two of his mother's paintings hung in a shaft of sunlight. He had feared that they had been destined for Amanda's attics. Or had they been hung because he was coming? But he did not believe she was a tricky woman.

His bedroom was small, but charming; he had never seen anything like it before, had never slept in a tester bed. It had its own bathroom.

'I'll leave you now,' said Maisie, accepting his grateful kiss, 'but don't be too long.'

Yet for a moment he stretched himself out on the bed, looking up at the flowered canopy, sprigged with green and pink. Outside the branches were stirring only slightly in the May breeze, sifting golden lights through the tracery of leaves. Somewhere a cuckoo was practising its minor thirds. 'The cuckoo sings all day at nothing In leafy dell alone,' he remembered. He thought it odd that Housman, so depressing, writing of suicides and hangings, should be so exhilarating when one was twenty plus.

He rose, straightened the bed, and unpacked his bag. He had dared to wear jeans and a cotton jersey for the trip down, but had brought his best suit in the pretty sure belief that it would be as well to change for dinner. He washed his hands, took a few stray bristles from his chin. If he had wanted it, he could have grown quite a thick reddish beard.

Maisie was waiting for him. 'What have you been doing? Dreaming?'

He smiled at her.

'Come into the garden,' she said.

'Maud,' he added.

10

At first it seemed to his dazzled eyes that there must be twenty or thirty people sitting on the lawn, which was spangled with the daisies Amanda would not have mown. Then he saw that there were about a dozen only. Nevertheless, he nearly felt shy, an emotion uncommon to him.

Amanda was sitting cross-legged among her court, wearing something like a djibbah in tones of orange and purple. The sun revealed the large pores of her skin, each containing a microdot of golden liquid. 'Come and sit by me, Toby, and in a moment I'll introduce you to all the people you don't know.' There were some he did, Crane, Peter Coxon, the critic Pollock, to whom he felt an impulse of unutterable gratitude, Adrian. 'I want to know right away how you felt you did. But mind you, we are not celebrating your results *at all*. We are celebrating because it's all over and you must be happy.'

He told her he felt he had done passably: 'Let's say that I think I'm unlikely to go down without a degree.'

She gave an incredulous crow. 'You've done splendidly. Don't pull the wool over my eyes. How's your dear Mamma? I hoped she would come down with you, but she wasn't to be flushed from coverts.'

Toby suddenly saw his mother as a vixen secret in its hole.

He greeted Crane and Adrian, was made known to the others. Some of the names he did not catch. However, there were several faces that he knew: an elderly and famous poet, a girl novelist who had recently achieved some notoriety, a minor film actor who played cads.

The cedar swept in its panchromatic magnificence over the grass. The may trees, red and white, were in full colour.

'I know your mother's going to have a show at the Arden Gallery,' said Pollock, 'I have my spies.'

'She owes it all to you.'

74

'Nonsense. She owes it all to herself. But don't let her be disappointed if London doesn't come up to Cambridge. There are more captious persons about.'

A manservant came out with a tray of drinks and served them all. 'Thank you, Scotch and water,' said Toby boldly.

'You see?' Maisie cried to her mother, 'I told you so.'

'No, honestly—' Toby began, but Amanda took no notice of him. 'Take your time, everyone,' she said, 'it's all cold food today, though I hope it'll be nice. And after lunch, Peter's going to read us the first chapter of his new book.'

Toby's heart sank a little. He was not good at quick aural comprehension, which was why he had attended so few lectures. He could listen to, and retain conversation though.

'And perhaps Edward will read us the first act of his play.'

'And perhaps Edward won't,' Crane said, 'saving your presence, Amanda. I read with extraordinary dullness. And anyway, you should know by now that I don't carry my collected works about on my person.'

She gave a shrug, and turned from him to Toby. 'Won't you miss Cambridge? It must feel a part of you by now.'

'Oh, I don't know,' said Toby, more talkative than usual, 'I've never made a large circle of friends – only Adrian and a couple of others – and I've had nothing to do with undergraduate activities. There are times when I feel like a pariah.' He pronounced it to rhyme with Maria.

Amanda at once, and without emphasis, corrected him. She was above all things an instructress. 'Pār'iah, dear. But I don't know why you should feel like that.'

Toby had blushed down the length of his neck. He had often believed that he would rather have been found in bed with a boy (in which activity he would not have had the slightest interest) than make a slip in pronunciation. This was why he kept a dictionary constantly by him.

'One says silly things,' he replied vaguely. He felt that they were all laughing at him; Crane, the serpentine Coxon stirring in his coils, even Adrian.

He tried to divert himself by noticing Maisie closely. She had come to sit beside him, and for the first time he knew that she was expensively dressed. Formerly, he had not been sure. She wore a black skirt, flared over the hips, narrowed towards the hem, a marvellous blouse of white silk and lace, high at the neck, secured by a huge jet brooch. All her eyes were for him, and he hated to think she was contemplating his mistake.

But there now occurred a diversion.

Out of the house came a tall, big-built girl with very fair hair tied in a pony-tail, wearing a white shirt and fawn jodhpurs. 'Hullo, everyone!'

'Where's the horse?' cried Amanda

'No horse. These are safer wear on a bike.'

She came across the lawn, her boots hard on the daisies.

'I think you know everyone,' said Amanda, when the girl had made her round of greetings, had kissed her and Maisie and Edward. 'Except Toby Roberts. Toby, this is Claire Falls.'

Toby placed her at once.

The girl plumped down by him. 'I've heard all about your super mother. I wish I'd been to the show. Daddy went.'

He saw that she was handsome, in a bold, almost equine way. She had large blue eyes, lighter than Maisie's, a finely-curved nose, rather a long chin. She accepted a dry Martini from the manservant, returned her attention to Toby. 'Of course, I don't know about pictures. But I love what Amanda's got. All those little girls in pink!'

'I wish you had come too,' he said, and she held his eyes. He noticed that she had finely shaped but rather large hands, and guessed that there was a horse somewhere.

'Are you at a university too?' he asked, making conversation.

'Me? Oh, I'm too dense. I was finished in Switzerland, and finished, I think, is the right word. No, I muck around a bit with antiques, and that's all.'

'I don't believe that.'

His mind was busy. She would be the Honourable Claire Falls, and he was not dishonest enough to pretend that this did not impress him. Llangain's daughter. A little older than himself? Perhaps a year or so.

Maisie said something to him, and he had to ask her to repeat it. The blue stare of those slightly exopthalmic and hypnotic eyes still held him.

'Yes, pet?'

76

'It was nothing.' But he saw that, just for the flash of a second, her face was open with dreadful astonishment.

'No, what was it?'

'Just something about Edward. I don't know what he's got to be so modest about.' She rose lightly. 'I must circulate.' She went to sit by Crane.

Claire called for another drink. She seemed a thirsty girl. 'Time for just one more,' Amanda called, 'then lunch. Edward, you?'

'Certainly.'

'Peter! Peter! Oh, I do wish I were Madame Verdurin and had a little bell to summon you all to order.'

Soon the maid came out to lay a big cloth upon the lawn, in which Amanda assisted her, and then to lay silver and glass. Next, the man, with one tray after another.

'Now this is going to be very rustic,' Amanda said, 'and if any of you have sore seats you can go in and get cushions.'

Toby felt that the spread before them was far from rustic. There was a great mound of *mousse de foie gras*, a lobster salad, garnet, coral and pearl between its leafy folds, two roast chickens, a raised pie of some kind, three elaborate puddings, leaking drops of gold. There were various salads of other kinds, and there was champagne, a drink he did not much like although he realised its ceremonial significance.

Maisie came back to sit beside him, but a little removed: Claire stayed where she was.

'Now the first glass,' Amanda announced, 'shall be raised to Toby and Maisie. All luck to them, but we're not celebrating the luck. We're celebrating that they have come through their trials.'

Claire, like Maisie, was a fairly hearty eater. After a while she said to Toby abruptly, 'You got any money?'

He was taken by utter surprise. 'Money? What do you mean?'

'I don't mean are you *starving*,' she said, as though scornfully (he did not see how he could be with all this abundance before him), 'I meant, have you any spare cash? Because I've got a very hot tip for the Derby. For Maisie, too.'

'You know I don't bet,' Maisie said.

'It adds to the excitement of life,' said Claire, 'and we could all do with that.'

Edward had moved in. 'I might take you up. I bet precisely twice a year, on the Derby and the National. Though to do the latter is ridiculous.'

She expatiated upon her tipped horse.

He wrote the name down solemnly in his pocket book. 'I may bless you or I may not,' he said.

After lunch, when they were all feeling satiated, they lit cigarettes and Peter Coxon was called upon to perform. Toby did not like the sound of his book at all: it seemed an improbable cross between Virginia Woolf and Kafka, and the hero was called 'S': very unattractive, he felt. The novelist, for all his slightness of build, read in a surprisingly deep voice, and seemed to love every word of it. During the reading Toby permitted his hand to rest on Maisie's. He felt vaguely that he owed her something.

'It's a remarkable thing,' Amanda pronounced, when the reading was done, 'it is like *nothing* else.' (It was.) 'Well, when we've had coffee, I expect you'd all like to go for a stroll. Stretch our legs. Oh, look how stiff you are! I told you you should have cushions.'

The unattractive relics of attractive food spread out before them were shortly borne away.

'I'll walk with you, Peter,' Maisie said vivaciously, 'I want to discuss your book. I like it, but it puzzles me.'

'It is meant to,' he replied darkly.

Amanda brought up the girl novelist. 'You must talk to Janet, Toby. Her name is on everyone's lips, isn't it, dear?'

Janet had a small surly face, a mane of beautiful black hair. 'They say I'm smootty,' she said (she had a broad North Country accent) 'but I don't see it. I'm only telling the truth. Just as Balzac did.'

They walked beneath the hawthorns, nothing in common between them. After a while Claire approached them. 'Getting on all right?' She was nothing if not direct.

'Fine,' Toby replied.

'Come down to the stream.'

He had not known that there was one, but there, right at the bottom of the garden, it ran between irises and kingcups, shallow, twinkling in mossy-gold over the pebbles. 'Of course,' said Claire, 'Amanda had it made. How you make a stream I don't know, but she did. Isn't she a marvel?'

Toby agreed that she was. 'And Maisie's a marvel too,' Claire added. 'She fixed up your show, didn't she? Daddy says so.'

Toby thought about her father. A merchant banker. It sounded very splendid. He wondered vaguely whether he would like such a career for himself, and wondered also if it always demanded a facility with figures. That might exclude him from any such dream. Mathematics had been his poorest subject, the mere sight of a figure in a telephone book hard to retain in his head, so that he would find himself consulting it again and again while dialling. It made dates hard for him to remember. 'She certainly did.'

'Tiddlers!' Claire squatted on the bank. 'I used to catch them in jam-jars, only there was nothing else to do after that but to put them back. Take them home, and they die on you.'

'I think fishing is cruel,' Janet said, 'just as cruel as fox-hunting. If you think the fox enjoys it, why shouldn't the fish?'

'My kind of fishing was harmless enough.'

'Have you ever gone hunting?' Janet asked, nostrils flaring. She was instinctively hostile to Claire.

'Of course I have. But I don't make a habit of it. Anyway, one so seldom finds.'

'Finds what?'

'A fox.'

'I don't know how you can.'

'You don't like me,' said Claire, 'some people don't.' She gave a wide smile, moved off.

'Hooffy,' said Janet.

All the guests drifted back to sit again under the cedar. 'We'll do something very old-fashioned,' said Amanda, 'we'll play Authors. Now, everyone try to find a writer beginning with A. There are more Bs, so you won't get far.'

They played the game until tea. Then, one by one, some of them got up to go, until at last nobody was left but Toby, Claire, and Edward Crane.

'Isn't Janet a bully?' Claire asked Maisie. 'I'm sure I'd loathe her horrible book.'

'You might give it a try.' Maisie was bland. 'Mother thinks highly of it, though she says it's a bit raw.'

'Claire! You're staying to dinner?' Amanda asked.

'Can't, thanks all the same. Mummy's got guests.'

Edward said, 'I'm staying overnight. If you like, Toby, I'll drive you back to Cambridge tomorrow. I've got to go there myself.'

Toby thanked him, though he guessed that Maisie would be disappointed not to take him to the station. The look of amazement that he had detected so briefly on her face now seemed like a hallucination. She was quite composed, relaxed.

Claire had another drink, then said that she really must go. She added to Toby, 'I'll be searching the papers for those results. And for Maisie's. You'll just see if I don't.'

She made her good-byes. Toby watched the iron set of her back as she made her way to the house.

'A nice girl,' Amanda said, 'not literary or artistic, but like a breath of fresh air. She just drops in and out of here as she pleases. Mind you, she's pretty tied. Moira's so slack that she has to entertain for Idris. Her brother's away in the Army of Occupation. I don't believe she likes it much, though she'd do most things for her father.'

The evening was quiet, and they played no further games. Edward spoke of his new play.

'When's it coming off?' Toby asked eagerly.

Edward grinned. 'You must never say that to a playwright. The last thing he wants it to do is to come off. You must say, "come on".'

'How silly of me. But then I am pretty obtuse.'

'Are you?' Edward asked, looking into his face. 'Do you know, I shouldn't have thought so.'

Dinner was a light meal, and for this Toby was grateful. He was still feeling a trifle bloated from his lunch. They listened to some music on Amanda's record player. Debussy: 'L'Ile Joyeuse'. Maisie sat cross-legged on the floor, seemingly absorbed. When it had come to an end she said, 'It's rapturous, isn't it? I don't know what they're going to do when they get to the Isle – something disreputable, I shouldn't be surprised – but very beautiful and exciting all the same.'

'Well,' Amanda said at last, 'I'm quite sleepy with all that fresh air. If you'll excuse me, I think I'll go up to bed. Don't hurry yourselves, though. Help yourselves to drinks. Toby, breakfast at any time from nine o'clock on. Tell Sukie what you want before you go up.'

She drifted away, sweeping the djibbah around her.

Now Edward was all attention to Maisie, of whom he appeared

extremely fond. How were . . . ? He mentioned friends of hers that Toby did not know. What would she do with herself now?

She said she had not the least idea. 'But I know what I'm going to do immediately, follow Mother's example and take to my bed. Good-night, both of you.'

'Good-night, pet,' Toby said boldly, and her eyes lit up.

'That's a charming little girl,' Edward said, when she had gone, 'if I were twenty-five years younger I should go for her. I should be almost tempted to do so now, if age and a sense of the ridiculous didn't weigh on me. Men never get too old to be attracted, you know, even though I suppose you believe that the capacity to do so ends at forty. I did when I was your age.'

'Maisie is sweet.'

'Yes, she is,' the other said gravely, and then said no more. Not much later, after one whisky, they both went up for the night, Toby taking a book with him – Janet's. He did not think he would sleep much.

He had been in bed no more than half an hour, when there was a gentle tap at the door, immediately upon which Maisie slipped in. She was in her dressing-gown. Her face was flushed, resolute, excited.

'Why, hallo pet!' Toby exclaimed, trying not to appear as if he thought this very unusual.

'Sh. Don't make a noise. Do you mind?'

'Of course not,' he said. She came to sit down on the edge of the bed.

'Listen, I want to talk to you. I have to do it quickly. Do you want me? Because if you do . . . You see, I've been thinking it must be that which has made you so, so odd lately. As though you were a million miles away from me. Perhaps you thought I was cold to you, but it wasn't that, I swear it. Do you want me?' She was trembling.

Of course Toby did. It was months since he had even had a casual pick-up. He was frightened, though; he knew he was to be the first with her. He stroked her gently along her spine and she quivered like a startled mare. 'Naturally. But are you sure?'

'If you're sure, I am.' She leaned over him and switched off the light. The moon was shining through a chink in the curtains, and he could see her taking off her dressing-gown. Then her nightdress.

He thought she looked miraculously beautiful, and his heart was pounding.

'Come on in then,' he said, opening the bedclothes, 'or you'll catch cold.'

It was frantically exciting for him to hold her in his arms; yet a colder part of his mind was calculating the consequences of what he was about to do. Should he, indeed, do anything *in Amanda's house*? He recalled old laws of hospitality. And if he did, would he not be hopelessly committed? His brain was racing.

'Mother's room is at the other end of the house,' she whispered. Her teeth were chattering.

'And where's yours?'

'Next door.'

Toby wondered. But he struggled out of his pyjamas, still under the tent of the bedclothes. It was irresistible.

They lay naked, their sweat commingled.

She said, 'You were pretending to like Claire because you thought I wouldn't. I know she likes you.'

Silly, Toby thought. Bad tactics.

'Silly,' he said aloud. But now he tried both to soothe and to rouse. He kissed her nipples and felt the shock of delight run through her. He stroked her down the length of her spine. She had a peculiarly sweet smell, like hawthorn flowers. Trying to forget the vision of Amanda bursting in upon them (though he did not think she would) he took her right into his arms, and rose above her. In the moonlight he could see that her mouth was tight.

After a while, because both were supple, he laid her side to side with him and made her put her leg over his thigh. 'Better?' He could kiss her now.

'I love you, I love you,' she said.

She gave only a small cry, both of pain and pleasure.

'Pet,' he said, as usual.

He drew away from her, and pulled her head on to his shoulder.

When she had gone, a sordid thought struck him, and he lit the lamp. But there were only, on the sheet, two minute specks of blood, which he did not think would arouse suspicion. The desire to think was upon him, but, more urgently, the desire to sleep. It was to the latter that he yielded.

He woke in the dawn, scared of what he had done. Maisie was far removed from the casual girls whom he had taken from time to time, merely for his own easing. Why had he been put next to her room? Was it conceivable that Amanda had wanted this? Surely not. If she had, why? He had nothing to offer. She might have been a pandar to one or to all of Maisie's longings. On the other hand, thinking that things had not gone far with them, she might have acted out of simple trust. He did not know how he was to face Maisie tomorrow. He did not get much sleep before seven o'clock, and from then until breakfast-time, when the maid came in with a tray (it had been given him to understand that he need not get up, nobody did) slept like a dead man.

II

When he went downstairs into the drawing-room he found Maisie waiting for him, eyes bright, a glow on her whole face like sunset over snow. She was wearing the same blouse and skirt as yesterday (for luck?). She put both her hands in his. 'Toby, Toby, Toby, Toby, Toby.'

'Dear,' he said.

There was no time for more, since Amanda came in with Edward.

'Another lovely day! You'll have a beautiful ride back.'

'We shall leave at eleven,' said Edward, 'take it easy and stop for a pint on the way. Will that suit you, Toby?'

He said it would suit him. He did not know whether he wanted to get away, or to stay for ever.

'Now don't you start worrying,' Amanda said, with the emphasis of a seer, 'everything is going to be *all right*.'

'I'm sure it will,' Maisie said.

When they left, he kissed her openly. 'Now you may kiss me,' said Amanda, 'I grant the privilege sometimes, though it seems to be more and more customary these days. Eighteenth century, isn't it?'

He put his lips to her porous cheek. What was to happen, he didn't know; but he felt a surge of euphoria, of the happy-go-lucky.

'I'll be in touch,' Maisie said. 'When are you going home?'

'When the lists come out. I haven't the guts just to ignore them as Bob does, but then, Bob's safe.'

He and Edward drove through the mild morning, under Constable skies. Edward talked about actors and actresses whom he knew; apparently he liked precisely three of them. He expressed the view that far too many tried to think, and that thinking was not their business; he much disliked the ones who would want a certain word changed because they 'could not say it'.

Toby, a little beglamoured by all this, was content to listen.

'Oddly enough,' Edward went on, 'I hate the ambience of the theatre. I hate rehearsals, though I think there might be the devil to pay if I didn't go to them. I hate going backstage afterwards, reciting polite insincerities. I hate the smell of grease-paint. I am only happy out front. And not often then.'

He was driving at a slowish, steady pace. He had obviously timed the whole journey. When they got to Linton he looked at his watch. 'What do you say to a drink now?'

They went into a small, unspoiled public house, into the saloon bar where no one else was about. Each had a pint of bitter.

'Now,' said Edward, in quite a different voice from the one he had used earlier, 'I am going to talk to you from the tower of my age. Let me tell you that I observe things. I've been observing you.'

Toby was alarmed. He said nothing.

'Are you fond of Maisie?'

'Anyone would be.'

'Don't deceive her, then. Break with her if you have to, but don't deceive her, because she couldn't bear that. I don't suggest that you do: but I do suggest that you might.'

'It isn't all that serious—' Toby began.

'To her it is. Look, I'm well into life. I don't call myself a wise man, but I've learned a thing or two on the way. Furthermore, I don't much mind intruding, when I think it is a good thing. Shall I go on?'

'Of course,' Toby said, 'but I'm not sure what all this is about.'

The sunlight sparked with orange the beer in their tankards. There was a strong smell in the air, of ale and soap and apples.

'Men can hurt women so terribly. I've done so in my time, though you may not think so. If the women don't cry, the men think they've got away with it; and if they do cry, then they regard it as intolerable behaviour which frees them from obligation.'

Toby felt all this was fascinating, but that it did not apply to himself, and he could not think why Edward should suppose it did.

'Maisie is a very delicate creature, and she's in love with you. As I inferred to you, if I had been your age I should have been in love with her. She wouldn't cry. She would go on smiling. But she would be unable to endure it. Amanda is quite different, a different kind altogether. Her husband, who looked frail and etiolated but was not, was consistently unfaithful to her; and when this fact dawned on her, which it did remarkably late, she merely took up other interests.

85

Hence her circle. I think it was a relief to her when he died, since she no longer had to worry about him at all. He left her very well-off, and she had her court, and she had her children, who, by the way, with the exception of Maisie, are Philistines and can't stand arty conversation. My wife was much the same, though she was extremely beautiful. But she didn't die, she left me for a stock-broker. That was before I had some success: I think she might have liked the glamour of what I had, though *I* didn't. But I've no idea now.'

'Edward—' Toby began, the name slipping out, 'I do appreciate all you've been telling me. But I assure you, I mean well by Maisie.'

'Try loving her, then.'

'Don't I?'

'I think not. Or not yet. I tell you, she seems serene always, but she is a mass of exposed nerve-ends. She wouldn't be, if she were reassured. She isn't likely to grow into a neurotic woman, if that's what you're thinking.'

'I wasn't thinking. At least, not about that. Maisie's sweet.'

'She is more than that. Well, we'd better finish our glasses and be moving on. I've got to be at King's by 12.45.'

They drove the rest of the way almost in silence. Toby knew there had been an intrusion, but mysteriously he didn't resent it. Or was it impossible to resent an intruder who didn't in the least mind whether he was resented or not?

When Edward had dropped him in the Market Square, he went off to have coffee and a sandwich. He had much to think about. The memory of the night was a delight. And a triumph. Yes, she was sweet! It was everyone's word for her. He wondered what Edward had seen, to make him say what he did. A fleeting look upon Maisie's face? But there had been no cause for it. He was glad to have the information about Amanda: he had wondered what her husband had been like. Thoughts of Haddesdon came thick and fast, like the daisies on the lawn. It was, to him, an enthralling place. But could other enthralments lie elsewhere? He knew the world was his oyster, though it might take a stiff oyster-knife to open it up.

The windows of the café steamed up, girls went by in premature summer frocks.

He had a sudden conviction that the word 'girl' was still magical to Edward, and wondered what he did for a sex-life. Of course the intrusion had not been without its underlying self-interest: or if not that, without an underlying meaning. He stopped thinking about Edward to think exclusively about Maisie. Perhaps Edward had done some good.

The thought occurred to him for a fleeting moment: he hoped Maisie would not become pregnant like Rita. But it was only for a moment. He doubted it, and he was not a worrier.

He went to supper next night with Rita and Bob. Mrs Champion had gone to a neighbour, her husband was on duty. Rita played hostess: she had taken much trouble. A lace plastic tablecloth, flowered mats, a vase of daffodils. Toby did not think she was looking particularly well. Her face was drawn above her body's bulk and, despite her hospitable airs, she wore a look of permanent irritation.

'Would you think he *still* spent half his evenings in that lab?' she asked him, as if aware that he had heard the exchange on the staircase, though he knew she could not be.

'I've got some work to finish, Reet,' said Bob, 'I'll soon be through.'

She said vivaciously to Toby, 'How's Adrian? I think he's such a lamb.'

'I saw him at the week-end. He's OK.'

'I think he's like a film star,' she said dreamily, as if she could imagine nothing better. Perhaps she could not, Toby thought, and he believed this marriage was going to be a calamity.

'I hope you can eat steak and kidney pud.'

'Nothing nicer.'

'Well, I hope it's nice. I'm not the cook my mum is.'

It was not very nice, but he was hungry.

'This is a poky place,' said Rita. Two up, two down. They would have to have the baby in with them. 'Sometimes I feel I can't stand it.'

'Well,' said Bob, 'you never can stand much, can you, Reet?'

'Is that meant to be a crack?'

'Not particularly.'

'Look,' Toby said, 'when Bob's results come through, and none of us are in the slightest doubt what they will be—'

'I am,' Bob said.

'—things will become much clearer for both of you. It can't have been much good up to now.'

'Mind you,' said Rita filially, 'Mum and Dad have done all they could. They've been angels in their way. But it drags on and on, the waiting. I feel like it will never end.' She meant her pregnancy.

'I'll wash up,' Bob said rather abruptly, 'and you two can natter. Then we'll play some records.'

When he had cleared the table and left them, Rita said, 'He always helps me – when he's in. Y'know, he likes washing-up. I don't mind cooking, but I can't bear getting grease on my hands. Is Adrian really going to become a priest?'

'Oh, yes.'

'I think it's a waste. He won't marry, ever, will he?'

'So far as one can see, no. But life has its surprises.'

'I don't think anything is ever going to surprise me again,' Rita said forlornly.

'Oh, come. You've an excitement to look forward to.'

'Cooped up with a yelling baby and all those nappies?'

He was as embarrassed as it was possible for him to be. 'I expect it will work out.'

Rita was smoking one cigarette after another. He was sure that it was bad for her.

Following his thought she said defensively, 'My doctor says I shouldn't make an effort to stop. It would only take it out of my nerves. Tell me more about Adrian. Has he never had a girl?'

'I wouldn't know.' His first impressions of her were entirely dissipated by now.

'I bet he hasn't. I bet you haven't, either,' she said with a fugitive gleam.

'You may bet,' Toby replied.

'Oh, you oyster! You are an oyster, aren't you, Toby? We all talk to you, and you just listen.'

He had listened to Edward.

Soon Bob came back, which brought an end to her probings. He put very loud rock-and-roll records on the gramophone, which effectively stopped her talking for some time. Then he brought in beer, and Rita took her full whack. She wore a reckless look, as if she wanted to impress upon them that she would do precisely as she pleased.

Toby was glad when the evening ended.

The day his results were due to appear was chilly, with a slight drizzle of rain. When he thought the time was near, he went to the Senate House to see the postings. There was a small crowd waiting, edgy, impatient.

At last the lists were up, and he pressed forward to see them. He studied the 2.1s, and his heart sank. His name was not there. Next, the 2.2s. Not there either. He re-read them frantically, thinking that in his anxiety he might have missed something. Then, at last, almost as a joke, he scanned the Firsts. There it was, Roberts, T. H. He could hardly believe it. Disbelief was so powerful an emotion that it obscured all others: even joy. A young man whom he knew congratulated him. So it had to be true.

He was released from the trance. He almost ran to the Post Office and sent a wire to his mother. 'Have got a First. Back tomorrow.'

As he had expected, his mother was not so much excited by the fact of his First as by the fact that he had got a degree at all. Nobody else in her family had ever had the chance. 'Well,' she said, 'well. Your dad will be on top of the world.' And indeed, Mr Roberts, returning at that moment from the shop, seemed to be.

'This calls for a celebration. Will it be in the papers?'

'In *The Times* tomorrow, I expect,' said Toby, who was by now feeling all the euphoria of success.

'Well, that's one thing we're never short of in this house, news-papers, I mean.'

They drank whisky that evening, and Mr Roberts marvelled. 'What a year we've had, eh? What with you and your mum.'

'Did you expect this?' Mrs Roberts asked.

'No. I didn't even think to look for my name up there, until the end.'

'Will it make a difference to your prospects?'

'I don't know. I shall go down and see Dr Hartford in a few days.'

The results were indeed in *The Times*. They brought, by midday, wires from Amanda and Maisie and, more surprisingly, one from Claire. 'I told you I'd be keeping my eyes out. Thrilled congratulations. See you both soon.' He supposed she meant him and Maisie.

The other results came out little by little. Bob, of course, had a First. Well, Toby thought, that ought to keep Rita quiet. But Maisie was another matter. By her standards, she had failed miserably. Only a 2.2. Toby thought guiltily that her involvement in the affairs of his mother had been much to blame.

He wrote to her. 'You're not to worry, pet. There is always another time, if you want to take it. I know what a disappointment it will be to you, but worse things happen at sea. It can't matter materially to you – though I know that's poor consolation – but it does to me. I'm going to be in Cambridge next week, seeing Hartford, probably Wednesday. Perhaps you'll join me there. I expect you saw that Bob did exactly what we thought he'd do. And it matters very much to him. Forget now about Lawrence, Jane Austen and George Eliot. About both Eliots. Cheer up now. I'll soon be seeing you. Adore you. Toby.'

'Adore', he thought, was always a weaker word than 'love', though he told himself that he had pretty well burned his boats. Of the wire from Claire, of course, he said nothing. But he could not help wondering whether, if the academic life was not open to him, Llangain might not be able to do something to help.

12

He met Maisie at the Blue Boar, where they were to dine. He could well afford this, since his mother had insisted on making him a celebratory present of twenty-five pounds from the proceeds of her painting.

Maisie was wearing the same blouse and skirt, but also a broad-brimmed hat with a black ribbon round it. Beneath it her hair curled tightly and close to her cheeks, looking, as always, as if it were slightly damp. The small round tendrils might have been newly washed, or else glistening with the sweats of night. She was filled with gaiety. 'Another great occasion! Aren't we having a lot of them?'

He had news for her. He had been that day to see Hartford, who had told him he thought the college would grant a research studentship, and had advised him to work at London University under Professor Tiller.

She exclaimed, 'Are you going to try for a PhD?'

'I don't know. It would take about three years, and I think I must make some money before then. A studentship might go some way, but not far enough. Besides, I'd want to move into lodgings of my own, somewhere near Gower Street.' This thought had only just a second before occurred to him.

'Your mother will be sad,' said Maisie.

'I don't think so. I shall go home as often as I'm used to doing. Look, pet, you'd better order. And do yourself handsomely, because I'm in funds.'

She took him at his word. They had half a bottle of Châteauneuf du Pape – 'Not a whole one,' she said, 'remember, I've got to drive.'

They had both settled down into something curiously like domesticity. Though he wanted her again, he could wait. But next time he would take no chances. He thought of Bob and Rita, and was disturbed.

The half-bottle did not go far enough, so he ordered another. 'You can have one glass,' he said, 'and I'll drink the rest. I'm feeling exuberant.'

Coffee was on the table before she told him what was uppermost in her mind. 'I've been thinking,' she began – which was obvious. 'Could we manage a week in Paris soon? I know a very cheap place, but very nice, on the Left Bank, in the Rue des Écoles. It wouldn't be grand, darling, but it would cost us so little!'

This, he told her, though the idea attracted him, he would not be able to afford.

'Please, please let me pay for it,' she said almost feverishly, covering his hands with her own, 'it would be just another celebration. Please let us go to France.'

He told her he would not let her pay for him. She had done too much already.

He was prudish about money. He would never have left a bus without paying his fare, if he had not given a coin on his behalf to his neighbour next to him. But also, he believed that the money of others had its lianas upon the spirit.

'If you're going to be silly about just a few pounds—'

'I am, rather, I'm afraid.'

'Because you know perfectly well that I'm not short of it. And if you prefer it that way, it can be a long-term loan.'

He smiled at her air of businesslike professionalism. 'What would your Mamma have to say?' he temporised.

'She might not like it much,' Maisie replied honestly, 'but she'd come round to it. She trusts you,' she added, rather naïvely. Toby wondered that Amanda should.

Paris and Maisie, of course, had their own allure. He had never been abroad before, except on a week-end trip with Adrian to Wimereux. 'Will you let me think it over?'

'Don't think too long! I want it so much. You do care what I want?'

'You know I do. All the same . . .'

He was, even now, resisting total committal with all his strength. But yes, he did want to go. They would sit on the café terraces. They would visit Notre-Dame, the Sainte-Chapelle, the Louvre, walk in the Champs-Élysées. See the Carnavalet, which might be helpful to him in his work, the Place de la Bastille.

Now he told her something he had hitherto kept back: he had written ten pages of *Saint-Just*. 'Mind you, I don't know whether I can keep it up. It may take me quite three years, and could be a flop even then. I expect it will be.'

'Then you've got to come to Paris! Sooner or later, you'll have to work there.'

He mused. 'I suppose I shall.'

'You can get grants for that, can't you, later on?'

He said that probably he could.

'I am so happy,' said Maisie. The wine she had drunk had flushed her cheeks with its own rosiness, making her eyes seem preternaturally bright. He wished he could have her that night.

She continued to prattle about Paris, weaving a glittering golden web of pleasures to come, but soon he stopped her.

'Let's shelve the thought for the moment, shall we? I promise I'll try to see my way.'

He changed the subject to Bob and Rita, and she was instantly absorbed and sympathetic. 'Is it really going to turn out so badly? Women are often very odd when they're expecting a baby,' she said, as from a world of experience. 'When it comes, things may be better for Bob,' she added. 'I do so like him, even though he *will* call me Maise.'

Toby said Bob was likely to have a brilliant career, which even Rita would be unable to lay waste, though she might wreck his personal life. 'She's taken a violent fancy to Adrian, too.'

'She'll get over that. Besides, it's not the slightest use.' She said suddenly, her mood souring, 'Oh, lives, lives, lives. What does it matter if we wreck them, if we can have some happiness along the way?'

'That's not like you, pet.'

'Lots of things about me aren't like me. You'll find out.'

The mood was only fleeting: soon it passed, and she was bright again. She lived on joy, Toby thought, and a spring of remorse, coming from some underground and mysterious well, for a moment chilled him.

When they came out of the hotel she stepped before him off the pavement and was nearly run down by a speeding car. She fell back into his arms; she was trembling. 'A close shave,' she said. 'Let me lean against the wall. I'll be all right in a minute.'

'Come back inside.' He, too, was shaken. 'I'll give you some brandy.'

'No. If I do, I shall make you miss your last train.'

'That doesn't matter. I want to make sure that you're fit to drive.'

He could feel the furious beating of her heart. Her teeth were chattering. 'I can always drive. I can't do much, but I can do that.'

She slid down to the pavement and sat with her legs crossed and her head low. People passing by looked at them curiously, obviously wondering if she were drunk. Toby stood above her, not knowing what to do. 'I could get you a room here for the night. You could telephone your mother.'

'I'll be all right in a minute. I'm sorry to present such a horrid spectacle.'

He knew how awful it would have been had he lost her, especially in this ghastly way. 'Come inside,' he reiterated. But she had recovered herself, springing up from her ankles with steadiness.

'I'm quite all right now. You must catch your train.'

He hugged and kissed her. Her whole body had quietened. When he took her to her car, he saw that the very sight of it was a consoling force. Yes, she could drive, whatever else she could not do.

'It's been a wonderful evening, darling,' she said, 'and we won't let the last bit spoil it. You will think about Paris?'

'About Paris and about you.'

He was only just in time at the station.

In the early dawn, he awoke from a horrible dream. Maisie was lying broken and disjointed in the gutter. Her big hat had rolled from her head and her hair was matted with blood. She seemed to have no face. There was no one in the street, and the hotel was dark.

He got half-way out of bed, thinking that he must telephone her; remembered that there was no telephone in the house, and that even if he got into his clothes and went out, the shop would be shut. Slowly, reality dawned; but he was still sweating with terror, and had to sit bolt upright till the dream's vivid impression had partly died away. He did not sleep again until it was light.

But in the meantime his thoughts had steadied. Paris? Perhaps, but not yet. He must put it off; there was the whole of the summer before them. There was his mother's show at the beginning of July, and there would be much to do. He could hear Maisie begging him,

94

'Please . . . please . . .' and even now she still seemed broken and bloodied. But his mind was made up.

Next morning he did go to the shop, where he telephoned to Haddesdon. Maisie answered him. 'What's the matter?' she said, sounding alarmed.

'Nothing, but I wanted to be sure you'd got back safely.'

'Of course I did. Why shouldn't I?'

'Well, you were shaken up.'

'And I unshook. I told you, I'm perfectly all right in a car. Darling, it was a lovely evening. Have you thought any more about Paris?'

He told her his decision. Late July, perhaps, if she had no other plans.

She said she would make no other plans. Amanda was going on a cruise round the Greek islands, and wanted her to go with her; but she would be acceptant enough if Maisie said no. 'She's always acceptant. That's why I feel I can't really do too much for her.'

This was the first indication Toby had had of the depth of her filial feeling; and he thought that was why she had been so absorbed in his own. Amanda had always seemed to him a woman to provoke liking, but scarcely love. She was agreeable, she was bossy, she was kind, but she was lacking in allure. What had she been like as a young woman? Handsome, perhaps, gipsy-like, her great load of hair untouched by grey?

When he had rung off, he went home for his breakfast. He had not realised that it was still so early, that it could not have been more than half-past eight when he put through the call.

Mrs Roberts was cooking sausages and bacon, and the smell was a comfortable one. She did sausages the way he liked them, just bursting.

When he was half-way through the meal Toby said, 'Mummy, I think I shall go off to Paris for a week when your show's over.'

'Who with? Adrian?'

'Maisie, as a matter of fact.'

She frowned, poised between disapproval and satisfaction. 'That seems a queer arrangement. What will Mrs Ferrars think?'

'There will be nothing to think.'

'I don't know that I should like it, if I was her.'

'Don't be Victorian, Mummy.'

'I'm not quite old enough to be Victorian, and you ought to know it. What about your old History?'

Toby smiled at her, but said nothing more at the time.

Afterwards he went upstairs for a thorough inspection of her new work. The paintings seemed to him charming, having a new authority which perhaps had come to her with her modest success.

She had, as she promised, painted the Backs, river and flowers and young men lolling on the grass. She was so adept now at giving her figures an impression of liveliness that the uninstructed might have believed that she could have made academic sketches if she chose. There was one rather large painting of a girl who might have been Maisie, sitting on grass, playing with some beads, another half-humorous one of herself at the stove, frying-pan in hand. Only two flower pieces, strictly decorative as geometrical blossoms represented by a Persian painter of long ago. A picture of the shop, with its cluttered windows, sweets, cigarette packets, paperbacks.

But Toby could not trust his own judgment. He knew, as the *cliché* said (and was it such an absurd one after all?) what he liked. But he wasn't Maisie.

He came downstairs again and congratulated Mrs Roberts. It was only then that he told her about the research studentship, the possible move to London. He added that he would have to find lodgings of his own.

She seemed neither surprised nor disappointed at the last piece of information. 'I suppose you don't want to have to go such a way every day. I expect you'll be coming home most week-ends, and in the meantime I can spread out a bit.'

'Well, don't let my room reek of turps. Otherwise you're welcome to it.'

In the June of that year, Rita bore a child, a daughter. Sitting honoured by flowers in the hospital ward at Mill Road, she was manifestly discontented and said so. 'A boy's *something*,' she told Toby and Adrian, 'but this is just a blob.'

Both of them tried to conceal shock. Bob, however, was enthralled. He took the baby from her mother and held her with infinite gentleness and perception, as if he were making a scientific study. 'Marvellous, when you come to think of it. Look at her little nails. And her toes. She's got Reet's eyes but my nose, God help her. Isn't she terrific?'

And indeed, the baby was very beautiful, with a fluff of black hair and a dark, unfocused gaze. The nurse came in to take her; it was time for her bottle, and Rita had not sufficient milk to feed her.

'We're going to call her Estella,' Bob announced. Adrian smiled: he had recently induced Bob to read a work of fiction, *Great Expectations*. 'Reet wanted Samantha, but she'd only get called Sammy.'

'I shouldn't so much mind Estelle,' Rita complained, 'but I don't want to call her anything from a book. Why it couldn't have been a boy, I don't know. We'd have called it Derek.'

'This is what I've got and what I wanted.' Bob sat down with a sigh. 'This is what happens to one.'

Shortly afterwards, he said he must go back to the lab for a couple of hours.

'You see? You see?' said Rita. 'Even now.'

'Don't be silly. I'll be in to see you again this evening.'

When he had gone she said, 'He'll spoil that kid to death, and then everything will devolve on me.' Belatedly she thanked the two young men for their flowers, violets from Toby, white roses from Adrian. She looked at the latter. 'How did you know I liked white ones best?'

'I just guessed. Who gave you the cyclamen, Rita? It's a beauty.'

'Oh, Bob. He knows pot plants die on me. No, I love those roses, but you should be giving them to some girl.'

'I am.'

'No, you're not. I'm just a mum. What a waste it's going to seem to them!'

'Who to?'

'All those girls.'

Adrian frowned a little, as he always did when she twitted him on his elected celibacy. But he said, 'There's no waste. I have to live my life in my own way.'

'And what a way.' She turned away from him, slipping back on to the pillow as if she were tired.

'Can it, Rita,' Toby said, in a manner not quite natural to him. 'If you don't, Adrian won't come here again.'

'I thought it was his job to visit the sick.'

'I never saw a sick woman look more blooming,' Adrian said in a mollifying tone.

97

'I feel sick. They're giving me stuff to take away the rest of my milk.'

Adrian blushed.

'And it makes me feel like suicide. I suppose it'll pass.'

'Everything passes,' he said, handing on this immemorial platitude as if it were a piece of new and deep wisdom recently invented by himself.

'Well,' she said, 'don't let me keep you two. I know it's not fun for you.'

'And it isn't fun,' Toby said to Adrian, when they were outside the hospital, 'and it won't be any fun for Bob.'

'You know, I think he'll manage better than you think. He's absorbed in his work, for one thing, and in the baby for another. I believe he thinks he's a lucky man.'

'What things we can think!'

Adrian smiled, and changed the subject. 'Have you seen Maisie recently?'

'Pretty recently. We may go off on a trip this summer, though I must get my mother's affairs settled up first. The show, I mean.'

When the show actually took place, Mrs Roberts refused to present herself there for more than half an hour. To Toby's astonishment, she said the strain had been too much last time.

'You didn't show it!'

'I show what I want to show. I didn't know how to get through the last one.'

'Then you're a wonder, as I've always said. You had me completely fooled. Cool as a cucumber, a *grande dame*. Congratulations.'

She smiled a little and patted his hand.

The opening was well attended, though the press only moderately admiring. Toby told her that she could scarcely expect things to be the same as at Cambridge, but she did not seem unduly put out. Maisie and Amanda had been there and she had boldly asked them back to supper, but with the air so much of one expecting a refusal that they made their excuses. Only four paintings had been sold.

'So I expect that's the end of my *meteoric career*,' Mrs Roberts said to her son, proud of the phrase.

'You wait and see what *is* going to happen. It's early days yet.'

And indeed, within a week, sales had picked up and there had been an article about her in one of the Sunday papers. She had allowed herself to be photographed in front of the shop this time, her husband at her side. 'You'd better come in for some of the fame, Stan,' she had said, 'such as it is.'

Letters of enquiry came in to her from the gallery. She had not had, as she had thought, a failure, but a modest success – no more. It sufficed her.

13

On the morning that he was due to set off for Paris, Toby had a letter from Claire. It was brisk and comradely. Would he like to come to Glemsford for the day, at any time in July? He had only to let her know. She signed herself, 'Yours, C.' No mention of Maisie; still, he supposed she might have written to her separately. He studied it thoughtfully, put it away in a drawer. It could wait till he got back.

He met Maisie at Victoria. Despite himself he was excited; and excitement was not a state of mind he really welcomed. She had made all the travel arrangements, had booked two rooms in the hotel. He had insisted that though each should pay separately for the trip and the accommodation, she must let him pay for all meals. He had borrowed some money from his mother, which he was confident of being able to repay. Things had been fixed up for him between Cambridge and London, and he was to work under Professor Tiller, with whom he had already talked several times.

It was not so much that Toby would have minded borrowing, but that it put him under obligations. He remembered how, as quite a small boy, he had longed for the day when his mother no longer had to pay his bus fares. He knew that his life was in part – though not wholly – solipsistic: he had to have his own aloneness.

The Channel crossing was rough, and Maisie went to lie down. He had known that he was unlikely to be troubled by high seas, and he was not. He drank some brandy in the bar, remembering to put a bottle of it and two hundred duty free cigarettes in his case, then went up on deck and enjoyed the wind and the spray.

Maisie emerged, somewhat green, just as they were coming into port at Calais.

'Feeling horrible, pet?'

'Not so much so, thank you. I'll be all right when we set foot on land.'

In the train to Paris they treated themselves to a rather expensive but delicious meal, and afterwards Maisie slept. Toby had brought some books to read, but could not tear his eyes from the landscape, the pastel-coloured houses, the men in their multiplicity of faded blues working in the fields. He felt that he really must read Proust, who had a great deal to say, he was told, about journeys.

His excitement rose as they took a taxi through the town, a tattered town at first, high and grey, then becoming more and more stately. At last they were in Montparnasse.

The hotel was shabby and narrow-fronted. The *patronne* greeted Maisie with a cry of pleasure. 'You're a stranger, mademoiselle!'

'How are you, madame? And how are Georges and Jean-Claude?' Maisie seldom forgot names.

They were shown up to their rooms on the fifth floor; the lift did not go beyond the fourth. Maisie waited till they were alone, then put herself into his arms. Her colour had returned, and she was gay. He could have taken her then, but he did not. He suggested that they should both unpack, and then go out to a café. 'Let's go to the Dôme,' said Maisie, 'it's where I always used to go.'

'Experienced traveller. How often have you been here?'

'To Paris?'

'No. To this quarter.'

'Well,' she said, 'only once. When I was with another girl I know. If I came with Mummy, it meant being rather grand on the Right Bank, and I don't like that so much.'

His room had a wallpaper of poppies and great black flowers, a little like crabs. There was a washbasin, a bidet. A bathroom along the hall, dragon-guarded. One paid extra. From the cinema next door came a blare of music, which he thought he might find trying.

Soon they went out into a magic night of Paris, into the *carrefour*, where the cafés were blinding with lights. Neither of them was very hungry, so they had *croque-monsieur* with a bottle of wine.

'Well?' she challenged him, 'was it worth it?'

'Infinitely, pet. And it is going to be worth far more.'

She had not spoken a word about any invitation from Claire.

That night, after he had been to her, he thought with what joy, even hilarity, she took the sexual experience. It eased him: he would have hated solemnity. This was how he himself liked to take a great part of life. He was deeply fond of her. Lying quietly at last – the blare of the cinema had ceased – he thought how pretty she had looked in the aftermath of pleasure, hair damp and curly, body relaxed. He no longer regretted that he had come.

All that week it rained, but they did the things they had come to do. The galleries, the museums, the historical places. 'Now after this,' she said, with a touch of bossiness, 'you can get on with *Saint-Just*. Doesn't it spark you off?'

'I might manage twenty more pages,' Toby said.

One night they went in a *bâteau-mouche* along the floodlit Seine. The rain pattered down on the roof and diamonded the river. The prow of the Ile St Louis rose in splendour. The enormous H of Notre-Dame. They were very content.

When it was time for them to return to England, both of them were sorry; but it was not in Maisie's nature, yet awhile, to grieve. She had not learned how.

They parted at Victoria Station. 'It was wonderful,' she said. 'Was it wonderful for you?'

'Of course. *Naturellement*. See what a linguist I've become under your tutelage.'

'Your French is far better than mine,' she said.

'I'll telephone you.'

'Do that. And thank you for all that wonderful food.'

'Little pig,' said Toby. He had only two shillings left.

When he had returned home, and had given Mrs Roberts (who was suspicious) a bowdlerised account of all that had happened to him, he took Claire's letter from the drawer and he answered it. Yes, he would love to come, though he couldn't make a precise date right now. He would get in touch with her. He signed himself, 'Ever yours, Toby.' He was a little ashamed of the pleasure he got in addressing the envelope. What was it like to have a title, even so modest a one? Did you get used to it after a time? Did the thought of it ever cross your mind, after you had used it for years?

The house at Glemsford would certainly be old, unlike Haddesdon. Half-timbering. Open fires, made from great logs. Shadows of firelight leaping over a great hall. Yes, some time he must go and see for himself, but the time was not yet.

He slept heavily that night and awoke to find himself missing Maisie. She had a curious little cooing noise, like a bird's, into which she subsided after the first cry of orgasm. She had been very light in his arms. He knew that this time he had put her into no jeopardy.

'Well, how's our wandering boy?' cried his father, who had not seen him the night before. 'And how was wicked Paree?'

'Not more noticeably wicked than London.'

'I bet you went on the town. Isn't that what they say?'

'They do. And to a modest extent, we did. Not night-clubs, though. Just cafés.'

'I wish I'd ever had a chance to wander,' said Mr Roberts. 'But your mother will be able to wander now if she likes. She's made a nice little nest-egg. That dealer's looking after all her work now.'

'Nonsense, Stan,' said Mrs Roberts, 'you know I don't want to wander. I don't like the idea. I just want to stay quietly and paint.'

'When's Maisie coming here again?' his father asked. 'I like her. She's a nice girl.'

'I'll ask her soon.'

Toby did, and she came to them to spend a day. Now that their relations must have seemed to her cemented, she was not taking advantage of the fact. She would not sit too close to him, took care not to mark their intimacy in her face. Yes, his father had been right. A very nice girl. *Jeune fille bien élevée.*

'I do wish you'd come down to Haddesdon, though,' she said to Mrs Roberts. 'Mother would be so pleased. You'd be another of her lions.'

'Oh, I'm a lion who stays inside its den. I might one of these days, though.'

'I shall pester you till you do.'

'I shouldn't know people.'

'What, with me and Mummy, and Edward Crane, and all those people you met at your show in Cambridge?'

'I was a bit too dazed to take them in.'

'She is telling me,' Toby said, looking at his mother fondly, 'that she was terrified on that occasion. I don't believe a word of it.'

'If I had your talent, Mrs Roberts, I'd be terrified of nothing and nobody.'

'Well, we aren't all alike.'

He did not make an approach to Claire that summer. It was not that it would have been an important matter: but out of something he believed was his moral nature, he did not wish to upset Maisie.

14

In August he found lodgings, which his mother made decent for him – he never minded her own particular kind of invasion – and in September went to work with Tiller.

This was a revelation to him. For the first time his studies began to take on a high seriousness, and during most of the evenings he got down to *Saint-Just*. He saw Maisie fairly frequently, and several times went to bed with her. But he knew there was something she longed for, something he could not as yet bring himself to give.

One night Adrian came to see him, and he was deeply troubled.

'Toby, would you say I was a vain man?'

'Good God, no.'

Adrian sat down. He seemed shrouded in a darkness of his own, face long, brows drawn together. 'I must talk to someone. Rita's being tiresome.'

This was the nearest thing to an unkind remark he had ever been known to make about anyone.

'That wouldn't surprise me,' Toby said, 'though I don't know how far things have gone.'

'She writes me letters. She's always doing it. Always asking me round, whether Bob's there or not. Often she says "Bob would like to see you," but it isn't Bob who would like it. First of all I wrote putting her off, then I stopped writing altogether. But she doesn't stop. Sometimes I think she's slightly unhinged.'

'Oh, come, you're a handsome chap. You'll have plenty of that kind of pestering when you have a parish of your own. Sighing ladies will hang round you tatting altar cloths.'

'Not if I know it, they won't,' said Adrian, for him astringently. 'I'm not getting into that kind of mess. Besides,' he added, 'things may not be easy for me quite at once, as you've helped to point out. I'm much as other men, and I have my temptations. But Rita isn't one of them.'

Toby guessed that, though low-sexed, he might indeed have his inner struggles before settling to a lifetime of celibacy. It was hard for a man who accepted it (unless he were homosexual, which Adrian was not) to have been given exceptionally good looks.

'The trouble is,' Adrian went on, 'that it does seem peculiar for me not to see Bob.'

'He keeps his rooms. Why can't you go there?'

'Because that would seem odd, too – as if I were avoiding Rita. I used to drop round to tea pretty frequently. By the way, Bob's got a DSIR thing. More money. He and Rita will move house soon.'

'Congratulate him from me. When did this happen?'

'A fortnight ago. There's been a delay.'

'I'll send him a wire. It will be hard to express total astonishment, though.'

'Perhaps it might seem rude if you did.' Adrian glimmered a smile.

'Do you think that when Rita's in the thick of house-moving, she might lay off you?'

Adrian looked doubtful.

'Well, if you want my advice you'll never, never see her alone. Just make sure that Bob's going to be around.'

'Do you think she's a nymphomaniac?' Adrian said rather naïvely.

Toby grinned. 'Now you're being modest. She just happens to fancy you, that's all.'

'I'd better go to supper soon. When Bob's there. That may keep her quiet.'

Toby heard the sequel a fortnight later.

Adrian had accepted an invitation, and had had a peaceable meal with them both. It was after it that the trouble began. Rita had begun to get increasingly fidgety, sighing, looking at the clock. Since it was only half-past eight, Adrian could hardly take all this as a signal to go home. At last she said to Bob, in a hard voice, that he might as well go out and buy himself a beer. She wanted to talk to Adrian privately. 'What about?' Bob had said. 'Spiritual matters,' Rita had retorted with a smirk. 'I need a bit of help.'

Adrian had protested, as he had done before, that he was not fitted to give anyone guidance.

'You never know till you try,' she said impudently, and stared straight at her husband.

Bob muttered, 'All right, I'll make myself scarce.' He was looking red and angry, as angry as he ever allowed himself, on the surface, to be. He had only just left them when the baby began to cry.

Rita swore. She had never known such a little wailer. On and off, all night. And Bob never helped with the floor-walking. 'I suppose I'd better go and see if I can shut her up,' she said impatiently.

She was gone for ten minutes, and the wails died away. When she returned she had combed her hair and put on fresh lipstick Adrian rose politely. She had told him to sit down, not to be soppy. She wanted to talk to him. It seemed to him that her prettiness had all faded during the months since her wedding.

'If you really want some kind of guidance,' Adrian said, 'I'm not going to give it you.' He tried to make a little joke. 'Next year, perhaps, when I'm ordained.'

She said that she did not believe he would go through with it. This seemed to him so preposterous a statement that he did not know how to answer her, and was aware that he was merely sitting with his mouth open. Then she said that she loved him. It was the first time she had ever really loved anyone in her life. She did not know what to do about it, she did not know what either of them was going to do. But she could not stand her life, and wouldn't be able to stand it better when she was the wife of a bloody don. She wanted Adrian. She wanted no one else, wanted nothing else.

Adrian concluded his four closely-written pages: 'So I rather lost my head. I told her not to be stupid, gave her a brotherly pat on the shoulder, and then just headed straight out of the house before she could stop me. And then, believe me, I ran, as if she and Bob and the baby were after me, all three of them. I have never felt such a fool in my life. So the question is, what do I do now? She has written twice to me since. I dread her writing on an envelope.'

Toby was less horrified than amused by all this: it had the character of farce, though he supposed it would be farcical neither to Bob nor to Adrian. He wished for Adrian a very remote and inaccessible country parish, something with a name like Pottle-in-the-Marsh. Then he sobered down. He wondered whether he should tell Maisie; he still listened more than he talked, but it seemed to him that her common sense might be welcome, that a woman's views might help in such a matter. So he asked himself down for the day to Haddesdon.

It would be, he knew, a quiet month there, for after the restless entertaining of the summer months, Amanda liked to take one of her rest periods.

He had, he said to Maisie, some rather disquieting news about Adrian and would like to consult her. It was not the first time he had asked himself down, and he had been in Suffolk several times recently. But this time she said no: she would come to him. Amanda, against her autumn custom, had acquired a string quartet, and they would be making the place impossible, not with their music (which was, she said, by no means bad) but with their chatter. In an earlier day, they would have been called rattles. She would be with him at five o'clock next Saturday.

'Poor darling,' said Toby when he saw her, 'a string quartet!' He kissed her. 'But it would be worse for me. You may have guessed that I'm not particularly musical.'

'Tell me the gossip,' she said, 'or, since it sounds rather solemn, we'll call it the trouble.'

He gave her a full account, even showing her Adrian's letter.

'Poor Father Stedman!' she said on a burst of amusement: her immediate reaction had been just like Toby's.

It struck him that the clergy were invariably regarded as funny, and he pondered, not for the first time, as to whether this was to the advantage of a society. An agnostic himself, he was by no means sure.

But she was soon sobered. 'It is pretty dreadful. Poor Rita, I wonder if she *is* all there?'

'All there,' said Toby, 'but in the first rage of love. I wouldn't say clubs cannot part them, because Adrian wishes to be parted. But it is real.'

'It can be very real,' said Maisie.

He had never used the word 'love' to her. It seemed to him too committal. He could say 'I adore you', and use his usual endearments: but not that: not just yet.

Maisie settled down to sort out the realities of the situation. She had a secretarial, a committee, air. 'We must see what's for the best. Of course, he oughtn't to go near her.'

'But she will be near him. Cambridge is a small town.'

'What would you do, chum?' she asked mimicking a catch-phrase of the day.

'What would I do? Go into retreat.'

'But he can't retreat.'

'Nevertheless he can keep out of the way. Do you know, I feel so sorry for Rita?' (She was, in a sense hardly realised, sorry for herself.) 'And, of course, for Bob.'

'At least, he has a future, I suppose. In fact, I'm sure he has.'

'And that will keep him going?'

'People secure in their work can always keep going.'

'And is that true of you?'

'Oh, dear, pet. I'm not really absorbed enough. Bob can be. And he will. He hopes to be a Fellow of the Royal before he's thirty-five – I know that. And I bet he is.'

'Then what would you suggest?'

'Answer no letters, however pastorally Adrian might intend it. Keep out of the way. He's a bit of a coot, you know.'

'The priesthood won't be easy for him,' she said wisely, 'I know. He'll be too soppy.'

'What do you mean?'

'What do you mean, what do I mean? It was just a thought.'

'You have a great many thoughts, pet.'

It was as if they had been quarrelling. Maisie changed the subject.

'How nice you've made it here! Nicer than when I came last.'

'You can thank my mother for that. She couldn't repaint the walls, but she did find me a carpet. The existing one was like damp, cold ham. I brought my bedcover and cushions back from Cambridge. And I have the glory of two of her paintings. You'd be surprised how often they are recognised.'

'Well, it's all very pleasant. And they damned well ought to be recognised.'

Even the mildest profanity was rare with her, and he knew that her mood had not yet passed. Rita: herself: love. She was brooding over it.

'Won't you make her come to Haddesdon?' she burst out.

'Make her? You could as soon make a mule do something it doesn't want to. She's a mollusc. Mixed metaphors, I'm afraid.'

'And so are you,' she said smiling.

'I'm grateful to your mother. But mine won't come out – almost literally. She goes to the shops, that's all.'

'And has none of this had any effect upon her?'

'Precious little. She's pleased with it, of course.'

'You should make her come out!' Maisie's face blazed. 'We'd make a tremendous fuss of her, you know that.'

'A fuss is just what she doesn't want.'

'Then we'd give her a quiet time. No more than that. She has only to say what she would like.'

'I'm afraid she won't.'

'A family of mules.'

After a pause Toby said, 'We're eating here tonight. You must sample my cooking.'

Maisie protested. She would like to cook for him.

'Gas-ring cookery. You wouldn't know how to begin.' In fact, he had two gas rings. He made a conventional fry-up, told her that she might, if she wished, see to the salad. They ate in amity, until she reverted to Rita. 'Anyone can see she's suffering. Doesn't anyone care?'

'She's not suffering. She's having a high old time, in her own way.'

'Of course, you'd always be on the man's side.'

'Perhaps I understand men better.'

'You certainly don't understand girls.'

'Perhaps that's what I was saying, pet.'

She looked mutinous. It seemed absurd to him that she should be identifying Rita with herself, but that was what she was doing. They did not sleep together that night, although his landlady, while not actively permissive, was quite uninterested in anything that went on so long as the rent was paid. After the meal Maisie insisted on washing up the few plates, and then he led her to the window, where they looked down upon the street lamps, lime-yellow in a rising mist.

'You'd better be getting back,' he said, 'it's going to thicken up, and though you may be the star of Brand's Hatch, for all I know, I don't like you driving in a murk.'

'Try to understand me,' she said

'Pet, what *is* this all about?' Though he knew, and did not at all want to be told. 'Aren't we happy?'

'It all seems so impermanent,' said Maisie, trembling a little beneath his arm.

He laughed at her. They were young. He was only twenty-one. Both of them had their way to make. It was the first time he had alluded, even indirectly, to marriage. 'Come on, be a cheerful girl. You always are. That's what I like about you.'

'I'm not always. I said you didn't know me.'

'I like very much what I do know.'

She began to cry, but in a moment checked herself, wiped her eyes and smiled with her normal brilliance. They talked of other things for a while, and then she left him, not protesting at being directed home earlier than usual.

When she had gone, he wrote a note to Claire. He would like to come to Glemsford one Saturday; Sundays were bad for trains. But it was two days before he posted the letter.

15

It was not she who met him at the station, but her mother: a woman of Amanda's build but not her colouring, since she was exceedingly fair. She bore down upon him with a kind of tally-hoing. 'It is Toby Roberts, I know, because as there's no one else here, it must be you, mustn't it?' Lady Llangain swept him into a big glossy car.

It was a chilly day with rain in the wind and a promise of more rain to come.

'Claire's the cook today. We have nobody at the week-ends, and anyway she loves to do it. My husband's met you, of course. He's playing golf, but he'll be back by lunchtime.'

The house was (this time) much as Toby had expected it would be. Big, rambling, it seemed to lean sideways as in a gale. It was half-timbered, yellow plaster with brown beams, set a little back from the road but, as Lady Llangain told him, with a garden behind. 'Idris says he could do with a bit more land, but I don't know, unless you let it out for grazing it only seems to make more work.'

She showed him into a stone hall with a great central staircase; and yes, because of the chill of the day, there was a log fire.

'Take your coat off – put it anywhere – and have a drink. Claire!' she shouted.

The strapping girl came from the back of the house, rather flushed from the stove, and she shook Toby's hand with a manly grip. 'Got you at last,' she said, 'and about time. I thought I'd never lure you.'

She was, he thought, indeed handsome in her own fashion, though he admired Maisie's style of looks more. He made some sort of excuse for his dilatoriness. He had been moving house, as it were. He had been working hard in preparation for the new term.

'Sit ye down,' said her mother. 'I can recommend vodka before lunch, but you can have anything else you like.'

Toby tried the vodka; he had never tasted it before. 'Do I have to down it in one swallow, or may I sip?'

'Of course you may sip. There's no need to follow Russian customs. Not in anything.'

'Prejudice,' said Claire. 'Russia's rather a good place, for all they say about it. I was in Leningrad last year,' she told Toby. 'It's a bit of a drag being with a large party, and the Intourist guides get fretful if you disappear, because they're held responsible for seeing you get to your transport on time, but it is possible to wander off for an hour and see marvels. Look after him, Mummy, I've got to get back to my birds. Grouse,' she explained. 'I hope you like them. I love cooking them and fidgeting with all the trimmings.'

Lady Llangain stretched out her feet luxuriously to the blaze; she was on her third vodka in about fifteen minutes, and Toby was surprised (and slightly shocked) to find that she tippled.

'You'll find us quiet here, after Haddesdon,' she said. 'Amanda always has such a crowd that I get muddled. Idris and I like to have one or two people just to ourselves. Mind you, she's a great dear and so is Maisie.'

He cordially assented.

'It's odd,' she went on, 'but I never had ambitions to be a hostess. I've always been hopeless with new names and faces. Even if someone has dined with me last week, I often find it hard to remember who they are the next.'

Toby said, with a touch of cheek which seemed to please her, 'Look hard at me, then. I have identifying marks.'

'If you mean an appendix scar, it's no use to me.'

'Nothing so arcane.' But this word she did not seem to understand.

'I live here all the year round,' she said, 'though Idris goes up to London a good deal. Heaven knows I find enough to do. And if I get in the doldrums, I go shopping in Bury. He adores the House of Lords, you know. How he can sit and listen to them droning hour after hour, I don't know. But then, I think men are better than women at doing that.'

At that moment Llangain came in. He threw down his clubs, greeted Toby, said 'God, it's cold. How is your good mother?'

So, thought Toby, with a spurt of resentment, he might have referred to the mother of a housemaid. This kind of thing always made him hotly protective towards her; though he was not so stupid as to believe that she was really in need of protection. If he had his privacies, so had she.

'She's fine, thank you, sir.'

'Remarkable talent. Even I can see that. Now tell me about yourself. How are you doing?'

Toby gave him a brief outline of what had happened.

'Now, let me give you a word of advice, because I'm on my home ground here.' Lady Llangain rose and gave herself a fourth vodka. She gave Toby a second, without asking him. 'If you're living in lodgings, don't be like most young men and starve yourself to death. It's quite easy to feed simply and well, if you take the trouble. Does your landlady do breakfast?'

He replied that mercifully she did: only tea and toast, but that was welcome because he was always somnolent in the mornings.

'Ah, a night-owl, then,' said Lady Llangain. 'I'm one myself. In this village, I should think mine is the last light to go out.'

'You're early enough when I'm here, Moira,' said her husband.

'That's because you can't stand me reading in bed, and I can't just stay up while you're snoring away.'

Llangain turned his attention again to Toby. What was he meaning to do with his life? Would he be a professional historian? An academic?

Toby replied that at the moment he just did not know. He would have to see how things developed. He did feel, he said, that the academic life might prove too much of a treadmill for him; he wanted to see more of how the wider world worked.

'Ever thought of going into business?'

'I've thought of it,' said Toby, 'but I don't really know how one begins.'

'Ah,' said Llangain.

Claire announced luncheon. They ate, not in a dining-room, but in a great kitchen; a beautiful smell pervaded it. Yet Claire was not the cook her mother had seemed to claim. The birds were dry, the bread sauce half-cold. Toby, who felt that with his recent experiences at Haddesdon he was becoming something of an epicure, had to make a pretence of enjoying it; obviously the other three genuinely did. Amanda, he thought, made no virtue of simplicity, did not delight in a kind of relaxed carelessness. The Llangains did. Claire talked to him little during the meal, but her eyes were much on him.

He noticed that she had points of real allure, a beautiful skin, a beauty-spot, oddly frivolous for her, it seemed to him, at the corner of her left eye.

'I'll wash up,' said Lady Llangain when the meal was over, 'you talk to your friend, Claire.'

Toby noticed that her speech was slightly blurred, and that she needed to retire for a while until it had readjusted itself. Her husband seemed not to notice. Soon he went upstairs to sleep.

Toby and Claire returned to the hall and sat side by side before the log fire, which she replenished energetically.

He said to her, 'I know so little about you. What do you like doing?'

'Oh, I don't really know. I worked for a while, but still I don't know. I ride a bit. I don't hunt much, though Daddy used to when we lived for a couple of years in Leicestershire.'

'Pity for the fox, I expect.'

'Just plain funk, really. Well, what else? I read a fair amount, but nearly always thrillers. And you may not believe it, because I have hands like hams, but I can sew.'

He noticed that her hands, though large, were excellently shaped. On the right one she wore an onyx signet ring.

'I make all my own clothes, except for shirts and slacks. That takes up a good deal of my day. I'm afraid I'm not very interesting.'

'I hope that is mock-modesty, because I don't think you ought really to be so humble. And I think you are very interesting.'

'I thought I'd ask Maisie down today, then decided I wouldn't. I hope she won't mind.' Toby fervently hoped she would not mention the matter to Maisie at all. 'But I'm a bit slow in getting to know people, and I rather like to have them to myself. Maisie's a dear, isn't she? Amanda I find rather terrifying. I'm always so afraid she's going to ask me an opinion about something and that I won't be able to answer. She does like one to speak up.'

'But she's fond of you.'

'Is she? Of course, Maisie and I have been friends for ages.'

There was much more he wanted to know about her, but he was always chary about asking more than the minimum of questions. Fortunately she talked on, about her schooling, how she had not been much good at it, how she wished it were otherwise. This was not just chatter for chatter's sake: her face grew wistful, her eyes had softened. Yes, she had dreamed of being a writer or an actress, or even a model girl: but for the first she was not sufficiently brainy, for the second she had appeared to have no talent, for the third she was just too big. 'I haven't an ounce of surplus fat,' she said, 'yet when I plucked up my courage and went to a model agency they told me I must take off a stone.'

'Most men hate skin and bones, whatever most women may think.' Toby was emphatic.

Since a thin sunlight had struck through the diamond panes, Claire suggested that they might go out to see the garden. It was a large one, though not comparable with that of Haddesdon. Toby was rather surprised, since he had not regarded Lady Llangain in the light of an enthusiastic home-maker, to find that it was beautifully kept. At the end was a small orchard of apple trees, now heavy with fruit.

'This must represent a lot of hard work,' he said.

'Oh, it's done by our rude and ancient gardener. "A haught, insulting man," ' she added.

'I thought you only read thrillers.'

'We did a lot of Shakespeare at school. And bits of it stuck.'

They passed between a height of golden rod, between borders of michaelmas daisies, faintly browning into the fall.

'Damn it,' she said, 'it's raining again.' They took momentary shelter under the apple trees. Suddenly she rose slightly on her toes and put her lips hard against him. It was not a sensual kiss, but it was a claiming one. Taken by surprise, he could only smile at her.

'There,' she said gleefully, 'your Maisie can spare me just that. And it makes a nice conclusion to the day.'

'Extremely nice,' he agreed.

She walked apart from him on their way back to the house.

Lady Llangain was lying on a sofa, doing a crossword puzzle. 'Been out?' she said unnecessarily.

'It rained again,' said Claire. 'It's a perfectly beastly day outside. Not inside, though. Let's help with the puzzle.'

Her mother read them the clues. Claire, obviously used to such exercises, was surprisingly quick. Toby wondered why she wrote herself so much down intellectually. He had been disturbed and excited by her kiss, surprised that she should take such a bold initiative. He believed that she was much used to young men.

After a while Llangain came down from his sleep, and they talked. 'If ever you get tired of what you're doing,' he said amiably to Toby, 'let me know. I might be able to suggest something.'

Claire went out, and brought back tea and dripping toast; the last Toby loved, though he believed his own mother thought it somewhat low. In any case, she never these days gave it to him. There was no refinement of cake. He was uncertain just how much he liked the household. It was cheerful, but ramshackle by the side of Haddesdon or even his own home. It made it difficult for him to place any of them. Was Llangain a rich man? He could have been, but apart from the size of the place, which must have needed considerable upkeep, there was no evidence of it. Still, it was comfortable, comfortable, and Claire, sitting with trousered legs crossed, was very much part of it.

Whatever happens, he thought, *I* did nothing. I didn't cheat Maisie. It occurred to him that men who found themselves kissed in this manner were slightly ridiculous; yet there had been nothing self-conscious about Claire's gesture.

The afternoon was closing into evening. The firelight fell on her fair head and upon her mother's. Llangain smoked placidly, saying little. His wife talked about her son. 'I'd like you to have met the boy. Perhaps you will some day.'

'Yes, you must meet Hairy,' said Claire, grinning. 'He's good value.'

'Hairy?' Toby asked, astonished by this nickname.

'Heir Apparent. That's what we call him. And he is rather hirsute, too, or as much as they'll let him be in the Army.'

Time to go. She drove him this time to the station, went with him on to the platform, and as the train came in shook hands. Her manner was once again strictly comradely.

'It's been fine,' Toby said, 'everything. Thank you very much.'

'You've got a spot of dripping on your tie. Try hot water on it when you get home. Well, I suppose we'll see each other some time.'

Neither of them made any further arrangements to do so.

16

Why couldn't he love Maisie? For he didn't. ('Yet' – he added mentally, by way of touching wood.) She was a lovely girl: a Miranda of a girl. 'The fringèd curtains of thine eyes advance . . .' How often had he seen that! He liked being with her, being in bed with her, engaged with her in all the subterfuges of love. But he needed to feel free to amuse himself with Claire, not because there would be anything serious in this, but because he liked to think he had a natural distaste for deception, which he thought of as 'two-timing'.

He had seen her once or twice, had given her dinner in London, taken her to the cinema. They had kissed lightly on parting, but not more than that. It seemed that Claire was in no hurry. She had great self-confidence. She knew not only what she wanted, but in what precise space of time she might reach out to grasp it.

Maisie he saw more frequently. The news of his visit to Glemsford had not leaked to her, and he could only imagine that Claire had enjoined silence upon her parents. Then, for a while, he was free of them both. Amanda and Maisie went to the Bahamas for the months of early winter, Claire by herself to Madeira. He tore himself from thoughts of the girls, and settled hard down to work.

He had submitted the idea of *Saint-Just* for a PhD thesis, which had been accepted by Tiller, and was only dismayed when he had discovered just how much upon him had already been written.

Meanwhile his mother was in a flurry of fresh production. She was selling her work pretty frequently now, and he calculated that she must be making quite a sizeable sum of money for it. He could not question her on such a matter, because she was as prudish about money as he was himself. He simply noted improvements to his home, new curtains, new china, a television set. Sometimes she bought new clothes, but they were always much like her others, fading into the background of her own personality. He could see that his father was rather bewildered. 'Dora's doing well, isn't she? I think she's got the magic lamp, like Aladdin in the panto. If I just say I'd like something, she goes and gets it for me. I don't know that I'm keen on the idea, but it seems to give her pleasure. She did say something about me being able to retire early if I wanted to, but I said, the hell with that. How would a man like me employ himself?'

Their Christmas was not more lavish than usual, since Mrs Roberts had always put great store by the feast, and had saved up for luxuries. Still, this time Toby did not have the awkward feeling that he was 'eating her out of house and home'.

In the New Year he went for the week-end to Cambridge; there were links there that he could not break.

He found Bob and Rita installed in Lensfield Road, behind the Catholic church, where they occupied half of a house. At first all seemed well with them. Rita was cheerful; they now had an *au pair* girl, a Swede, who took the baby off her hands a great deal. Their home was quite pleasantly furnished, and the plastics had largely disappeared. Bob had bought some nice objects, a set of crystal wineglasses, a pair of silver candlesticks, a graceful console table. He had, it appeared, acquired an eye for antiques, and had not paid too much for any of them. Indeed, he had bought the candlesticks in the market-place. 'Filthy, they were,' he said, 'but nothing the wit of man couldn't deal with.' He was openly pleased with his relative prosperity.

He suggested that they should go to see Estella put to bed.

'Oh, Toby would be bored silly,' said Rita.

He disclaimed this.

The baby was just out of her bath, lying on a pink towel across Ingrid's knees, smiling like a sun at them, displaying two teeth. 'I have to admit she's forward,' said Rita, with some vestigial display of pride.

'Get away with you,' said Bob, 'she's a bloody marvel.'

'Blow your own trumpet,' said Rita, and gave a lubricious giggle.

Bob had tentatively anticipated, also, some donnish habits: white wine in the new glasses before the meal, a decent claret with it. But the meal itself was far from donnish, toad-in-the-hole, in fact, with some gravy stiff enough, Toby thought, to stand up by itself. Rita did not care for cooking, and it was no part of Ingrid's job. The latter ate with them, a plain girl with downcast eyes, uncertain enough of her English to remain in silence.

When it was over, when Ingrid had retired to her studies, and they were drinking coffee, Rita said suddenly: 'And where's your po-faced friend?'

'Who do you mean?' Toby asked, though he knew.

'Adrian, of course. He hasn't been near us for ages.'

'He hasn't been near me. I think he's been in retreat.'

'You're telling me!' Rita crowed. 'When you see him, you can tell him we're missing him. Not that he's a live wire, exactly, but he soothes me, doesn't he, Bob?'

Bob said nothing.

Toby almost expected him to beat a retreat himself, to the lab: but he did not. He was watchful over Rita these days, not perhaps out of love, but in a kind of anxiety.

'He ought to be on television, I told him he ought.'

'The last thing he'd want,' said Toby. 'He needs a quiet life.'

'And I don't,' said Rita, on a spurt of irritation, 'but I get it all the same. I never get to go dancing; Bob hates it, and anyway, he's all over my feet.'

'Then you shouldn't want me to do it,' Bob said. He said it with good humour, but he was troubled.

'And he eats in Hall about three times a week,' Rita went on, 'gay for me, isn't it?'

Toby pondered on the distance between this girl and the demure young creature at the wedding. He wondered how long this marriage would last, whether, the child apart, Bob would want it to. Was she interested in other men besides Adrian? He thought probably not. Adrian was a mania with her. And she might as well have cried for the moon.

'I'm going to put on some records,' she said, 'that kid's wailing again, and I've had about enough of it for today.'

'Don't worry, Ingrid will cope.'

'Poor her.'

Toby was coming to detest Rita, with a detestation he felt for very few people. It was his habit to like, and to achieve reciprocity.

Oddly enough, she did not play the pop records which she liked, but chose them to Bob's taste. He was, in an uninstructed way, musical. Vivaldi. The prelude to *The Meistersingers*. The Polovtsian dances, from *Prince Igor*. As Bob listened, the worried look was swept from his face. The lab: the music: his daughter. They would be enough for him.

When it was time for Toby to go, Rita sweetened towards him. 'It's been so nice to see you. Why do you make yourself such a stranger? I tell you, I love seeing people. I'm alone a good bit, you know.'

The irritation returned to Bob's face.

'Mind you, this is a nice enough place. But Ingrid's no company. My mum looks in when she can, and my dad when he's off duty. But the hours are long,' she added, in a tone rather out of key with all the rest of this, wistfully, and with her head cocked to one side. 'By the way, how's Maisie?'

'Still away. She'll be home soon.'

'Where is she?'

'The Bahamas.'

'Fancy being rich! I'd like to travel round the world.'

'When the College takes me in,' Bob said, 'I may take you. Keep on hoping.'

She kissed Toby good-bye, lightly, on the cheek. He thought he would try not to accept another invitation.

In the following week, he had a letter from Edward, whose new play was opening on Tuesday. He enclosed two tickets.

'Come or not, just as you like. I'm afraid this one is going to "come off", as you haplessly put it; something's gone wrong all through rehearsals. But if you would like to attend a first night that may go off at half-cock, it might amuse you. Perhaps you and who-ever you bring will have supper with me afterwards. I don't care to hang around the dressing-rooms, and I try to avoid first night parties, especially when they're likely to suggest that a wake will shortly follow.'

Toby accepted, and thanked him. He was curious. He telephoned to Maisie to ask her to go with him, but she was not yet home. He wondered that she had extended her holiday so far. Could he ask Claire? But he sensed that Edward would be suspicious if he did so. The latter's antennae were a little too delicate for his taste, and he had not forgotten the conversation in the pub at Linton.

Adrian, who was back in circulation again, was eager to go with him. Neither of them had ever been to a first night before.

The play was once more historical, *The Conjurors*, dealing with the witch-cult surrounding Eleanor, Duchess of Gloucester. The audience was fairly glittering, or at least the stalls glittered. Edward sat in the front row of the dress-circle, but did not approach them; he simply waved a hand.

And it was obvious at once that something was wrong. Not so very wrong; but the play was only likely to be a half-success, half sustained by Edward's name. Both Toby and Adrian were troubled by the contagious atmosphere of the house; they liked the play themselves, and were prepared to be enthusiastic. They went out to smoke in the interval; they did not order drinks, because the prices of the theatre bar were too high. Edward had disappeared.

They noticed that nobody about them was discussing the play. Discussing everything else, but not that. They were impressed by the various celebrities who swept past them, recognised from television and from newspaper photographs. The celebrities were not discussing the play, either. Both Toby and Adrian began to fear that the reception would be positively hostile; but it was not. It was polite. There were five curtain calls. Edward did not, of course, answer the cries of 'Author'; that was not customary now, and had not been for some time. But when the crowds were drifting from the theatre, he came to seek them out.

'Well,' he said, 'the critics will be courteous tomorrow but no more, and that's not good enough. You'd better come round behind with me, and then we'll make our escape as soon as possible.'

They were excited by this. Neither of them had ever seen the back of a stage. They blundered through the darkness and dust, over cables, between looming shapes of canvas, into a warren of draughty passages. Edward knew his way about. He led them first to meet the leading lady, introduced them to her (how coarse, Toby thought, she looked, still in her make-up) and said so mechanically that it seemed like irony, 'You were wonderful, darling.' She pressed gin upon them.

She was, in fact, far from being unrealistic. 'Well, Edward dear, I think we've just got away with it. But it was a cold house.' She turned to Adrian, always the cynosure for women's eyes. 'What did you think of it?'

'I liked it immensely. I thought it was impressive. And that you were.'

'So did I,' said Toby.

Next they visited the leading man and several other actors; the director, who was looking downcast. Several more gins.

'You're coming to the party, Edward?' the director said, but not in any particular tone of hope. He knew Edward's ways.

'I'm afraid I can't. But we'll have a post-mortem tomorrow.'

Edward disengaged himself from them all, and took the young men to a small restaurant not known for a theatrical clientèle.

'Well,' he said, 'that's that. We shall run for about three months, and that's all there is to it. Let's talk of other things.'

He questioned them closely about their careers, initiated some gossip about various friends in common. Amanda? Maisie?

'Still abroad,' said Toby. Perhaps emboldened by the gins and the wine – Edward had been drinking rather hard and had pressed wine on them – he mentioned the Llangains.

'Oh, them,' Edward said carelessly, 'they're as rich as Croesus. Far better heeled than Amanda, only they don't so much enjoy showing it. Not that that's meant to be a criticism. I love Amanda because she does show it, and makes one share.'

But he was not so sunk in drink and disappointment that he failed to cast a sharp glance in Toby's direction. 'You know Claire, of course? Yes, of course you do. And you do, of course, Adrian. She's an odd girl. You're too young to have heard of a character called Lummox. But that's what she pretends to be half the time, and it's all nonsense. She's as sharp as a needle, and she always gets what she wants. Maisie gives me the impression that she seldom gets what she wants, though quite what it is I don't know. Have you seen any more of Claire?'

'I saw her once. She's good-looking in a big sort of way,' Toby said, and with more than a touch of depreciation.

'I'm sure you think so,' said Edward.

The conversation again moved on.

17

He began to see Maisie regularly again, sometimes at his home, because his mother asked for her and would have thought it odd if she were not invited more often at his lodgings. He also saw Claire from time to time: and since he was frightened that Maisie should find out about it (though she had shown no sign of doing so), he told her a half-truth.

'I ran into Claire in the street the other day, and took her for a cup of coffee.'

'Oh.' Maisie was silent for a moment. Then she said, 'She didn't mention it to me.'

'It was only last week.'

'But I saw her last week.'

'Pet,' Toby cried, trying to laugh, 'I expect it was after that. Anyway, what does it matter?'

'It doesn't, I suppose. Only I hate not to know things.'

'But there's nothing to know. She was just up for a day's shopping. We talked about Mummy's painting most of the time. She's a nice girl, but a trifle on the stalwart side.'

'I can't lay claim to being that,' she replied, for the moment appeased. But his soul was wary.

'You have a stalwart spirit,' he said, and she smiled.

But later she said, 'Which day was it that you saw Claire?'

'Thursday, Friday. I forget which.'

'What was she doing in Gower Street?'

'She wasn't. I met her in St James's Square. I'd been getting some books from the library.'

'It's odd, though.'

He said, gently, 'You mustn't suspect me of nameless crimes.'

'I don't. I only said it seemed odd. Of course, there's nothing to stop you from seeing Claire.'

'Darling, it was only that once.' (Though by this he might be landing himself in deep water.)

'I don't own you,' Maisie said, without expression, and as he made no reply, mentioned Claire no more on that occasion.

Meanwhile, Edward's play had been forced to transfer to another theatre, where it had closed after six weeks. All much as predicted. Adrian was preparing for ordination. Of Bob and Rita, nothing had been heard. His own work was going steadily, though he had an uncomfortable idea that Tiller did not think much of his capacities.

Only Mrs Roberts really seemed to flourish. Her name had crossed the Atlantic – there had been a small picture in *Time* – and her work was selling, if not dramatically, with some frequency. Even her husband had urged her to leave the house and get a proper studio, as an artist should, but she was adamant. She did not propose to change her way of life. The back of a chair made a good enough easel, and they were comfortable where they were, weren't they? This refusal to budge attracted the attention of a few reporters, who made occasional descents upon her, as usual coming away with precious little. She forced her generosity upon Toby.

'You know I don't like to take your money,' he said.

'And what else should I do with it? I know young men, they like to make a splash now and then.'

He had been able to buy himself a small second-hand car: it was his pride and his independence, yet somehow he was half-humiliated by it, too. He was able to drive Maisie about, able, upon occasion, to drive Claire. Both these affairs seemed in a state of stagnation. Life with Maisie went on as before, and he was too attracted by her, and needful of her warmth in bed, to contemplate any sort of break. With Claire he appeared to make no progress at all, since she had given him that first firm kiss. She liked going out with him and said so, but no more. He wondered whether he had been wasting his time.

In March a blow fell, not upon him directly; but on a friend. There were semi-sensational headlines in the newspapers. A young Cambridge scientist had pleaded guilty to an assault upon his wife: strained past bearing, he had beaten her up with his fists, whereupon Rita had gone straight to her father. She asked in court that Bob should not be allowed to molest her. He was ordered not to do so, and fined fifty pounds with costs. Rita's appearance in the witness-box with a black eye had been impressive to all her female friends, but Bob's own friends had sided – if not too openly – with him.

They knew too much. Rita obtained a separation order. She remained in Lensfield Road with Ingrid and the child, and Bob returned to rooms in college.

Toby drove straight down to see him, and found him in a broken state. He had never seen a grown man cry, and was embarrassed.

'Tobe, I've never hit a woman before in my life. But she kept on about Adrian, Adrian, Adrian, and the kid cried, and if she sues for divorce I'll have lost Estella for good. I can't stand it. But with my record, they're bound to give her custody outright – and even if I had it, what could I do? They've been decent to me here. I don't dine in Hall, I lie doggo. But this can't go on for ever.'

Toby fetched him a drink from the cupboard; he could think of nothing else to do. He noticed that Bob now kept a supply of whisky.

'Believe me, I think I had a kind of brainstorm. I don't remember much, except socking her the first time. I feel a sort of monster. I think I always shall.'

Toby said slowly, 'I think all of us knew that she was asking for something. It worried everyone who knows you. As for Adrian, he just had to back out.'

'Christ knows, I'm not blaming Adrian. Reet had a crazy thing about him.'

'I think you ought to get out and about a bit, and be damned to everything.'

'All she's got to show for it now are a few bruises – no, I can't. God, if only one could put the clock back! I'd give my eyes for these few weeks to be wiped out. I wasn't tight or anything, you know, it happened after breakfast, just as I was leaving for the lab. It's like a nightmare now,' he added, unoriginally.

Toby gave him a handkerchief, and Bob looked at it as though it were some artefact the use of which he could not fathom. However, after a few minutes he did put it to its proper purpose, and went off to rinse his face. When he returned, he drank about three fingers of whisky neat.

'Help yourself,' he said. He reverted to his misery. 'I can't keep my mind on my work. I've already mucked up an experiment I was doing. I feel I'll never get over it.'

'Look,' said Toby, 'people know that she asked for it. But you mustn't let it interfere with your career, whatever else you let it do

125

to you.' He said this so emphatically, for him, that Bob was startled momentarily out of his misery.

'It won't, not for ever. But just now – bloody hell, you can't imagine what a swine I feel. It's as though somebody else did it, not me.'

'I can understand how you feel at the moment. But it will wear off. It must.'

'Must it?' Bob's voice was dreary. 'You tell me.'

Toby, finding out that he had not eaten all day, did induce him to come out for a snack in a back-street café. Having done so, he was pleased to see that Bob was ravenously hungry, wolfing down the food as if he had nothing else in mind. 'I could just do with that,' he said at last, 'it was what I needed.'

A lab acquaintance who happened to come in greeted him with cheerful normality. Bob gave him a lift of the hand, a half-smile which looked as if it had been wrenched from him.

When he had lit a cigarette, he said to Toby, 'What does Maisie think?'

'I haven't seen her since I got the news. I know what she'd think, though – as everyone does. Look, there's no point in imagining you're a leper. It will only do you more harm. You've got to pull yourself together.'

'I don't know how I'm going to face Maisie.'

'She'll be a tower of strength,' said Toby, though of this he was by no means sure. He knew where her instinctive, transferring sympathies would lie. 'She knows a thing or two.'

When he returned to London, the landlady told him that Miss Ferrars had telephoned, and would ring again. She did, within ten minutes. He did not much care to speak to her in this way, as the telephone was at the foot of the stairs; and though the landlady was incurious, he disliked the thought of being overheard.

It was plain from Maisie's first words that she was not going to be a tower of strength so far as Bob was concerned.

'Have you heard about Bob and Rita? Isn't it beastly?'

'I was in Cambridge today. I saw him then. He was awfully cut up, pet.'

'So he ought to be! Did you ever think he'd be the kind to be violent to anyone?'

'Rita has brought it on herself, you know.'

'I don't care. Will it affect his chances?'

'No. Most people's sympathies are with him.'

'Well, mine are not. Toby, I don't know how you can!'

But at that he said mildly, 'Pet, don't let's talk about Bob and Rita. We shall never agree, and I hate to be at loggerheads with you, of all people.'

She was silent for so long that he thought the line had gone dead. Then she said, 'All right, we won't. Though I can't imagine how you – never mind. I'm sorry. I was really ringing to ask you if you'd come to Haddesdon next week-end. Mother hasn't opened up to her circus yet—'

Perhaps a less filial note than usual?

'No string quartet. There will be Edward, I suppose. Possibly Peter Coxon, though he may be still in New York. Shall I ask Adrian?'

'Not just at the moment.' Then, an old curiosity overcoming him, he asked about Edward's wife.

'Don't you know? She divorced him ten years ago. They had a baby once, but it died. It was a girl.'

'I'm sorry.'

'Never let him know I told you about that. He hates to be pitied. What are you doing this week?'

He never liked being asked his movements, where he had been, where he was proposing to go. 'Working, I expect.'

'I shan't see you before Saturday then?'

'Better not.'

'You're not angry with me, for what I said about Bob?'

'No. But we won't talk about it any more. Shall I come down by train?'

She said yes: the drive was a long one anyway, and she would meet him as usual at the station. She did not sound happy.

But when he did go to Haddesdon, he found something of the old Maisie, serene, lively, the smile curling over her lips which were naturally pink. She hugged him right in front of the stationmaster, and Toby wished she wouldn't. He was still clinging to what remained of his secrecies. It occurred to him that not much did.

'Too much of a stranger!' Amanda cried, as she welcomed him. She was like a galleon in full sail, and he saw for the first time how handsome she must have been before her youth faded, a Cleopatrawoman, needing only a barge. 'Edward's here, but no one else. Now, you two do what you like. I'm busy.' First she asked warmly about his mother, then she bustled off upon some mysterious pursuit.

The day was fine, so Toby and Maisie walked in the garden. He could feel as he took her arm that she was yielding; her whole body yielded. 'I love the start of spring,' she said, 'it makes me feel there are new starts for me, too.'

He looked for a buried meaning in this, but found none. When he kissed her, he knew that she was all softness. There should be no contentious subjects between them that day.

Edward came over the grass to join them.

'Is it warm enough to have drinks out here?' Maisie asked. 'We might, mightn't we?'

'Just about. I'll buttle. I know your tastes.'

Edward seemed to have cheered up considerably. But all at once Toby knew that he was a lonely man, lonely by his own choosing. There was something about Amanda which drew him to her, some-thing far from sexual, but compelling enough to make him a regular visitor. Was it purely her ebullience, her life-giving quality? Amanda was not a brilliant woman, not an intellectual, though she had taste, and kept abreast of all forms of contemporary art. Edward, Toby guessed, was highly intellectual, though reluctant to make a display of this. He did not keep abreast of contemporary art, and had no intention of doing so.

'He's so soothing,' said Maisie, 'or so I find. Don't you?'

But Toby, though he assented, in reality did not. Edward saw too much. Far too much.

He came out of the house, carrying a tray. 'Here you are. Tell me if I've put in too much water, Toby. I couldn't bother to bring the jug out.'

The buds were just greening on the trees, a sooty, bloomy green. There were dwarf daffodils along the margin of the stream. It was unseasonably mild, and the sky was a pale blue, washed over by a silvering of sun. The sort of weather appropriate for Maisie; it should be her inner weather always.

He was astonished, when they went indoors for lunch, to find Amanda had acquired yet another of his mother's paintings, this time the sardonic one of Mrs Roberts in the kitchen, which had not been sold at the show. 'When did you buy this, Mrs Ferrars?'

'Only last week. I looked in at the Arden and liked it. Then I went away. Then I went back again. It was tugging at me, do you understand? I wish I bought for investment, which I don't, because I think your mamma's paintings might be very profitable some day. Of course,' she added realistically, 'she may be just having a temporary vogue; with this kind of work one can't say. But what does it matter? I like it, and that's all that matters to me.'

He repressed the unworthy thought that she was not quite sincere, that she was more eager to lend support to himself and his family than to acquire yet another picture. Yet she seemed so open, so honest, so frank. He could not really bring himself to doubt her.

After lunch Edward said he would have, as he put it, a 'snooze', and Toby and Maisie went for a drive through the villages set in the folds of hills so gently undulant that the casual observer might have thought it was flat country around them. They stopped to see a little church, ancient, with painted tombs and rich armorial bearings. A knight and his lady slept, feet and hands neatly together. Reds and golds.

'I'd like to sleep like that some day,' said Maisie. She was holding his hand.

'You'll sleep in a different way tonight, my girl.'

She turned up to him her blissful face.

When, at tea-time, they returned to the house, it was to find Claire waiting for them. Toby was jolted. He knew he had coloured, and he hoped that Maisie had not noticed. He cursed the fineness of his skin.

'Fancy finding you here,' said Claire, giving him her manly handshake, 'nice, too. I only dropped in for the brief cuppa,' she told Maisie. She turned to Toby. 'We're pretty near neighbours, you know.' As if he did not know it already.

He was filled with unease, grateful to see that, if only for the moment, Maisie still remained untroubled.

The girls chatted for a while, about clothes, films, friends in common. Then they went in to tea, where the conversation turned to gardening.

'Horrible old Rudkin is ill,' Claire said, 'and mother is having to do the work. She hates it.' She said to Toby, 'You know our orchard?' Then she added swiftly, 'No, of course you don't. You haven't been to us at Glemsford. Maisie must bring you over some day.'

'Yes, I must,' Maisie said evenly. But her face again wore the look of shock that he had seen before.

'Something's got at the trees,' Claire went on, 'and Mummy doesn't know what it is. Daddy certainly doesn't. They keep on spraying in a mad sort of way, but it does no good.'

Maisie went upstairs, and stayed away for some little time. Claire, Edward and Toby went on talking; about what, Toby could never afterwards remember. When she re-emerged, it was with a vivacity that never left her throughout the course of the evening.

Claire got up to go. 'Do make Maisie bring you,' she said to Toby, 'before the garden goes to pot altogether.'

For him, the rest of the evening hung with appalling heaviness, though Maisie and Amanda were lively, and Edward placid as usual. After dinner they played *bouts-rimés*, capped quotations. Maisie performed brilliantly. Then she put on the gramophone. She did not play classical records this time, but tunes of the nineteen thirties, Cole Porter, Astaire and Rogers' songs. Her eyes were very bright. Toby thought of Noël Coward's remark about the potency of cheap music, and found it profound. He drank rather a lot that evening.

At last they all went up to bed. He waited for Maisie, but she did not come to him. At last he went to her, tapping first at her door.

She was sitting up against the piled pillows, the light still on. She said, 'You've been to Glemsford.'

He came towards her quickly, smiling. *He could see his own smile*. It was more like a rictus, hilarity overlying deceit. 'Pet, don't be silly!'

'Claire gave the game away. Do you suppose I didn't notice?'

He made up his mind with speed. Coming to sit beside her on the bed, he put his arm around her shoulders but she drew away.

'Listen, I did go, once. She badgered me into going.' (This was ignoble and he knew it.) 'I didn't tell you because you get jealous, and I can't bear people to be jealous of me.'

'You should have told me.'

'I suppose so. But it was so unimportant; the whole thing is unimportant. You can't believe that Claire means anything so far as I'm concerned?'

'Why was she so quick to deny it? Oh, it makes me look a fool, such a fool!'

'Because she saw the look on your face,' Toby said. Again he attempted to embrace her, but she put him off.

'I don't mean anything to you,' said Maisie, 'or nothing serious.'

'Darling, you mean a very great deal. Are we going to quarrel about something so casual – so casual—'

'I have been lied to.'

'Maisie, Maisie. If this piece of nonsense has hurt you, I'm sorry. What more can I say?'

'It's better for you not to try.' She burst out, 'You've destroyed what self-confidence I had. And you always knew I hadn't very much, didn't you?' Tears shone in her eyes, but did not fall.

'Pet. Let's forget it, shall we? I want you. She's just a nothing to me.' (Ignoble again, but in for a penny, in for a pound.)

As if exhausted, she rested her head on his shoulder, and he was able to kiss her, delicately, tasting her as if she were a fruit. When he made love to her, she responded with an eagerness that was almost febrile, but he knew that all was still not well. It would not be well. Then she turned over on her side and went straight to sleep. Fearful of disturbing her, he did not go back immediately to his room but lay wakeful – this was rare for him, who usually went into a kind of stupor after sex – until the dawn was breaking.

18

For a fortnight after that ill-starred week-end (the Sunday had been, for Toby, an almost intolerable strain) he heard nothing at all from Maisie. Then she wrote to him.

'My darling,

'I thought I'd better stay away for a little while, just to get my breath back. If you tell me to trust you I will do so, but the shock was a bad one. I realise that I may have been making mountains out of molehills. Come to Haddesdon again soon, perhaps when Mother has opened her "season". I think' (she could not resist adding) 'that Claire is unlikely to drop in again unannounced.

'I am working in an antique shop in Lavenham – I must do something. The job is mostly dusting dangerously fragile objects and waiting for the customers who don't turn up. Perhaps when the holiday season starts, we shall get the tourists. It isn't much of a job, but it is all my miserable Second has fitted me for. I could make more money as a secretary, if I knew shorthand and type-writing, but I can't face taking a course. However, I am quite all right, and missing you. I'll be in touch again soon, but I do need to be alone for a while.

'Forgive me if I was annoying you by being jealous, but I think one couldn't be in love if one wasn't.'

This, he thought, was pretty moderate in tone, for he knew that she was a passionate girl. He replied briefly, and with affection.

Then, shortly afterwards, Amanda telephoned to him. She would like him to lunch with her, if it wasn't breaking into his work. Her voice was cheerful and robust; yet this wasn't a mere casual invitation. It was a command. He said he would be pleased to come and, not putting off the evil day, named the day following. 'Good,' she said, 'meet me at the Jardin des Gourmets in Greek Street, one o'clock.'

He was there before her, disquieted, but determined not to seem so. She came in a little late, a hat of white feathers surmounting her great bun of hair. She looked, as always, a little mad – which she was not – but impressive. He could tell that the waiters knew her. She was carrying a novel of Montherlant's, *Pity for Women*.

'This wasn't the table I wanted,' she told the head waiter, 'it's too much in the open. We'll move to the other side.'

When the move had been achieved, she greeted Toby cordially, ordered apéritifs, and went straight to a verdict upon her book. 'Why do women like this man? He loathes them. Pity for women, indeed! He hasn't got any. Yet they go for him. I expect we're all masochists at heart, though we don't like to think so. I'm certainly not aware of being. But he's such a pure stylist and he does get on with the job. How's yours, by the way?'

'Ticking over,' Toby said. He did not again thank her for the week-end, since he was punctilious with his bread-and-butter letters.

'Poor Edward,' she said when they had ordered, 'I'm afraid he's taken a terrible toss. Not that he ever shows it.'

Toby could remember the time when he had.

'I thought it was a fascinating play. What's wrong with people these days? What do they want?'

'I suppose one gets out of phase with current fashion. And then, by doing nothing different whatsoever, one gets back again.'

'Sage remark,' said Amanda, 'very sage.'

She told him fervently that he must bring his mother to Haddesdon at all costs. 'She's still a great lion.'

He noticed that she had said 'still', as though a little of the glory had already departed.

'Honestly, Mrs Ferrars—'

'I think you might call me Amanda.'

'Thank you. Honestly, she's unbudgeable. It surprises me now that I even got her to Cambridge.'

'But she was superb that night!'

'She says she was petrified.'

'No, she wasn't,' Amanda said positively. 'But it makes a good excuse for, as you say, not budging.'

'She's had a very sheltered life.'

'Well, she's made the shelter for herself. I realise that. I once had a hermit-like period, only I don't suppose you'll believe it.'

'I admit I find it hard to.'

He was apprehensive. He knew perfectly well that she had something to say to him, but not that she was herself fearful of doing so. She was simply biding her time.

After a long and eye-protruding inspection of the sweet trolley, she said she would just have coffee. Toby said he would have the same.

'Oh, you must have some of this goo! You're not slimming, are you? Because there's not the slightest need.'

Politely, he refused.

'I suppose you've heard about Maisie's job? It's very boring, but she felt she couldn't hang about at home all day. Perhaps she'll get something better soon.' Then she plunged straight in. 'She's unhappy. Do you know that?'

'I'm sorry,' said Toby, 'but no, I didn't know.'

Amanda looked around the dining-room, lowered her voice. 'I want to talk to you. I'm not one to beat about the bush.'

His heart shrivelled.

'Go ahead,' was all he could say, with as much lightness as he could muster. Since she was silent for a few moments, he had time to contemplate her self-confidence, her air of slight vulgarity, her formidableness.

'I know you've been sleeping with her. I always know what's going on under my roof.'

This phrase he hated, feeling himself the betrayer of her hospitality, which in fact he had been.

She went on, 'I don't like it, of course; no mother would. But you can't oppose young people much these days: they'll do what they want even if you try. Well, aren't I right?'

Toby said, 'I am very fond of her. And I'm sorry it was in your house.'

'Yes, you are very fond of her. But she's in love with you, worse luck – I wouldn't have said that once. It's a very different matter. Have you two quarrelled?'

'Oh no.'

She said, with an air of exasperation, 'Why do people think I'm as blind as a bat? Of course it was about Claire. You went to see her at Glemsford, and didn't tell Maisie.'

'It was silly. But I assure you, Claire is nothing to me.'

'I must tell you this. Even when she was a little girl, Maisie hated surprises, even when they were nice ones. Even before her birthday, she wanted to know what she would be given. She would rather know the worst of anything, than not know. Sometimes I think you're being dull, not to notice that. It wasn't Claire she was upset about, it was Claire *knowing that she didn't know*.'

'There has been a great deal of ridiculous fuss over Claire,' Toby said, recovering himself. 'Maisie will get over it.'

'Do you realise that some girls of a certain type never get over some things fully at all? She'll forget in time, but then she'll sometimes remember. Look here, Toby – drink up your coffee, it's getting cold – if you don't mean anything serious with Maisie, it would be better if you cut the cable. I learned to do that when I was young. I like you, but I won't have Maisie upset. Or rather, I'd prefer that you upset her once and for all, than see her in this state. She hasn't said anything to me, of course. She seldom does, though in a way we're close.'

Toby pondered all this. He was surprised, as he had been with Edward, that he resented her interference so little. The most tormenting thing had been to him, the phrase 'under my roof'. It was a trifle grandiose, but it had rung true. Meanwhile she had changed her mind about the sweet trolley, and was eating cherry flan.

He said finally, 'Amanda, I'm awfully sorry about this. But I promise you that I won't upset Maisie again. I've made an ass of myself, I know.'

'Perhaps rather worse, but we won't go into that.'

'I can't really do without her, you know.'

'Not for the moment, probably you can't. And yes, you have made an ass of yourself, but then, young men do.'

She finished the flan, carefully wiping away a stain of red juice from her upper lip. 'That's all,' she said. 'That's all I'm going to say.' And she meant it. She talked for a while about her new 'season', still hoped he might coax Mrs Roberts into coming down.

When she had paid the bill and they had risen to go, he asked if he might get her a taxi.

'Don't bother, dear. My car should be here by now.'

It was. The moment they emerged, it drew up for her. No parking problems. 'Can I drop you back?' Amanda said.

He replied, 'That's kind of you. But I want to go round to Foyle's, to look for some books.'

When she had driven off among her parcels he thought: how angry had she been with him? He could not tell. He believed not very; she was too intent upon what Maisie wanted not to be at least pretty complaisant. However, he made up his mind that he would not sleep with Maisie at Haddesdon again.

He did not get the chance. His invitations were for the day only. Luncheon parties. Teas. The circus as usual though Edward was in New York, seeing whether his play would have more luck there. (It did, in fact.) He got into the habit of seeing Maisie regularly again, and once more she was temperate and sweet. What she knew about what her mother had known, he had not the slightest idea. Like all apparently open people, she had her heart-hugged secrecies.

There were some new faces in Amanda's circle, the string quartet, who seemed to him very dull, twittering like sparrows, an abstract painter, two or three young men whom he hardly identified, one of them being a baronet of twenty-four. Toby thought how enviable it would be to be a baronet at that age. A place to stand? Of course, of a sort. He realised that to these young men Maisie was attractive; and though not jealous in her sense, was resentfully conscious that they would have more to give her than he.

Amanda greeted him with her usual effusion: the meal at the Jardin des Gourmets might never have been. But he thought she was watchful. What did he know of her? Precious little. What there was, was very much on the surface. Had she felt like a tigress-mother, protecting a cub? Or had her libertarian principles dominated her? He began to think, perhaps for the first time, that he did not know very much about anyone. Anyone at all.

He saw Maisie in London with fair regularity. Their bodies fitted so beautifully that when she was with him, he could scarcely contemplate a life without her. She was both ardent and accomplished – she had become so. She no longer reproached him, for she knew now instinctively what it was that he most hated. Once he went down to Lavenham, to see her pottering around the antique shop, dusting, as she had said, rearranging, trying to make a more effective window display. 'I'm learning,' she said, and seemed to load this with a deeper meaning.

Then, in the summer, Claire wrote asking him to a May Ball. She had a couple of tickets, but no partner – 'or none that I care for. Can you come with me? I don't know whether Maisie would mind, though I'm afraid she would. We're harmless people after all, aren't we, you and I?'

But he wrote refusing this: in Cambridge they would be too conspicuous, though this thought he did not convey to her. He wouldn't be in England, he would be in France. He hated to miss the chance, but that was how it was. She wrote briefly: she was sorry but – that was how it was. She would have to take some awful weed with her. 'A sad life, Toby, as it so often turns out.'

He was filled for quite a week by a sense of virtue, of temptation overcome. Besides, he was not quite ready for her yet. He would have to lie quiet, because he was not going to France at all; perhaps he would do so, with Tiller's encouragement, for a few months in the autumn. So, during May week, he did not even see Maisie. She might talk, though he knew her intimacy with Claire had much abated. But one never knew.

Then, towards the end of term, something happened which much troubled him. He returned from a long day at the British Museum to find Professor Tiller pacing his room, a little, plump man with hot eyes. He was holding so much of the thesis as Toby had let him see.

'Look here,' he said, 'this won't quite do. There's a lot of work in it, but you simply don't know enough. You may have to make a fresh start. Sit down, and don't get in a state.'

Toby sat, dismayed. He was not accustomed to set-backs of this order. 'Well, what shall I do?'

'My immediate thought is that you should go to France and spend next term there. You can slog it out in the Bibliothèque Nationale. I think you've milked the BM dry, in so far as you can. Is that a possibility for you? We could raise some money, I dare say.'

'Yes, I could go.'

'Anyway,' said Tiller, looking more appeased, 'you'd have quite a good time. And it would do you good to get abroad for a bit.'

It was agreed.

When he had gone, Toby looked at the rejected thesis into which he had put so much labour – and, despite himself, so much hope. The laziness induced by the prospect of new beginnings for the moment swamped him. How much could he salvage? Something, surely. Well, he would go to France and if he still felt – as he did now – a failure, he would have to turn his mind to other things. He thought he knew where he might turn it.

19

He went down to Haddesdon in August to say good-bye. It held the promise of a scorching day, Amanda's tutelary weather, and he guessed that there would be a picnic; an uncomfortable meal. He would rather have eaten at a table indoors. He took an early train, so that he could have an hour with Maisie before the 'circus' arrived.

When she met him, she was as he most liked to see her: she did not look unhappy, but filled with the promise of a day of pleasure; she was smiling and calm. She wore the white blouse in which he best remembered her, this time with a white cotton skirt sprinkled with yellow flowers. 'Let's drive,' she said, 'let's not get back too soon. The string quartet's coming, and Peter Coxon, and several others whom you don't know. And you remember George Pollock?' This was the critic who had been so kind to his mother.

'Of course I remember. By the bye, Mummy's having a seven minute programme on television soon. She resisted every attempt to let them bring lights and cables into the house, so they'll have to do it in the studio, with some of her paintings in the background.'

They drove round and about. 'I shall miss you,' Maisie said, with something of a stoical look, he thought, though perhaps he had become hypersensitive, 'but I'll come over to see you.' The light breeze of their passage fluttered her pretty hair. He thought he had never seen hair so pretty, or come to that, a girl so pretty. She had grown on him. 'You'll have to listen to Haydn this afternoon,' she warned, 'shall you mind that?'

'He's not my favourite. But I can wander off if I like, I suppose. People do, and your mother doesn't appear to resent it.'

'My dear,' she said quaintly, 'it would be quite against Mummy's principles to resent anything.'

He was not so sure of that.

They stopped for half-an-hour at a small public house, where they drank some beer and played shove-ha'penny, a game at which Maisie proved singularly adept. It all seemed to him idyllic, a pleasant, unstressed manner for the saying of farewells. The bar had a sanded floor, and smelled of tobacco and ale-slops. Such customers as there were ignored them, except for one old man who was casting a covert glance at Maisie's skill. 'Nobody likes us here – us newcomers, I mean, though we've been here for eight years – and nobody ever will. One gets to terms with it. Let them keep to themselves. So shall we.'

They returned to the garden where Amanda was presiding in some batwinged garment, over her first guests. She reintroduced Toby to the quartet, who seemed indistinguishable from one another, except that the fourth was a girl, and to several persons whose names he had heard of, but which he knew he would forget. Edward Crane was not there.

The meal, of course, was lavish as usual, Amanda dominant over it. She was in one of her most queenly moods, obviously in that state of enjoyment which only this kind of entertainment could induce. Toby talked to Peter Coxon, whom he was learning to respect, no longer critical of his small stature, his snake-like head, his pink pussy-bow tie. Since his return from America, where he had considerable success, he seemed far from inflated; indeed, his gushing manner seemed to have left him. He seemed all set for a life of greater dignity.

Toby had read half of his new novel, and had been impressed. He was not sure that the effect of subtlety was not produced by letting a character express what he thought, and then by letting him act in a manner precisely contrary to it. He did not know whether this was an old literary dodge or a new one; still, he no longer wrote Peter off.

The book was restrained; it showed not the slightest trace of the homosexuality which had characterised the first. Men and women suffered in it, through one another. Transference? There might have been some, though he did not think so. Anyway, to transfer the sexes, Toby thought, must be far more difficult than innocent people thought. He expressed his admiration.

'I hope it's all right,' Peter said, 'but the moment I see a book of mine actually in print I'm plunged into despair. I always feel I could have done so much better.'

'I suppose Michelangelo thought so, when he had a good final look at the Sistine Chapel,' said Toby.

Peter gave something as near to a grin as his sober features would permit.

'It must be wonderful to have a success.' Toby meant this.

'A bit of a success. Don't let's exaggerate.'

'From what they tell me.'

'Oh, they'll tell you anything.'

The rest of them were in casual clothes, but Peter in a dark suit, trimly-waisted. They sat down under a tree (though the grass was wet from the day before, and Amanda had had to have rugs spread for the picnic) until the quartet was finished.

When they went back to the party, Amanda had gone into the house.

'She's finishing your book, Peter,' Maisie said, 'you know she can't bear not to keep up.'

'That gives me a feeling of terror. I don't know why.'

'You needn't. Mummy went back to it because she couldn't resist it, not because she was in a critical mood.'

The heat of noon had not departed. They were all beaded about their foreheads and their upper lips. They talked in a desultory fashion and awaited Amanda's re-emergence.

She came at last, when tea was almost over, bat-winging from the house, the book clasped to her bosom as if it might have been the Book of Kells.

'Listen, all of you! Peter's book ends with a parable. I want to read it to you, Peter's Parable. Now make yourselves comfortable, because this is important. You don't mind?' This last was addressed punctiliously to Peter himself.

'If you'll give me time to make myself scarce, Amanda,' he replied, and strolled off towards the stream.

Her guests sat beneath the blue-green tent of the cedar tree, now filtering only a slant or two of gold between its branches.

'All well?' Amanda demanded. 'Smoke now if you're going to, because I don't want anyone lighting up while they're listening.'

She herself sat in a garden chair, rather like a throne, beyond the shade, the sun on her abundant hair. She began to read in her loud, plummy voice.

'"There is a country where there is no marriage nor giving in marriage. A husband and wife who have loved, may continue to love profoundly and with infinite tenderness: but without sexuality.

They may walk in the majestic gardens, where all the flowers bloom at the same time, in the courts with floors of jasper, shaded by willow-trees, and bright with fountains springing lean and silver as mercury in a thermometer to spill in bounty over their alabaster basins: but there is no marriage nor giving in marriage. Everyone is happy without fear of endings. The lord of the country passes through his domains sometimes, greeted cordially and without fear: but even he cannot think about everything at the same time.

' "Now there came from her own country a woman who had been pining for seven years for her husband. There she had loved him with a rending ache, and had longed to be reunited with him. When she came to the other country, he was the first person she saw, awaiting her with brilliant face, his arms open wide. She went to him as to a home. Yet there was no marriage nor giving in marriage.

' "It seemed that a change had come over everyone, except herself; she was a sport, a freak. She knew it, and even in this marvellous country she was filled with secrecy and guilt. The lord, in passing, spoke kindly to her and his eyes were keen: but he asked her no questions.

' "She spent all her time – there was sunlight and moonlight but no division into hours and days – at the man's side. They went out into the forests, where there were all manner of wild animals and insects; but she was terrified of none of them, as she had been in her own country. They were the lord's creatures and comfortable in his sight, and therefore in the sight of all his people. The man who was once her husband was content to be with her, but she – the freak, the sport – was not content. There was no marriage nor giving in marriage. But her love had been so overmastering that she wanted him still. It had transcended the gift of eternal bliss. So she continued to ache and to implore, and he to love her and to smile. But, he said, all the rest was over, like a dream forgotten. Surely they existed on the summits of happiness, untroubled, upon the exquisite plateau? He was, of course, faithful to her, seeking no other companion (as he not infrequently had in the other country) because, as with everyone else here, desire had no part in him.

' "So, for this woman, the country became not a paradise but a torment. All the flowers faded and gave out an evil odour, the bird-song wrought upon her nerves like the Chinese water torture, the fountains laughed like the tittering of idiots. Only her body begged and beseeched. The lord of the country came by one day, and he knew at once that a mistake – the only one in a multiplicity of worlds – had been made.

' "In darkness she was taken to the edge of the sparkling sea, which was the empyrean, and there floated gently out, to sink forever downwards through the vastness between the stars, sink neither in pain nor in bliss, but in comfort as on a feather-bed. She had few thoughts as the aeons passed by her, except for one: It has all been worth while." '

When Amanda had finished reading, Toby saw the great tears standing in her eyes, and he guessed that she, too, who had never spoken of these things, had loved like that. Maisie, with head bowed, was plucking like the dying at the folds of her dress. For himself, the parable had enabled him to catch a glimpse of the future: when he might love not boyishly but in maturity, and know pain. But this, he realised, was not yet to be. Had Peter written it with a man or a woman in mind? Perhaps it did not matter very much.

'I don't think that needs much comment from me,' Amanda said at last, to a somewhat meaningless and even sycophantic chorus of praise.

Peter came back across the lawn.

'It was wonderful,' she told him.

'I hope it was all right. If I didn't, I shouldn't have written it. But it may be *kitsch* for all I know.'

'There are more things in *kitsch*, Horatio—' Maisie began, then laughed. 'No, I thought it was good.'

After tea, most of them rose to leave, but Maisie insisted that Toby stay.

'It will only be pot-luck,' Amanda warned them, not looking overly pleased.

'We're going for a sandwich in Clare,' Maisie said. 'Toby's leaving us for months, and I want the time that's left.'

So they went off together, Amanda first kissing him lightly on the cheek. The early evening was still hot. As they drove, Maisie said to him, 'It won't be for ever. You'll be able to do great things. And I shall drop over to see you – that is, if you want me to.'

'Of course I shall want you to, pet.' And indeed, he felt that he was going to miss her. She was in her prettiest mood, showing no sign of strain; doing everything she could to please him. She said only one disturbing thing. 'I couldn't really bear Peter's parable. It was a bit near the bone.'

'I suppose all our bones are more exposed than we think.'

'I could almost wish yours were.'

'Ah, you don't know.'

It was more convenient for him to catch the train back from Cambridge, so Maisie drove him to Clare station. They waited in the glowing light, not speaking much. Then they saw the train signalled, the puff of smoke from not so far away.

Now she clung to him. 'Good luck, darling. You'll write to me?'

'Copiously, I expect.'

'Go to some of the places where we went.'

'Of course I shall.'

'Eat *croque-monsieur*, and remember me.' She laughed. The last thing he saw from the window was the radiance of her laughter.

20

He had just time before he left for France to see his mother's tele-vision broadcast. It had been pre-recorded, so he was able to watch it with her and with his father.

She appeared on the screen sparrow-like but at ease, wearing the dress she had bought for the private view in Cambridge, even though it had been warm for the time of year.

'Fancy me,' she said, taking a bemused look at herself.

'Yes, fancy you, Dora,' said her husband, moving closer to her side.

She was asked whether she were not something of a recluse.

'Oh, I wouldn't say that. I just like my home, that's all. I'm not good at meeting people.'

'May I ask,' said the interviewer, 'when you first began to paint?'

'Well, I suppose I've always dabbled. But seriously, only during the past five years.'

'Do you paint from life?'

'Not really. From the window, sometimes. But mostly out of my head.'

'You've attracted a good deal of attention, you know. If I may say so, very well deserved. Do you never feel like enjoying the fun of it?'

'I like people to like my pictures.'

Several of them were shown, not looking so impressive in black and white. Lastly, the picture Amanda had bought, of Mrs Roberts in her kitchen.

'Why did you paint that?'

'Why not? It just seemed something to do.'

The interview soon came to an end, with Mrs Roberts as un-communicative as usual.

'Well,' said Mr Roberts, switching the set off, 'that I should live to see the day!'

Toby kissed her. 'Congratulations, Mum.'

'I couldn't think of anything to say. And they did ask me about people I didn't know about. They would call me a Primitive; I thought that was some kind of ape.'

'Not exactly,' Toby said, 'and you're not an ape. You're wonderful.'

'I think,' said his mother acutely, 'that I'd have made less of a stir if I'd wanted to go out and about. They don't understand that I like it here, and that I don't like meeting new people. It puzzles them.'

All the same, it had made a difference to her life. Neighbours who had occasionally dropped in now did so no longer, but she did not mind. 'I have to get on with my work,' she said, 'and if I'm always having to make cups of tea it interferes.'

And so Toby went away. He spent most of his days at the Bibliothèque Nationale. Maisie came to see him once, and they tried to reconstruct (which is never a success) the days of their happiness. But she seemed content at the time. He acquired a casual girl, a student whom he had picked up in a café on the Boulevard St Michel, and she supplied his needs. When they parted, it was without much feeling on either side.

He was not especially happy these days. Paris had lost some of its charm for him by familiarity, and his work was not going well. He had been working hard, of course, but was getting sick of constant research. *Saint-Just* remained unrevised; he simply did not know how to begin.

A fortnight before his return he wrote to Claire. It was an ordinary, friendly letter and seemed to be without point: yet it had one. 'I am beginning to feel more and more that I'm not cut out for the academic life. I'd like to dabble in a wider world, find out something of how the world ticks. If I do chuck it up I shall disappoint everyone, including my mother and father, so I dare say I shall go through with it after all. Still, I am a bit down in the mouth and if I have much more of the French Revolution I think I may go a little off my head.' Nobody was less likely to go off his head than he, but he was, as he put it to the most honest part of himself, 'rattling the tin can'.

Her reply was all he had hoped for.

'I think you're a coot to throw up the opportunities you've got. Still, who am I to be preachy, when I do damn all myself? But if you want any advice, I'm sure Daddy would give it you – I think he said he would. Shall we talk about this when you get back? I shall have something to consult you about, by the way, so you must be the wise old man of the tribe. Give me a ring. Love.'

He returned to London on a bleak morning in November. The air smelt of dampness and, mysteriously, of chrysanthemums; the leaves on the pavement were sodden underfoot. He went at once to his lodgings and did not immediately make contact with Tiller. He was not sure what he would find to say to him.

The first person he rang was Maisie, but he found, to his surprise, that without a word to him she had gone off with Amanda to share the latter's annual escape to the sun. 'I think Miss Maisie will be home before Christmas, though,' said the housekeeper, her voice holding a note of encouragement.

So he telephoned Claire, who greeted him brightly. Yes, they could meet. Why not? He could come to Glemsford, couldn't he? There would only be her father and herself at home. Her mother had gone skiing in the Austrian Alps – 'and I do wish she wouldn't, poor darling. She's so badly adapted for it, and she usually breaks something. Not large fractures, little ones.'

He went down on a Saturday. She herself opened the door, wearing slacks and a dark blue turtle-necked sweater. She kissed him casually, now, as if he were an old friend to whom these formalities meant nothing, and led the way into the hall. It was draughty, as usual, but the log fire was high, and they seated themselves on a long stool before it.

'Before we get down to brass tacks,' said Claire, 'we need a drink.'

She poured whisky for him, gin for herself. 'Now then. You're looking well, Toby, despite your doubts and hesitations.'

'So are you.'

'Probably you ought to get out more. Do you, much?'

'I walk between my lodgings and the university, and to the British Museum. That's all.'

'I wish you rode. Sometimes I think we must teach you. How's Maisie?'

Toby said he did not know: she had gone away.

'She didn't tell me. But then, she doesn't tell me anything since I made that boob about you coming here. So silly – her getting so remote, I mean. But it was silly of me, too. I don't think much before I speak.'

Toby believed that in fact she thought a good deal. She was a subtle girl in her own way, though it was her pretence not to be so.

She questioned him sharply about his work, how things had really gone in Paris.

'As I told you, so-so.'

'That will need some thinking about. Don't do anything hasty; you may just be in temporary dumps.'

'I may be. But I don't think so.'

'You're not getting much lunch today,' she said abruptly, 'only sandwiches, but plenty of them. I thought we'd have them before the fire. Pour yourself another drink. We never manage to keep warm in this house, and the kitchen and the dining-room are both perishing.'

When she had left him, he thought about her. She seemed at times very nearly beautiful, but not quite. Did she lack temperament? If so, so much the better. But if temperament she had, she kept it to herself. On the surface an open-air girl, comradely, a little horsy, her interests limited. She would be peaceful, her nerve-ends deeply buried. Though, he suspected, not a good home-maker (as his mother would have put it) she had the knack of making things around her pretty easy and relaxed.

She came back with the tray. 'Help yourself. Now I want to talk.'

But she ate in silence for a while, and so did he.

At last she said, 'I am *thinking* of getting married. Note that I underline the thinking part. What do you think?'

It was something of a shock to him. He had not expected this.

'How can I think before I know more of the facts?' he temporised.

'Well, let me give them to you. His name is Alec, and he's a youthful Bart: his father died two years ago. You may have met him at Haddesdon – he knows Amanda well.'

'I think I did, once.'

'He is nice, kind, quite clever, but he has no chin. I wonder whether I could forget about that? It oughtn't to matter, but somehow it does.'

'He might grow a beard,' said Toby facetiously.

'I can't bear whiskers. No, I'm being unkind to him. But do you

147

remember how Anna Karénina' (she pronounced it with the accent on the penultimate syllable) 'suddenly noticed that her husband's ears stuck out?' This from Claire, who claimed to have read nothing except thrillers. However, she was adept at picking things up. 'He hasn't got much money, but that doesn't matter. I'm beginning to feel that if I don't settle down soon, I shall begin to wither on the vine. Anyway, that's what he implies.'

'How old are you?'

'Twenty-three.'

'That's no age for withering,' said Tony, feeling a certain coldness in his stomach.

'Still, it might be a good thing, mightn't it? What do you advise?'

Perhaps it was because her bold frank look was not so frank as usual, it dawned on Toby that she was not serious about this marriage at all.

'Then I should settle for him,' he said, 'chin and all. If we're fond of people,' he said sagely and with a degree of deliberate pomposity, 'we tend to like them because of their defects, not in spite of them.'

She went on eating as if she were ravenous; there was something stagey about this, as if she were an actress compelled nightly, with matinées Wednesdays and Saturdays, to consume a sizeable meal before an audience. Then she stopped and pushed the tray away. She replenished the fire.

'You wouldn't mind, of course,' she said.

Toby said warily, 'I should think all the men who knew you would mind.'

'I liked you, you know. The first time we met, I behaved in a very fast manner. Did you like it?'

'Of course I did.'

She kissed him again, and this time he responded with some ardour. He did desire her, if it is possible to desire with caution.

'Daddy won't be in till three. We've got time.'

She meant, to go to bed. In a dream-state he followed her upstairs to a vast cold room, where there was a four-poster hung with faded damask. He could not believe that this was happening to him. The room was so bleak that she undressed very rapidly and slipped at once between the sheets, waiting for him to join her. He caught only a glimpse of her body, which was broad and muscular but, as she had said before, with no surplus flesh.

When he took her, it was with ease and delight. Unlike Maisie, she was far from inexperienced. 'Oh, yes,' she said at last, 'I've been around. But always with discrimination. I have been discriminating over you. By the way, you don't have to feel that this has meant anything.'

'But if I want to?' He wished at once that he had not said this. It augmented his betrayal. If Maisie, of course, had not gone off without a word to Jamaica, it would never have happened.

'Come on, old thing,' she said, 'time to make ourselves proper again.'

They were very proper by the time Llangain came in from golf, to wolf the rest of the sandwiches which Claire had forgotten to cover for him.

'Good to see you, Toby.'

'And you, sir.'

'I hear from my girl that you have doubts about your future.'

Toby considered his reply rather carefully. Claire was watching him. 'They're small doubts as yet. I have to do some thinking. But sometimes I feel I don't want to be locked up.'

Llangain frowned, and went on with the sandwiches. 'Stale,' he said, 'but acceptable.'

'Daddy, you know you had lunch at the club.'

'What they call lunch. It's getting worse and worse.' He turned to Toby again. 'When I was at Oxford, at your age, I used to dream of being "locked up", as you call it. I used to dream about "dons on the dais serene". But I wasn't brainy enough. Now, you are. What's wrong?'

'I think I want to see how the world works.'

'Perhaps better if you didn't,' said Llangain, lighting his pipe. 'Far better. I never like what I see. But if you'd care to take a look into my business, I could arrange it for you.'

'That's very kind of you, sir.'

'Don't call me sir. It makes me feel decrepit. I may be getting on that way, but I don't like it rubbed in. You could see Clive Baumann, one of our junior partners. He's a bright lad. He'd put you in the picture. Just let me know if ever you think that might be a good thing.'

'Thank you. May I wait a bit?'

'Wait as long as you like. The offer's there. But whether you'd see the world any better from our side of things, I don't know. I envy you the chances that you've got. Claire isn't brainy, either,' he said simply, without pejorativeness and without, it seemed to Toby, the slightest idea of what she was really like, 'or I should have steered her that way. Switzerland – all spit and polish.'

'No spit, Daddy,' Claire said, 'just polish, morning, noon and night, till our skins were raw.'

She had been listening to the dialogue with a kind of inner glee, not in the least disturbed by her father's reflections upon herself.

She said to Toby, 'Hairy isn't too brilliant, either, but he'll make something of himself. Or if he doesn't, something will be made of him.'

She was revealing herself more than she knew. The pose of horsy stolidity was wearing off; she was proving to be good fun.

'Well,' said Llangain, with an air of concluding the subject, 'mind you let me know what you decide. All the time in the world.' He said to Claire, 'Can we have tea early?'

'But you've just eaten all those sandwiches!'

'Is there any of that cake left? The one Mrs Dodge made?'

'I dare say I can find you a slab.'

'It was the orange cake,' said Llangain, 'it was good. I dare say Toby would like some too.'

While she was getting the tray ready he said to Toby, 'I hope my wife isn't breaking any limbs this time. She always does, you know. She's only fit for the nursery slopes, but she's ambitious. Your mother ever go in for this sort of nonsense?'

This astonishing example of forgetfulness took Toby aback. But he said, 'It hasn't been at all in her line.'

'Oh, yes, she paints. Jolly good too. Tell her so from me, if the praise of an ignoramus is any good to her. In fact, I do remember telling her that myself.'

Claire brought tea and the orange cake. She was looking more vivid, more excited, than Toby had remembered seeing her.

He left soon after the meal; he was driving back.

She came out on to the steps. 'See you soon.'

'I hope so,' said Toby, putting the car in gear.

Then she called after him, 'If I don't marry Alec, I might always marry you.' She grinned and waved her hand. Before he could think of a reply she had gone into the house, shutting the door behind her.

21

As he drove home, Toby had, of course, very much to think about. It had been a day to bewilder and to enchant him; yet had it meant very much to Claire? Her last flippant remark had startled him, but had it been altogether flippant? He decided that it must have been.

He told himself that the whole thing had really been Maisie's fault, all of it. If she had bothered to write to him, he would probably not have gone to Glemsford, certainly not have gone to bed with Claire. He could be sure of that (or couldn't he?) He felt for a second like Macheath, and he grinned to himself; but it was with discomfort.

The night was sharp, and for him it had still the smell of chrysanthemums. Such weather would henceforth be for him Claire's weather.

He found a letter from Maisie awaiting him. He did not open it at once; he was in too great a perturbation of spirit. It was unlike him, at this hour, but he felt he needed a drink. He drank a gin and tonic, slowly. Then he opened the envelope, which was postmarked 'Haddesdon'.

'Dear, dear Toby,

'I think you must be home by now.' (She had miscalculated; he had been back in England for some time past.) 'I expect you have wondered why I haven't bothered you with letters. For one thing, I don't think you like to be bothered too much. For another, I have been thinking about our last time in Paris. It seemed all right, but it wasn't really, was it? Something was wrong, and I can't put my finger on it. You were rather remote, when you forgot not to be, and that's not like you. Dear, if you think we're coming to an end you must simply *tell me*, you know I hate not to know.

'It has cost me a lot to write this, and I dare say I shall have to post it in a rush, not thinking at all, before my courage goes running away at my heels. But I love you too much – you have never said this to me, you know—'

He knew.

'—to cling on to you, if it's not what you want. I could almost want for you what you want – I say "almost": it's all I can manage at the moment. I think only a saint could wish it totally, and I'm very far from being that.

'I was thinking about Peter's parable. It wasn't very good, was it? So Biblical, and it didn't fit the rest of the book. But I think I might love like that, and I also think it isn't the way you want to be loved.

'If you want us to meet, let me know. Please let us, even if it's only that I shall hear all your news. I am writing this late at night, which is the worst time for it. I should have written it about nine-thirty in the morning when my head was clear.

'Jamaica wasn't much fun. I got too sunburned, and it is boring lying about beaches all day. It was all right for mother, she was unfashionably reading Trollope's political novels from end to end, so she was occupied.

'None of this is what I really meant to say. I don't know if I did wrong not to write before, or whether it was quite the opposite. I only wanted you to feel free. Write if you like, or telephone.

'For ever, Maisie.'

He read this again and again. It was a sacrificial letter, wasn't it? Or wasn't it quite? For a moment he had a sense of absolute freedom, succeeded by a sense that he was still bound to her. He was, he told himself, as before, young, young, young. He had little money, at present no prospects, though he fancied Llangain might put some in his way. Why should he be forced to make decisions? He was overcome by a restless irritation. He had enough problems of his own, unconcerned with girls. He would sit through another term under Tiller, and then see how he felt about things. There was plenty of time, the Lord only knew there was plenty of time, but people were trying to make him telescope it. He thought he would put off making contact with Maisie for a day or two, and was not at all surprised that he should have a restless night. He blamed her for that, as well.

Next day he had an unexpected visit from Adrian, who had recently become ordained, and who now wore, with a somewhat unsuccessful struggle against pride, a clerical collar. It made him look more handsome than ever.

'Father Stedman,' Toby said, smiling, 'and now we shall all mean it.'

Adrian looked pleased, but said nothing. After he had asked about Toby, he told him that he had been offered an assistant curacy in a small parish near Wragby, in Lincolnshire. 'It was all very quick. They seem to sweep us up the moment we're available. It would be ungrateful of me to look down my nose at Lincs, though it's rather more remote than I'd hoped for. Still, it is going to give me the experience I badly need, and simply haven't got.'

He would only accept a cup of instant coffee. When it had been made he said, as if wanting to get something off his chest, 'I've seen Bob and Rita. I thought I ought to. Have you?'

'No. You mean, separately?'

'Didn't you know? They're back together in Lensfield Road. Rita thought twice about having a divorce and Bob wanted to be with the child, so there we are. I don't suppose anyone could imagine that they were happy, but it seems better than nothing.'

'Why did you think you should go?' Toby asked curiously.

'Rita wrote to me again. She said she was sorry she'd been a bit silly in the past, but that she did want us all to be friends. What else could I do?'

'So it was a kind of pastoral duty on your part.'

'You could call it that. They were both subdued, Bob especially. I don't think he will ever get over what he did. Perhaps it's better for him not to.'

'That sounds to me a bit hard,' said Toby, 'coming from you. Even you must have some inkling what started the trouble in the first place. Surely the poor sod – sorry, Adrian, I must watch my step now – ought to be allowed to forgive himself.'

'We're all forgiven. Forgiving oneself is quite another matter, and I'm not sure most of us achieve it.'

'I hope Rita's going to leave you alone now.'

'Everyone will leave me alone,' said Adrian, with a glimmer of a smile, 'when I'm installed in Lincs. And I shan't mind. The present incumbent is old and, I'm told, bone idle. So I shall have plenty to occupy myself.' He drank the coffee, passed his cup to be refilled. 'Now tell me all about Maisie.'

Toby hesitated. 'There really isn't very much to tell.'

'I'm allowed to marry couples now, you know,' Adrian teased him, 'I hope I may one day perform the office for you two.'

'Perhaps. Nothing's very settled, though. We seem to have been drifting a bit.'

'I'm sorry.'

'And of course, I'm unsettled myself, as I told you. I don't really know what I'm going to turn my hand to in the long run.'

Gently he nudged Adrian into talking about himself: and Adrian talked. He seemed to feel the need for this. He was full of doubts – not religious doubts, for he had none – but doubts of his own capacities for the work that lay ahead. He felt unequipped, unfit, for any kind of pastoral work. He would be too young to have much influence. He had prayed for help (Adrian never minded talking about prayer) and the answers had always seemed reassuring for an hour or so, until the worry began again. Besides, apart from all that, there was the problem of his mother. He told Toby, for the first time, that she had had a stroke seven years ago and was partially paralysed. 'She used to be a friend of Amanda's and go to Haddesdon quite a lot, but she won't now, even when Amanda proposes to send big cars for her.' He couldn't leave her, he said, he had no one to leave her with. He proposed to take her with him to Lincolnshire if a place suitable for them both could be found – she had some money of her own, so that wasn't the problem. But the old priest wanted him to live at the vicarage, and if he insisted – which probably he would – he could only hope to have his mother cared for locally, perhaps in a small place with an SRN in charge. He went on and on, and Toby listened. As usual, Adrian did not know when to go home.

He did so at last, spurred by a half-hearted offer of more coffee, and when he had gone left Toby depressed. Adrian might not have felt good at giving people guidance, but Toby certainly was not.

Next day he wrote to Maisie, though it was some time before he could put his pen to paper. He was aware that she had given him a means of escape, if he really wanted this (he was yet unsure) but was ashamed to take advantage of it. Yet he could not help but feel that much of what had happened had been her fault, the result of her too delicate scruples.

'Yes, Pet,' (he began) 'you should have written. I couldn't quite understand it when you didn't. I would have written myself, but I thought your housekeeper was on the reserved side, and "Maisie, Jamaica" didn't seem to me a wholly satisfactory address.

'I didn't feel anything was wrong with us in Paris. Things when you try to repeat them can never be quite the same, but who expects them to be?' (Though he knew she had expected this.)

'I have quite a lot to talk about, mostly connected with my future plans, and I'd welcome your advice. Can you come here? I shan't be going home till December 23rd, just in time for Mummy's Christmas orgies. I have a lot to finish up here. *Saint-Just* hangs fire, I'm afraid, and though I have collected a whole mass of notes, I rather dread trying to collate them. I shall stick out the next term with Tiller, though if things don't look up for me, I shall really have to think again. I have another iron in the fire, but I'll tell you about that when I see you.

'My mother prospers. Her prices have risen; she can get, for a large painting, from between £75 and £100. How is yours? Give her my love. I hope you haven't burned yourself black, because you have such a pretty skin. Sorry this is so brief, but I can't think properly yet and it would be better to talk. Can you manage Friday? Love, as ever.'

She telephoned to say that she could; she would be with him about six. Her voice sounded laboured, as if she had just received a stiff dose of novocaine at the dentist's.

'Sufficient unto the day is the evil thereof' was one of Toby's favourite aphorisms. Yet he did dread seeing Maisie, because he was still half in love with her; but only half. He did not now think he would ever be wholly so. Her physical appeal remained considerable; but so did Claire's. He found himself inventing conversations between Maisie and himself, was realistic enough to abandon this exercise. One might indeed say what one proposed, but there was no guarantee – indeed, there was not the slightest likelihood – that the other would answer as anticipated. So he tried not to think at all until he saw her.

When she arrived at his digs she seemed unflustered, and she kissed him warmly as usual. She was, indeed, much browned by the sun but this was not unbecoming to her. She said at once, 'I'm afraid we have made a muddle of it. About writing. But I thought you'd like to be undisturbed.'

'You didn't go the right way to undisturb me,' he said, 'however, that's over now.'

He had bought wine, and food from a delicatessen. 'Soup will be hot,' he said, 'I thought we needn't go out.'

'Then you're going to be serious,' she said, 'I almost wish you weren't.'

'There's quite a lot to be serious about. As I told you, my work's in a mess, or I think it is. Tiller isn't congenial, but that's because he really doesn't approve of me. It might have been better if I'd gone to work with someone else.'

She took off her thick coat to reveal a dress of white tweed. Toby, accustomed still to count pennies, wondered what the costs of it would be at the cleaner's. He still made some of the calculations that his mother would make. But he said, 'Very pretty.'

'Thank you,' she said, as always responding courteously to the slightest compliment.

'Did you enjoy yourself out there?'

'I told you, I was rather bored. So many boiling bodies, so many fat ones in bikinis. Mother wore a very decorous beach dress; she says bathing suits are not for her these days. Really, you'd think she was a hundred from the way she talks.'

'I'd have thought she'd have looked magnificent.'

Beyond the window was a dark December day, the sky a packed and solid grey threatening the rain that had not yet fallen. Toby turned on the brightest of his lights, a converted oil lamp with shade of jade-green glass, a present from Maisie. 'More comfortable?' He gave her a drink, poured one for himself.

They sat side by side on the sofa, which was large and rather handsome but had defective springs. He put his arm round her waist.

'I did go to Glemsford once,' he said without preamble, 'but less to see Claire than her father.' He felt her body stiffen. 'He says he thinks he can help me, which is the iron in the fire that I wrote you about. How would you like me to be a merchant banker? I don't know how one does it, of course, but I could find out.'

She muttered something he did not quite catch.

He went on, talkative for once in an attempt to make her relax, 'It sounds preposterously grand. I suppose if they did take me on I'd have to start by licking stamps, if they do lick stamps these days, all my ideas on the subject are pretty Dickensian. But I'm not taking any action yet. What do you think?'

'If it suits you,' she said, her voice sounding ventriloquial as if it came from the far corner of the room. 'It isn't for me to judge.'

He kissed her. 'Stuffy. Don't be. What's the matter?'

'Nothing. What you do is your business.'

'And a little of yours, too. I'm fond of you, you know.'

'I don't think I do know, any more.'

'Pet, don't be a tragedy queen. There's nothing to be tragic about, honestly. Come on, drink that up and have another while I lay the table.'

'I'll do that.' She broke free of him. She knew where everything was. He watched her as she went with irritable precision from drawers to table, took plates from the small dresser which had come to him from his mother. He could see that she was not far from tears, but that she was determined not to let them fall. He knew now that a break must be made, but did not want it to be sudden; the more gradual the better. He believed it would be easier for her if he managed to extract himself little by little, still making love to her on occasion till they both slipped out of the way of it. He was far from feeling happy, but he was almost without a sense of guilt, having persuaded himself that if she had indeed written to him during all those months, things might have been quite different.

'How was Claire?' she asked, her back turned to him.

'Hearty. Much as usual. It would be better for her if she had a job, like you.'

'I had to give mine up, of course. But I can always go back to it. Of course, nobody else wants it.'

Now that the table was laid, her manner returned to something more like normality. He believed, ever-hopeful as she was, that his casual reference to Claire had given her some comfort.

'Are you driving back tonight?'

No, she said, she didn't care for the two hours on the dark roads, she had told him that before. She was spending the night with her sister. He nodded approval; he was protective towards her.

'Hungry?' he asked.

'Only so-so.'

Yet she seemed eager, as always, for food. He repressed the thought, which momentarily shocked even him by the callousness of its humour, that she was probably the one condemned man who would really make a hearty breakfast. Nevertheless, it cheered him to see her eat. He believed that, for the moment, the worst was over. He would not let her wash up. He had always made a guest of her and she had once loved to be so. He stacked the plates in his small kitchen, and brought the rest of the wine over to the sofa.

The green lamp shone, round and soft.

'I gave you that,' she said.

'Do you think I don't remember?'

She burst out, 'Oh, can't we talk?'

He hesitated. 'Better not, just now. We're nice and contented, aren't we? We've been exchanging tricky letters. Better forget them first. Tell me all about Jamaica.'

But he had heard the alarm-bell ring in his brain. She was trying to enter his mind, which he had only to a certain extent permitted. He wanted to take her to bed. This would at least delay the evil hour of *talking*. Oddly enough, he had never been so conscious of her golden prettiness. He rose to turn on the top-lights, fearful that the single green one would prove too evocative. Then he went back to the sofa and he caressed her in the way in which she had always hitherto delighted. But she no longer did so. She pushed him away, with a sharp, uncharacteristic movement.

When she spoke, her voice was authoritative. 'Toby, you can't *hide* for ever. Are we going to go on?'

'I don't see why not, quite. Why aren't we?'

'Because things have changed. I don't deceive myself. I never have. That's what you don't like about me,' she added shrewdly.

'I like everything about you.'

'But what is it all going to end in?'

'Pet, don't you think it's early to talk about ends?'

'No, I don't. I gave myself away when I did write to you, didn't I? And you gave away not a single thing. You never do. If I ever disliked you, it would be because of that. I'm at a hopeless disadvantage. I have told you how I feel. And I think you have told me how you don't.'

'Quiet,' Toby said, 'there's not much in all this.'

'Yes, there is,' she said, the tears now standing in her eyes, but still not falling, 'you're not in love with me, and I am with you.

What a confession to make! Mummy would say it's degrading, but she doesn't understand much.'

'I can't say big words,' Toby said slowly, 'but I thought you understood me better than that. I adore you, in my own way. But I can't come to decisions. I'm not ready. For giving up history, for adventuring with merchant banks, or anything else. I simply must be free to sort things out.'

'And you think you've left me free?'

'We both are, to an extent. But I want you, and I want you now.'

'I'm not a place to run to,' Maisie said, 'not a place to hide in. You must believe that. And for God's sake don't tell me you're young! You've done it so often that I've visualised you in rompers. I want some security, I need to know where I'm going. And I don't think I'm going anywhere with you.'

He told her she must give all this time, that she was tending to rush things, and that he could not bear.

'You're rushing away,' said Maisie, 'and that *I* cannot bear. But if I can, I must. I can't go on with a farce.'

This was so unlike her that he permitted himself to laugh: for the first time that evening. 'Come, darling,' he said – and he used this term rarely – 'I think neither of us has been feeling farcical. Hasn't there been much ado about nothing?'

'I may have done wrong,' said Maisie, 'but it was only because I thought it was what you would like.'

(She was right, he had liked it.)

'Come to bed,' he said.

'I won't. I don't want to.'

'I think you do.'

She flared up, not Maisie at all. 'How dare you tell me what I want, or don't want?'

'Quiet, quiet.'

'I shall be quiet. I'm going now. This is the end, isn't it?'

'Not if you don't wish it.'

'You know damned well I don't, but you do.'

'And you shouldn't really tell me what I want and don't want, should you? I'll be in touch with you, and then perhaps we can talk more sense. Sense hasn't been conspicuous this evening, don't you think so?'

He was still hoping that she would stay with him. But she

shrugged herself into her coat, carefully adjusted her hat before his one small mirror. When he kissed her she responded but not with warmth.

'Don't be so silly' was the last thing he said to her.

When she had gone, he switched off the green light.

22

For Christmas he sent her a jacquard scarf, she sent him an expensive boxed volume of *Les Très Riches Heures du Duc de Berry*.

Both wrote in mutual acknowledgment, and then Toby wrote again. He asked her to tea at his home, badgered into this by Mrs Roberts, who was hard with suspicion. 'Is there anything wrong between you and Maisie?' she said. She was nothing if not direct.

'Why, no, not really.'

'What do you mean, not really?' She was, for her, belligerent. He knew she loved Maisie, would have liked her for a daughter-in-law.

'Perhaps people tend to drift away from each other a bit. It can't be helped.'

'I hope this isn't your fault.'

'Listen, Mummy, I think this is my affair.' At the same time as he said it, he put his arm around her waist. 'Perhaps it will all come right in the end. But don't expect me to say so. I suppose we're both in a delicate situation.'

'Ask her here.'

'If you like.'

'Because *I* want to see her.' Mrs Roberts' demands were few, but when she made them it was with some emphasis.

So Maisie came, and everything was wrong. To his mother she was as sweet as usual, gentle, interested in all she was doing. But she seemed to look at Toby as little as possible.

She chattered brightly enough. Edward had a new play coming on, and he had high hopes of it. It was a modern play this time, but defiantly far from the kitchen sink, which was having its critical vogue, as he had predicted. It was, she said, based upon a successful *salonnière* – 'suggested by Mummy, of course, but taken a long way from her. His heroine's not at all like that. He did ask Mummy if she minded, and she made a token fuss, but really she was thrilled.'

Maisie examined all Mrs Roberts' new paintings, expressed her delight. She listened quietly to all the small indications of what might possibly be a larger success.

Mr Roberts was warm to her. 'You shouldn't make yourself such a stranger. It's months and months since we've seen you. Have a cigarette. And now I suppose you're going to take yourself off with Toby, as usual.'

But she did not, making some cogent excuse to get away.

When she had gone Mrs Roberts said sadly, 'I suppose I've seen her for the last time.'

'Oh, I shouldn't think so,' Toby said breezily.

He and Maisie met several times over the next two months, but seldom in his lodgings. They went to places of public entertainment, the cinema, the theatre. This was expensive for him, since Maisie, now withdrawn into her own thoughts, did not make her usual attempt to pay her share. Edward's play, *The Hostess*, was well received, and continued to draw the crowds. He had asked them to the first night, but they did not go. They waited till it had been on for a week.

They had, as Toby had said, been 'drifting'; their fingers were ceasing to touch across the river against whose tide they had been making their difficult way.

Then, one night, when they were leaving a cinema, Maisie said, 'I want this to be the end. Don't write again. I must put a stop to it now, or I shan't be able to bear it.'

'But pet—'

They stood together in the garish streets of night.

'I need the last word to be mine,' said Maisie. 'I shall feel better that way.' She was speaking rapidly, gasping a little as if she had been running. 'This is the thing *I* can do, *I* can say that it's all over.' She smiled at him then as she had not smiled for weeks: sweetly, her lips curling upwards. Her moist-looking hair glittered in the light wind.

'You're being silly—'

'You can't love me, and that's all that matters. I shall make a life for myself. But to see you gives me far more pain than joy, and I see no sense in putting up with that.'

They were jostled momentarily apart by three youths walking abreast, who had no intention of giving way. She staggered a little, and he caught her arm to steady her.

'I'm going to Anne's.'

'I'll see you back there.'

'No you won't.' The cinema crowds were pouring out into Leicester Square; they themselves had not quite seen the film to the end.

'Darling,' Toby said, 'I've never been so fond of anybody as I have been of you.'

'Past imperfect. Let's say good-bye and do it quickly, because this has cost me a lot, and I can't bear any more.'

She kissed his cheek. Then, swiftly, she turned and made her way towards Coventry Street. He looked after her, not believing that this was really the end, half-hoping that it was. She had been brave, far braver than he could have been. Left to him, the affair would have etiolated itself for a good while longer. Would she write to him, asking him to forget all that she had said? Would he write to her?

But he knew that it was over, and was more saddened than he thought she would have believed. But parts of one's life inevitably came to an end, and then life tacked and veered and went off on another course. What course would it take?

The Haddesdon period was necessarily over. He would not be able to go there as a casual guest, remembering what Amanda knew. He did not sleep for a long time that night, lying awake with the light on, feeling miserable. He tried hard to blame her for her silence from Jamaica. Without that, he would never have gone to bed with Claire – or so it seemed to him. He thought with an up-rush of regret of all the nights with Maisie, joyful ones, their bodies twined, her fair head lovely on the pillow, the delight in her eyes. Would he be able to do without her? How badly had he treated her? All might have been well if she had not tried to poach upon the preserves of his spirit (he did not like this ugly image as soon as it had occurred to him), but her customary sensitivity had let her down here. Maisie, yes, darling Maisie. He would miss her.

And he did. But she did not write to him again, nor he to her.

One day in March, he received a stately invitation from Rita to dinner at Lensfield Road, which he reluctantly accepted. On the morning of his going he saw in a popular newspaper a photograph of Claire and her baronet at a first night, and it did not make him feel any more comfortable. He had never seen her *en grande tenue* before, and it occurred to him that she could look very imposing. The baronet was a short young man, not lacking a chin, so far as he could see, but having a small one somewhat reduced by a large dimple. Toby thought he looked sickening. He had, of course, seen him before, at Haddesdon, but had scarcely noticed him.

He went to Cambridge in a state of gloom.

Bob and Rita looked as if nothing had occurred to sow dissension between them. The little girl was still up and toddling about. Rita seemed to take more interest in her, now that she could dress her up in frills. Bob was doting.

When she took Estella away to put her to bed (they no longer had the *au pair* girl) he said as much. 'I don't know how I'd cope without that kid. I'd like another, but Reet's not keen, and anyway, we're not doing all that well. Not badly, but not well enough to start another family right now. Who do you think she's like?' (He meant Estella.)

'A bit like both of you.'

'We never seem to see anybody much these days. We haven't heard again from Adrian, but then, I suppose, he wouldn't want to write much. How's Maisie?'

Toby said, 'That's over.'

Bob stared. 'Over? I thought you two were like kittens in a basket.'

'Over, all the same.'

'I'm sorry.'

'So am I. But it wouldn't have worked.'

Rita came back. Dinner was nearly ready, she said, she had made a risotto. Toby dreaded it, knowing Rita's cooking.

They drank white wine, as before, in the stately glasses. 'It's a Montrachet,' Bob said with proud casualness. He was learning some names.

The leopard, Toby soon discovered, could never change its spots. During dinner, which was horrible, Rita could not keep the conversation from the subject of her discontents. Bob was an old stick-in-the-mud. It was hardly worth her buying new clothes, since he never seemed to notice them. 'I bet you notice Maisie's,' she said. She had not heard the earlier conversation.

He smiled. 'One tends to notice things without saying much,' he said, to mollify her.

'If it wasn't for Estella, I'd go and get another job. There's nothing much to do here, hanging around the house all day.'

All unhappy families might be different in their own fashion, as Tolstoy said, but it seemed to Toby that there were a good many unhappy ones like this. He disliked the way in which Bob was always trying to propitiate her, but he knew the reason. He, at least, had a guilt he wasn't able to shift. And moreover, because of her, a police record. He had developed a smile, when he spoke to her, which Toby could only think of as 'smarmy'. She had lessened him as a man.

She, of course, spoke no word of Adrian, but she looked at Toby as if there was a complicity between them. For he knew, and she was sharply aware of it. He was relieved when the evening came to an end.

Early on Tuesday morning Edward rang up. Toby had seen nothing of him since the first night of *The Conjurers*. His voice sounded thick and strange, as if he had been drinking, which he could not have been at that hour.

'This is urgent. Can you come round to see me this evening? About six o'clock?' He gave an address in Hertford Street.

'Of course I can. But what's up?'

'I can't tell you over the telephone.' Edward hung up the receiver.

Toby spent an uncomfortable day, though why, he did not know. He climbed the two steep, graceful flights to Edward's flat and rang the bell.

The bulky, grey-haired man answered it, but his face was also grey.

'Come on in.' He led the way into a handsome but somewhat derelict-looking drawing-room. 'Sit down. I have to talk to you. Maisie tried to commit suicide on Sunday night.'

Toby opened his mouth. Had he been given a chance to say anything he could not have done it.

But Edward went on, 'Let me do the talking for now. She's all right, I can tell you that. But this wasn't one of these suicide attempts which are fakes, with the expectation that rescue will arrive. Amanda's away for a fortnight in Paris and only Peter and I were staying in the house – at the far end of it. Maisie seemed much as usual. Then she went up to bed and swallowed a great many aspirin tablets. Far too many, in fact, because they only made her sick. She was found by Sukie in the morning when she came in with the tea, lying in her own vomit and breathing like an animal at the end of a race. They called me.'

Here he stopped, and poured drinks for them both. 'We may need this. Anyway, I do.' He sat down heavily.

'I called the doctor and we brought her round. Amanda is not to be told, not by Sukie, not by the doctor, not by me. Peter never was told, and when he senses something wrong he tends to sheer out of the way. *Nobody is to know.* Maisie's adamant about that, and so she should be. But I thought you ought to hear about it.'

Toby tried to pull himself together, but the horrible image of Maisie 'lying in her own vomit' had shaken him too severely.

'But I don't see why—' he began.

'Oh, I think you do, I think you do.' Edward took a great swig of whisky, turned upon Toby his prescient eyes. 'Secrecy,' he said, 'that's got to be for ever.'

'Of course. But—'

'Don't think I blame you entirely. We can't choose whom we shall love or whom we shan't – or can we? Oh, of course we can. I believe there's always a fatal second of choice. But while she was in a weakened state – and I took a shameless advantage of it – she told me a great deal. Maisie has been through much.'

'Look, sir,' Toby said, in his agitation reverting to an older form of address, 'it was she who finally put an end to things.'

'Yes, to save her own pride. She's young enough for that kind of damned nonsense.' He said, more sympathetically, 'This must have been a blow to you. But of course, you being you' – a little less sympathetic – 'it won't be for long. Nothing is for long with you, is it, Toby?'

'I'll go to her.'

'That's just what you won't do, if I can possibly stop you. It's the last thing she wants. In a queer way, she didn't feel she'd made a positive end with you: and now she does. I've been fond of Maisie since she was a child, and I won't have her more troubled than she has been. I told you this precisely so that you might resist any compulsion to reappear now and then in a nice light-hearted way.'

Toby sat silent, his glass, still untouched, on the ash-strewn table before him.

'Go to Claire, if you like.'

Claire? What did this man know? Toby fancied, dreadfully, that he knew, that he had always known, all about him, even from the frail days of his social pretensions, now for ever exploded by his mother's publicity. But Edward, surely, could actually know nothing positive.

In an attempt to distract himself, he looked for the first time around him. It might have been a derelict room, the upholstery shabby, the paintwork faded, but there were some pleasant pictures on the walls. He saw one of his mother's. He believed this was the way Edward liked to live, and that he would live in no other fashion.

He said, 'Maisie was always deluded about Claire.'

'Possibly. But she told me about your visits to Glemsford.'

Toby felt a sharp sense of sex-betrayal. How could she have told all this to this elderly man? Edward bulked in his chair, more relaxed now.

'I don't think she's far wrong. She may be. But anyway, it was that which broke her.'

Toby said, passionately for him (which was not very passionate), 'Is she quite all right now?'

'All right, and on her feet. But she must not be disturbed, now, do you see?'

'Then why did you tell me at all?'

'Because,' Edward said heavily, 'I thought you ought to take your share in the business, blameless as you are. Yes, blameless. I've been unfair, haven't I? I often am. But Maisie, though you may not fully have realised it, is someone special.'

Toby said, 'Of course I realise it.'

'Not as people do who have known her as long as I have.'

Edward relapsed into silence. He swilled the remaining whisky round and round in his glass, making a golden focus of hypnotic light. Then he said, 'I'm telling you all this so that you might be more careful what you do to people next time. But no, you won't be able to *will* love, not at your age. That comes later.'

'But I can write to her.'

'No. Not unless she writes to you. Which I don't think she will. Don't you see, she's achieved a degree of real emancipation from you?'

Toby could only see the vomit congealed around Maisie's face and matting her hair.

'Try to be kind,' said Edward. 'We learn to do that pretty late, if at all. Sometimes we learn it, and then, in our age, forget it again. What the hell's the use of giving the wisdom of years to youth?' He seemed to lose the thread of what he was saying.

They sat together in the none too bright room, most of the light coming from the neon-strips above the paintings.

'Be happy with Claire if you can,' Edward said at last, 'that is, if she wants you. I think she does. You're free now, do you realise that?'

He rose, dismissively, and Toby rose with him.

'Good-bye,' Edward said abruptly, and he closed the door behind him before Toby was half-way down the stairs.

23

Toby was miserable for quite a long while. To assuage this he worked hard, earning grudging appreciation from Tiller. He thought he might as well now carry on to the end of the academic year, or even beyond.

Stung by Edward's censure (for it had been censure, and he wasn't fool enough not to realise it) he searched his conscience. What had he in fact done wrong, that was really wrong? Well, during the winter months he had seen Claire three times in secret, but on each occasion – he consoled himself – at her command. Twice they had dined at obscure restaurants. The third occasion had given him pause, for he feared that it would not be so obscure. A friend of hers was opening a new restaurant in the Fulham Road, Toby and she were both to be his guests, if Toby would like that. It would be fun. There was no need to dress up, it would be quite informal. He hesitated before replying, because he was afraid of publicity, of photographers; but he did so very much want to accept.

He went at last. It was a somewhat chaotic evening, overcrowded, with some celebrated faces from the entertainment world, the drinks lavish, the food pretentious and poor. There were cameramen, who photographed Claire talking to the proprietor: Toby had managed to slip away into a corner. He had got away without trouble, this time: and yes, he had enjoyed himself.

But that was in February. Now, at the beginning of April, when he was beginning to feel that he might recover, he received a letter from Bob containing, for once, good news. Bob had finished his thesis in two years, and could not submit it for his doctorate until the statutory three were up: but he had been elected a Fellow of his college. Even Rita had seemed pleased. It would mean far more money for him than he had ever had; they would move, as soon as they could get a new house.

Toby read this with pleasure: this must surely augur happier times for his friend. And he was fond of Bob.

He was now free to see Claire as much, and as openly, as he wished; but it was usually she who did the wishing. She seemed eternally occupied, though by what, God only knew. But when they met, she claimed him as though everything were settled between them, though Toby did not dare to assume that it was.

A letter came from Wragby.

'It is hard going here at first. My vicar, an excellent old man, though prepared to delegate almost everything, has a large house and is prepared to let my mother have a room in it. I have found a nurse in the village, who comes in most days.

'I am kept busy. What do I say when I visit old people who are desperately ill, or young ones who have got themselves into a mess? I don't know. You're not a believer, Toby, or I think not, but in a queer way you'd do better at this sort of thing than I do. We are a bit "high" for the local people, but they are getting to like it, after a fashion. Sometimes I feel very lonely and incapable.

'I heard Bob's news, but not from him. I am glad of it. It will probably keep him away from Rita more than ever, but, Heaven help me, I can't feel altogether sorry for that. I can't condone what he did, but I think I can understand it.'

If you think you can understand the impulse to hit out at an intolerable woman, Toby thought, then you can think anything.

'The more I ponder about things in general though, the less I feel I know. Perhaps it will come with time. In the meantime I go about the parish chores, and make my visiting rounds – when people will let me in, which believe me, they very often won't – and try to do what I can. I have never questioned my vocation, though it does seem to me that I am *bad at it*. Sorry. I am in a darkish mood, but I expect I shall soon surface. Love to Maisie and yourself.'

But the angel with the fiery sword had closed the doors of Haddesdon against Toby, though not the doors of Glemsford which, though less fun, did contain Claire. He began to go there regularly.

'You are an old ditherer,' she said, 'you simply can't make up your mind. Why not chuck the whole academic thing and let Daddy lend a hand? He would, you know. He always does what he knows I'd like.'

But he replied, 'Let me wait a while. I may still become an Acton or a Macaulay, for all you know.'

Just as he had concealed much of his life from her so, until recently, she had concealed parts of hers from him. For instance, he had only just discovered that the Llangains had a London house, in Chelsea, where Claire slept after evenings out with Toby (he had always assumed that she stayed with friends) but which her parents rarely used, hating to leave the country unless they could help it. Here Toby and Claire now went frequently when they wanted to make love.

With her, each time, he found it a new experience. She was made gleeful by intercourse; energetic; not for her, 'every animal is sad after coition'. Far from it. It was in these aftermaths that she was most eager to talk.

Toby said one night, 'I expect you'll marry Alec.'

'Why? Do you think I should?'

'If I were you I wouldn't. But I'm in no position to judge.'

'You're in a position at this very moment where he could judge you,' said Claire, with a robust giggle. She added, 'But there's no need for anyone to get into a tizz, is there? All the time in the world.'

'And during that time you may slip away,' said Toby, who could have said this to nobody else.

'I don't suppose I shall. It's so nice with you.'

'You remember what you said when I was driving away from Glemsford that day.'

'My dear old boy, I have total recall, as my very few intellectual friends might say. I even remember that hideous blob I made at Haddesdon about the orchard.'

But she should not have said this, for Toby could not – for brief periods at any rate – think of Maisie without melancholy. He compared the marmoreal Claire, lying so jubilantly at his side, with Maisie lying so small.

He said he must get up and go. He rarely left her later than midnight, for there was a resident housekeeper here too (doing incredibly little, he thought, for her money) and even Claire, despite her gallant swagger, practised a degree of concealment.

'Oh, don't. I'm so snug. If we ever did marry, Toby – mind you, I'm making no promises – would you like that?'

He replied, still lying on his back and staring up at the ceiling, 'You know I haven't tuppence to rub together.'

She said impatiently, 'But I have. What rubbish all this is about money!'

'It's only rubbish when you happen to have it.'

'Anyway, I'm not proposing to you, and don't you think it. We're having a lovely time together, aren't we? And who wants more than that?'

'Who indeed,' Toby said, out of his manifold uncertainties.

'You must meet Hairy. He's coming home on leave soon. If you can stand the shock of that, we shall still go on having lovely times.'

As he drove home, he thought how much she puzzled him, believed she went out of her way to do so. Maisie had never done this: there had been nothing devious about her. But Claire's concealments both irritated and fascinated him. Always he was wishing to learn more about her. Why, for instance, did she pose as so ill-read, so indifferently educated? Certainly she was not an intellectual, but she was far from being a fool. He had discovered that she spoke French excellently, and had read a good many of the French classics; he supposed some sort of results must be achieved from expensive Swiss finishing schools. Why did she seek him out so boldly, and then treat him with a kind of affectionate flippancy? She did not seem in the least to care what she said – but there were a good many things that she did not say. It was scarcely thinkable that she really considered marrying him, yet Toby could not help but be beglamoured by the life which she might offer.

She was costing him a good deal, but indirectly; for her part, she always seemed to have invitations in her pocket in which he was included. Yet he had been forced, for the first time in his life, to buy a dinner jacket, and he now possessed what he could only call a 'best' lounge suit, of a speckled greenish tweed with side-slits. She had told him that he looked very smart in it.

He decided that night that he must be honest with her: she must know where, and how, his family lived. He supposed she would react to SE1 with the nonchalance with which she reacted to everything. But he was not so sure how his mother would react: she knew nothing about Claire as yet, though she was aware (he had bitterly disappointed her) that his affair with Maisie was over. He would go home at the week-end and prepare her: it would not be easy.

'Mummy, I want to bring a girl to tea.' This, he thought, would be a safe meal. He had already trained her to cucumber sandwiches.

'What girl?' Her voice was sharp with apprehension.

'You'll like her. We've been seeing a good deal of each other. Her name's Claire Falls. She's pretty tall, and very good fun. By the way, you met her father at the Cambridge show.'

'Who's her father?' Mr Roberts put in.

'I can't remember everyone I met,' his wife snapped.

This was not going at all well.

'Come, you talked to him for quite a time. Lord Llangain.'

'Good God, lords!' his father exclaimed. 'What do you suppose that sort of crowd are going to make of us?'

Toby said this was an attitude of another day and age. Claire was the simplest girl on earth; they would like her.

'Well,' Mr Robert said, not without shrewdness, 'we've got your mother to be proud of, anyway.'

'I've got everything to be proud of,' Toby said, 'both of you. And Mummy's quite a big noise. Claire knows all about her. Who doesn't?'

He went on to mention, as if casually, that Lord Llangain was prepared to help him if his academic work didn't quite come off.

'Why shouldn't it come off?' Mrs Roberts demanded. 'What have you been doing wrong?'

He tried to laugh at her. Nothing wrong. But he liked to have avenues open to him; one never knew what one might want.

'So perhaps you like this girl because of what her father might do?' (Sympathy between them had momentarily failed, and he was disconcerted.)

'I wouldn't trust a lord further than I could kick him,' said Mr Roberts, with some grandiloquence. 'He won't lift a finger if ever the time comes, you mark my words.'

'Really, Dad, you know nothing about him. He's a simple tweedy type, without the least side about him.'

'Everyone in this business seems to be simple,' said Mrs Roberts. 'Well, I can't stop you bringing her, if she'll take us as we are.'

'Mummy,' Toby said, with a degree of justified exasperation, 'will it never dawn on you *what* you are? It's dawned on everyone else.'

'Fix your day, then,' said his mother, 'and I'll take a look at her.'

But when the day came and Claire, blandly unruffled, arrived at the house, he found that his mother had taken a curious way of getting her own back on him for her distress over Maisie. There were no cucumber sandwiches. There was a marvellous high tea, planned with all her skill, and it was laid in the kitchen.

'You must take us as we are, Claire,' she said almost at once, 'we're too old to change.'

'Why should you change?' Claire said, 'my parents never do. And you're a celebrity.' She looked round her. 'It's awfully nice here.'

And indeed, owing to the artistry of his mother, the kitchen was indeed attractive. There were new orange curtains at the windows, a cloth sprinkled with orange flowers covered the big table, on which there was a blue bowl full of zinnias. Mr Roberts did not appear: he had left his apologies to be conveyed.

'He has to mind the shop,' his wife said, almost between her teeth. 'He can't get away at all hours.'

Claire nearly approached Maisie's standards in doing justice to the meal. 'Now I shan't want to eat for the rest of the evening, and Toby, you mustn't try to make me. You're a wonderful cook, Mrs Roberts. I must take some tips from you. I am perfectly terrible.'

'There's nothing difficult about it,' said Mrs Roberts, 'it's all a matter of plain common sense.'

'I'm a bit short of that,' Claire remarked, with one of her wide smiles.

She asked later if she might see some paintings, but Mrs Roberts said she had nothing finished. Toby knew this to be untrue.

Claire expressed no disappointment. She merely said, 'Better luck next time.'

'And anyway, they're up in the bedroom. I use Toby's room as a sort of studio, when he's not here. I know he thinks I ought to move house, but I'm set in my ways.'

Her manner was quite different from the one she had displayed to Amanda. She might have been caricaturing herself. Toby was embarrassed.

Claire deliberately set out to please. She had done so before, but now she was doing it with concentration. How did Mrs Roberts work? Did she make preliminary sketches? Had she ever worked except in oils? (She sounded as knowledgeable as Maisie might have done.)

Mrs Roberts could not help replying with some interest. After all, since Toby had tended to stay away more and more, her painting had become the most important part of her life.

'I'm dreadfully sorry you can't show me anything,' Claire said, 'I'm a boob about these things, but I do love the pictures of yours that I've seen.'

Mrs Roberts seemed all at once to make up her mind. 'Well, I'll show you just one. No – don't you get up – I'll bring it down.'

She disappeared.

'I'm honoured,' Claire said, 'I'm glad she's relented. I like her so much. She's awfully like you, isn't she, on a much smaller scale?' She added, 'She doesn't like me yet, but she will. People usually seem to get round to it. With a few notable exceptions, of course.'

Mrs Roberts came back with a canvas which she held with its back to them. Then she turned it round, and propped it on a chair.

It was the painting of a golden-haired girl in a meadow, less the representation of a girl than of a smile, and it was a smile that Toby knew. She sat wearing a daisy-strewn dress, among daisies. Behind her was a bright blue sky sprinkled with small puffs of white cloud, as if it were with cannon-smoke.

'Why, it's lovely!' cried Claire, who had not, and could not have, recognised its inspiration. 'It's perfectly lovely! Mrs Roberts, could you just conceivably let me buy it?'

'Sorry, it's bespoke.' Toby's mother turned its face to the wall. 'I'm glad you like it, though.'

'I do, I really do! Please don't put it away just yet.'

'Does no good to look at any picture for too long.'

Now Toby had never, not in his whole life, known his mother to be cruel, and he was deeply troubled. She had deliberately raised a ghost, though how near this had been to a metaphorical truth she could not have known.

Claire, who had seen nothing, remained gay and comradely till a quarter to seven, when she and Toby went off to Shepherd Market to meet her brother there. 'No,' she said thoughtfully, as they were on their way, 'I am not liked. I suppose it is still Maisie for your mother.'

'Let's not talk about it,' he said in a voice which surprised even himself.

Claire, as usual, seemed not to take the slightest offence. 'Then we won't, darling. All things shall be as you please.'

They were greeted in the low-ceilinged, stuffy pub by a young man who seemed to absorb most of the available space. He was very tall, well over six feet, blond, moustached, handsome. The mannishness, vestigial in his sister's looks, could only be advantageous to him. He wore the uniform of a captain; he was going on to a regimental dinner.

'This is my brother Ivor,' Claire said in her positive voice, 'he hates his nickname but everyone comes to use it sooner or later. Just let him get used to you. Hairy, this is Toby Roberts, my current boy friend.'

Hairy shook hands. 'Claire tells me you're a historian,' he said. 'I wish I knew one damned thing about history.'

'I don't know much. I'm really a beginner.'

When Hairy went to the bar to order drinks she said, 'He is much sought after.'

'I don't doubt it.'

'A title,' said Claire promptly, following Toby's own train of thought in her uncomfortable manner, 'and ultimately splosh, though Mummy and Daddy are extremely *fit*. I don't know what I'd do without either of them. But you see, they won't mind in the least what I do – I often think they'd have cheerfully exposed me on a hillside – but Hairy has to do as he's told. He has to carry on the "line", you see. By the way, he was at New College, reading Classics, so don't you be too foxed by his pretensions to idiocy. He stopped at Honour Mods, where he got a tolerable Second, and winged it off – somewhat belatedly – to Sandhurst, where he was as happy as a bee in clover.'

Before Toby had had time to laugh at Claire's imagery, Hairy returned with half-pints of beer.

'Sköl,' he said.

He looked over the foam at Toby, with intent blue eyes. 'You're doing a PhD thesis,' he said. There seemed nothing that Claire had not told him, and he supposed they were in regular correspondence.

'If I ever finish it.'

'You must,' Hairy said with surprising force. 'Bad thing to start something and not finish it. I know. But I've managed to make the Army my life, though I know there's not much hope for it in the future.'

'The Peninsular Wars would have been more reassuring,' Toby said, and Hairy gave a broad smile very like his sister's.

'We're killing time now in Germany. They don't need us any longer. We dress up, and we parade. But it's all about something which is over.'

Claire sat back as if admiring her brother, which perhaps she did.

'You know,' Hairy said (and if he did pretend to be cretinous for the benefit of others he was not playing this game with Toby), 'I was in the Far East for a short time. I remember brooding in a cemetery in Malacca, full of names of soldiers, doctors, clergymen, traders. And it struck me suddenly that, with all their shortcomings, one's grandfathers were better men than we are. More guts – misguided, maybe, but guts, yes.'

'I remember,' Toby said, though he still found it hard utterly to detach his mind from the events of that day, 'seeing a late-night show guying the Victorians. And a chap near me shouted out – he was a bit drunk – "Oh, shut up! How many of us are worth half so much?"'

'Still,' said Hairy (Claire seemed content to listen), 'we mustn't sentimentalise too much. We blew people from guns. There was General Dyer and his Crawling Order. But before that we built roads and railways, we irrigated the soil, we produced a workable Civil Service. I rather like to think that when we made our ceremonial exit from India they cheered not just to see us go, but just a bit to acknowledge what we did at best. I may, of course, be wrong.'

He looked at his watch. 'Just time for another half, and then I have to go and wallow in a steam-bath of sentimentality. I'm glad women aren't allowed. I shouldn't like to see the look on Claire's face.'

This time Toby bought the beer.

He liked Hairy very much. What sort of a picture did he present to others, that made them regard him as dense? This was a family of disguises. Only Lady Llangain seemed to wear none.

24

A long letter from Adrian.

'Dear Toby,

'I am having rather an awful time here, and feel I must tell some-body. One usually tells things to you, because you're so good at taking them in, which must result in your being imposed upon by your friends – which I suppose I'm doing, though I don't want you to rush up to Lincs or anything absurd like that.

'This is a parish of some seven hundred persons, but we have another two parishes within our charge. Old Father Seaton is, I think, very ill, though he tries to conceal it. Anyway, he takes one service on Sundays, and that's about the size of it. I do everything else, and I tell you – though I know it's a weakness on my part – that I would about give my ears to have just one morning a week lying in bed till nine.

'Luckily, there is a very old car and I go further afield, if I'm wanted, in that, though locally on a bicycle. My mother is behaving like a saint, and I think they'd make her one if she could manage a miracle or two. She is alone nearly all the time, except for little chats with Fr Seaton, if he feels like it, and she seems to be reading the London Library dry.

'The most comic of my troubles has recently been this, though my conscience gets to work when I call it funny. I don't know whether I should. One of my parishioners, a Mrs Allen, has recently got it into her head that she is possessed by the Devil. It seems that she picked up some paperback thriller in a jumble sale, dealing with the subject, and since then nothing will do for her but that she must be afflicted in the same way.

'She got me to visit her, gave me some tea and seed-cake (you know that parsons will eat anything at any time, since they can never be sure where the next meal is coming from) and then sug-gested that I should exorcise her! Of course, I told her that I was unfitted to do any such thing, but that I would pray with her if she liked. So I did, but she kept squinting at me all the time between her fingers, and it wasn't pleasant. The fact is, that I didn't believe that anything was wrong with her. I knew something of her history, that her husband, an agricultural labourer who had married somewhat above him, had been playing around a bit – platonically, I gather, with the local girls. It seemed, from what she said, that her "fits" only occurred when her husband came home from work, so I thought they might be a handy way of taking it out of him.'

Reading a letter from Adrian, Toby thought, was just like listening to him: no reply seemed necessary. But it was quicker to read him than to hear him and that was a good thing.

'She started on this exorcism business again, but she knew well enough that I was sceptical. Suddenly she gave me a demonstration. She hurled herself acrobatically backwards against a rather fine Welsh dresser, bringing all the plates down, but they were pewter so it didn't matter. I wonder if she would have done the same if it had been the dresser in the kitchen. Then she sat on the floor and bubbled – I don't mean frothed, because it wasn't froth. I didn't know what to do. I just sat there till she seemed to feel a bit better. Then I got her to her feet and she spat at me – missing, however, as in *Uncle Vanya*. That seemed to satisfy her, because she sat down again, and said, "*Now* are you going to exorcise me?" I said I would get in touch with the Bishop; it was all I could do. I believe he has a certain canon who specialises in these matters. She said, "I should be obliged, Father," but I could see she was disappointed that I hadn't performed these rites on the spot. Anyway, I managed to get out of the house, and have never been so glad to climb on my old bicycle in my life.

'Father Seaton was having a nap when I got in. I told him the story. All he said was, "Well, I'm sure you know the drill, dear boy." I did, so far as it went, but I asked him whether it wouldn't be better if he approached the Bishop. He said, No, he thought I would do it very nicely. So there the matter rests, except that I had a visit next day from her husband. He said, "I know all about Annie and her fits. You don't want to take much notice. She can stop them all right if she likes."

'Of course, I felt horribly guilty.'

You would, Toby thought.

'I may have been wrong, but I don't think so. There was such an atmosphere of fraud, and her dramatic demonstration seemed to me an absolute fake. But there, I'm a sceptic about these matters, and always shall be.

'As I said, that was more or less of a comic interlude. But I have a worse plague, another parishioner who is called Mrs Flixby. She is in her late thirties, and rather pretty. She calls on me almost every day, telling me she is in awful trouble with her husband, and what shall she do? (Her complaint seems to boil down to one thing, that he always goes to the pub in the evening and won't take her with him, which I fancy she would like.) She is desperate, she says, and so unhappy. Shall she leave him? What use is there in going on with such a miserable life? She weeps copiously, and I have to wipe her up and give her handkerchiefs. She never seems to carry a handkerchief of her own. Shall she divorce him, she asks. What for? I ask. She replies, "Mental cruelty, you can get one now," all the time fixing me with her eyes, which are a rather odd light blue. I simply don't seem able to get rid of her, and when she goes, I feel drained, as if a vampire had been at me. She usually says something to the effect – "If only I could have met someone like you—" and all I can do is to give her the Christian view of marriage.

'The fact is, Toby, though it sounds repulsively conceited, that I think she has taken a fancy to me.'

And she won't be the last, was Toby's silent comment.

'I know this does sometimes happen, in these remote places, when a woman's bored and lonely and the parson seems the only man she can go to, because I don't think Mrs Flixby would contemplate an affair with any of the locals, even if there was one available. I am really at my wits' end over all this. I feel increasingly lacking in charity, since a woman like this does really seem to be suffering, but I can't feel it *for* her. I have suggested that she might do some church work to take her mind off things, but you can imagine how that went down.

'Sometimes I think I can have no vocation at all, that it has been a mistake, that I'd be of more social use if I were a bricklayer.

'Thank you for putting up with all this. I have written it late into the night, because it is about all the time I get. How are you, old boy? Late in the day to enquire, I know. But I do think about you. Love to you and Maisie.'

Toby thought Adrian was entirely right to give priority in his worries to Mrs Flixby rather than to the demonic Mrs Allen. He turned over the last page.

There was a postscript. 'Rita still goes on writing. I wish someone would exorcise *her*.'

Toby wrote back with sympathy, but naturally he could not be helpful, except to suggest that Adrian tore the letters up unread, or, alternatively, sent them straight back: but this he thought the more dubious course, since it might lead to Bob finding out about the whole thing. Rita, he said, was a pain in the neck. He had never met anyone with quite such an obsession. Of Maisie he said nothing.

After this, it was a relief to dine with Hairy, who had invited him to his club. It was the first men's club Toby had ever entered, and he was fascinated. He liked the quiet, the fuggy-smelling leather chairs, the implication that here no Rita – or Claire, come to that – could ever enter. He had always been fond of women, but he didn't want them around all the time, he had by now concluded. The invitation intrigued him: evidently he had passed muster with the entire Llangain family. This laid a flattering unction to his soul.

Hairy arose from the depths of a sofa to greet him. 'Hullo, good of you to come. Takes the edge off the tedium, as it were.'

'I don't see why this should be tedious, Ivor,' Toby said.

'Oh, drop the Ivor,' said Hairy rather gloomily, 'you'll come round to the other disgusting appellation in time. They all do. Well, it's tedious because I feel I have to spend a couple of evenings here per week when I'm at home – God knows why – and every-body seems so old. Increasingly so. I like a bit of cheery gossip sometimes. Claire sends her love.'

Toby had not seen her for about ten days.

'Give mine to her. She's busy, I suppose.'

'What on earth should she be busy about? Why she doesn't get a steady job, I don't know. Mother can perfectly well cope without her.'

'She doesn't have to work, of course,' said Toby, flying a kite.

'Oh, not in that sense,' Hairy replied. 'She comes into her Trust fund next year. I've already come into mine.' He was the most open of men. 'But I don't like to see her loafing around.'

He asked Toby what his own plans were.

'Well, I shall work at the university until the end of the year. Then I'll really have to make up my mind about things.'

'Claire says if you get bored, the old man could probably put something in your way.'

Toby was astonished that this particular family should exert such pressure on him – for pressure it was. He thought about SE1 and the only distinguished member of his family, his mother.

Hairy suggested that they should go and eat, and they went into the dark panelled dining-room. 'Not many people here,' he said, 'they all come at lunchtime.'

Toby noticed an absence of ash-trays, which was to save him from a *faux pas* later on.

'Try the anchovy butter, if you like it. It's good.'

Throughout the meal Toby turned the conversation to Hairy himself and induced him to talk about his life in the Army. Apparently he enjoyed it, but could not see where the future lay. He only anticipated small wars, and wasn't sure whether he was keen on them. 'Still, I suppose that's what I've been trained for. I shall have to go through with anything that crops up.'

Afterwards, he suggested that he and Toby should go 'back to base' in the library, and here the business of the evening seemed to begin.

Over coffee and brandy, he confided that he got on well with his sister. 'Some brothers and sisters fight like cat and dog,' he said, 'I've seen it. Horrible sight. We don't. Claire always cheers me up.'

'She'd cheer anyone up, I should think.'

'We've always done things together. She writes me long letters when I'm away in Germany. My father doesn't, and my mother sends picture-postcards. I expect she thinks I have to be reminded of England. St Paul's, the Tower, Buckingham Palace, I've had the lot.' He made a great stirring in his coffee cup. 'Claire seems to have taken a fancy to you.'

'I've a fancy for her, come to that.'

'Mind you, she's taken a fancy to a good many chaps. But more particularly to you. I shouldn't want to see her let down,' Hairy said, looking for the first time like the potential head of a relatively noble house. (Anyway, Toby calculated, the first title must have been conferred long before the days of Maundy Gregory. This thought amused him, but he was apprehensive.)

'None of my business, I know,' Hairy went on, 'but then, you see, I'm never sure what my business is. I just think about a thing and I say it.'

Toby wondered what was coming next.

'Look,' said Hairy, 'if anything ever came of this, we on our side would have no objection. What about yours?'

This was so like the proposal of a royal alliance that Toby was taken thoroughly aback. He was not used to dealing with men quite so straightforward as Hairy, who indeed appeared to say the first thing that came into his head, and he could not help the recrudescence of a trapped feeling. He looked around the picture-hung walls, so like those of his own college, at the few somnolent members talking over pints of beer or riffling through *The Illustrated London News*. He said at last, not giving a direct answer, 'I won't let her down. But you mustn't think that either of us is really decided.'

'Oh, Claire is. And usually she gets what she wants. Seen anything of Maisie Ferrars? I used to go over to Haddesdon sometimes, but the atmosphere was a bit highfalutin for me. I was always scared stiff that someone would ask me something I didn't know. I always felt like the brutal and licentious soldiery.'

Toby grinned. Anyone less brutal and licentious than Hairy he could not imagine. Yet this whole conversation, to him, was taking place in a kind of dream.

'I don't see much of Maisie these days.'

In fact, he did not see her at all.

'Claire's a bit funny about her,' Hairy said. 'They used to be pretty close, but not now.'

It was warning enough.

'Pity,' Toby said. The conversation was allowed to drop, and to change to other things.

Toby went through with it in the same dreamlike state. Why should this have happened to him? Money in plenty was his, if he wanted it. His brother-in-law would one day be a peer. Llangain would find him a job, no doubt, if he wanted it. He would quite like to marry Claire, as much as he wanted to marry anyone – yet. Time seemed to sit below him like a bolting horse. Why should anyone want him so much? He had nothing to offer, and he still wanted to be able to give. It was, he supposed, his own integrity, of a sort.

For the rest of the evening he turned the talk to Adrian, telling Hairy the whole story.

'Poor sod,' said Hairy, at the end of it, 'poor sod.' He added, rather acutely, 'You say he thinks the old vicar's pretty ill. If he dies, what's to become of your friend? Will he take over, or is he too young? Will they put someone else in over him? I don't know about these things.'

'Nor do I. But I expect Adrian must hope that they will.'

'Hard luck for a chap to have all those looks,' said Hairy, 'it always makes for trouble. Or for a girl too, come to that. It's not an unmixed blessing.' He looked at his watch. 'Sorry to break things up, but I've got to be up early in the morning and go on my way. Thank you for helping me out with my lonely life.'

They went out from the club into a sharp clear night, the stars high above the rust-red glow of the London smoke and neon lights. 'See you next leave,' Hairy said. 'Enjoy yourself.'

25

In mid-June Toby was astounded – and made apprehensive by – a friendly but cool letter from Maisie inviting him to a luncheon at Haddesdon to celebrate her mother's fiftieth birthday. Amanda wanted, she said, to have everyone about her.

For a moment he had forgotten that he was not supposed to know of Maisie's suicide attempt: no one did, except Edward, the house-keeper, the doctor and himself. He thought about the whole thing. He imagined that Amanda must believe his affair with Maisie had blown over: which, to the best of his belief, it had done by now.

Maisie was urgent about only one thing: this time he *must* per-suade his father and mother to come with him. Her letter concluded with the usual platitudes, enquiries about his health, his career.

When he told his parents what she had written, his father said, 'Catch me. Who do they think's going to take care of the shop?'

But Mrs Roberts said, to Toby's amazement, 'If they're all that keen, I'll go with you. I wouldn't mind seeing this wonderful Haddesdon for once. And I want to see Maisie again.' She added that she supposed he would drive her down. 'Mind you, I'll be a fish out of water, but if all these clever friends of Mrs Ferrars can do something, at least I can paint.'

By this time she was established in a modest position, and the dealer was making a respectable profit out of her.

He wrote to tell Maisie that they would both come, but by road, so that nobody need meet them at the station. This brought a cordial note from Amanda herself. She was so thrilled that he was bringing his mother! She had almost lost hope of it. She must not be shy, because everyone would be thrilled to meet *her*. 'You must get that firmly planted into her head. We're all friends at Haddesdon.'

It was not, this time, Amanda's weather. A biting June day, the rain lashing the trees and battering the flowers into the earth. Mrs Roberts said, 'I'm glad I put on a woolly vest.'

Again, as on the occasion of her show in Cambridge, she showed no nervousness. There was resolution in her demeanour: it was Maisie whom she had come to see.

Toby, whose apprehension had increased during the long drive, was wondering about himself, how Maisie would greet him. But why should he be awkward? She had probably forgotten the past as he had – almost. The scents of Cambridge and Paris were still with him. Her green lamp still stood on his table.

They were a little late, and by the time they arrived the whole company seemed to have assembled. Both Llangains, Moira clutching her glass of vodka and – this was troubling – Claire. Peter Coxon. Edward, cordial but remote. A Scotch girl painter who had had a recent success. The string quartet. The art critic. A pianist who had made a name for himself in an international competition in the Soviet Union. One or two of Amanda's more elderly and anonymous friends.

It was Maisie who greeted them, a calm little girl wearing slacks – he had not seen her in them before – and a light sweater. She kissed Mrs Roberts, kissed Toby brushingly on the cheek. Then Amanda descended in a flurry of scarves, and caught the reluctant Mrs Roberts to her bosom.

Toby's mother was warmly greeted by everyone whom she knew, though her response to Claire was reserved. The Scotch girl flew at her. 'You're a mythopoeic figure! I'm so excited to meet you.'

'What's mytho-what?' Mrs Roberts asked.

'Well, like someone out of a legend. I never really thought you'd turn up.'

'I'm not going to introduce you to everyone,' Amanda boomed, 'you'll get to know all of them in time. You need a drink – no, you don't drink – but you'll have something. Tomato juice?'

Mrs Roberts settled for tonic water, which to Toby seemed for her almost sophisticated.

They sat in the big drawing-room, made pleasant by a coal fire. Claire, he felt, was being deliberately cool to him that day, and he understood the reason. In fact, he admired her tactfulness.

He brought out his present, which was a small box for pills in a Wedgwood design. 'Many happy returns,' he said.

'How lovely!' Amanda cried. 'I always carry aspirin, just in case. Many happy returns? How many? We're not a long-lived family, but perhaps I can count on twenty.'

'Nonsense,' said Edward, who had barely spoken, 'you'll make a magnificent eighty-five.'

'Bless you, my dear, what a nice thought!'

The party tended to break into separate groups, members of each drifting one to the other. Only Mrs Roberts sat stiff in her chair, seemingly unmoved by her surroundings, though Toby had caught a gleam of pleasure in her face on entering the house and seeing her own paintings in the hall. Thus she became the cynosure of a group for herself alone: Claire, Llangain, Moira, Edward.

Toby talked to Peter Coxon. No, his book had not gone down so well here as in America. 'They didn't like my parable,' he said, adding, with the twitch of a smile, 'Two reviewers thought it very false theology, though what the devil either of them could know I can't imagine.'

Maisie joined them. She might have been any girl, chatting to any two young men. She was sorry, she said, that Adrian couldn't be there. It seemed that for him to leave Lincolnshire was impossible.

'He's having a rough time,' said Toby.

'What about Bob and Rita?'

'I've a bit lost touch. Perhaps it's as well.'

'I know about Adrian,' Claire called across the room, 'Hairy told me.' She was not having much success with the enthroned Mrs Roberts.

'Oh, you know Hairy,' Maisie said to Toby, 'I like him.'

'Praise of my son is pure bliss to me,' said Moira.

Llangain said, 'Had any second thoughts, young man?'

'Dozens,' Toby replied, 'but they haven't crystallised.' He felt, rather than saw, his mother glance at him sharply.

They went into luncheon and here Amanda, having made sure of her *placement*, took charge. 'Children,' she announced, 'after we've eaten, Philip' – the pianist – 'has consented to play for us. He says you may order, as from a menu. Entirely *à la carte*.'

Great delight was expressed at this.

They ate plovers' eggs – Mrs Roberts was suspicious of these and Toby thought they were dull – a crown of lamb, blackcurrant ice-cream and cheese fritters. He noted that nothing had impaired Maisie's appetite and, as usual, he was relieved. Not much conversation passed between the two girls. Edward was unusually silent.

Toby heard his mother remark to Llangain, on whose right she was seated, 'With a steak-and-kidney pudding, it's all a matter of getting the proportion of suet and flour right.'

Amanda was toasted three or four times. At the end of the meal Edward rose formally to his feet.

'I want you all to drink to Amanda once again. We're deeply fond of her. But I doubt if we recognise how much she's done for artists of all kinds, especially for young ones. As for me, she has comforted me in my hours of tribulation and cheered for me in happier times – there are such times for us all, you know. Even happy times happen: don't you forget that. Her house – and, I may say, Maisie's – has been open to us all. Life is growing more bleak, less generous. I don't think I much like the life I see ahead of me. This is the relic of an older and more golden life. So I ask you once more to drink to Amanda on her birthday. And may we be drinking to her thirty years from now.'

He raised his glass. They all rose. Then he sat down abruptly, as if afraid that the chair might be jerked out from beneath him.

Amanda responded with smiles and tears: tears came easily to her when she required them. They were all wonderful, they were all dears. She had done nothing, except to please herself. It was they who gave the pleasure.

When they had returned to the drawing-room, the pianist played to them. Nobody had asked for anything in particular, preferring to leave the choice to him. He was a magnificent performer: even Toby could understand that. As for Mrs Roberts, she seemed endowed with the gift of appreciating any kind of art. She sat quite still, her head slightly cocked, as if she had been listening to this quality of music all her life.

Philip played French music, Debussy, Ravel, Fauré. The concert lasted for an hour. Then he rose, and with a curiously decisive, even discourteous-seeming gesture, he shut the piano.

He had been so good that nobody really knew how to praise. 'That was a treat to me,' said Mrs Roberts to Maisie.

'You've made my day, Philip,' said Amanda, 'you and dear Mrs Roberts between you.'

Afterwards, the conversation became general; nobody objected to shouting from any point in the big room. Mrs Roberts whispered to Toby that she would like to go to the bathroom. He said that he would take her, and after that, if Amanda did not object, would show her the collection of English water-colours in the study. 'I doubt if they'll mean much to me,' his mother said.

Amanda's permission readily obtained, they went upstairs. Claire was just coming out of the bathroom as Toby showed his mother towards it. When the door had closed, Claire touched his hand briefly.

'Not to be sad, sweetie,' she said, 'so momping-mum.' She knew her Gilbert and Sullivan. 'I know this is sticky.'

She went downstairs, elegant in cream silk slacks and shirt. He had never seen her looking so large nor so elegant. He hung about until Mrs Roberts emerged.

She looked at the Birket Forsters, at the Coxes, the de Wints, the Sandbys, with a bleak eye. 'This is what I don't understand. They seem insipid to me. Don't you tell Mrs Ferrars that.'

'As if I should.'

'Fancy wanting to paint with a kid's paint-box,' she said, her ecumenical taste in art deserting her, and so the inspection was not a success.

They went downstairs together, into the hubbub of talk, into the smoke, the mysterious radiance, of Haddesdon. This may be the last time for me, Toby thought: and indeed, he thought that they had already made him something of a stranger. He felt himself distinctly unpopular, by the old standards: but at least he knew why he had been asked. It had been for his mother's sake, and he was proud of her for that.

Afterwards there were the usual intellectual round games, in which Mrs Roberts did not join, but Peter Coxon distinguished himself. He was quick-witted, he had a compendious memory. Edward took part, but with no more interest than was courteous to Amanda. The string quartet brought out their instruments and played till tea-time. Mrs Roberts whispered to Toby, 'They do expect you to stuff yourself here.'

Then it was time to go, in a flurry of compliments for Mrs Roberts. Amanda kissed her, and Edward said he would like to if he dared. He was not given permission. Claire and her father came up to shake hands. It was Maisie who showed them out, her eyes very bright, Edward lingering behind her as if in protection. It was queer, Toby thought, but this time he really did not expect to see her again, and it gave him an unexpected pang. After all, who was so delightful as she? As fresh as springtime, as neat as a new pin – all the clichés. Yet he had been unable utterly to love her. Perhaps he came nearer to it now than at any other time. 'We'll see you soon,' she said, though he doubted it, 'and, Mrs Roberts, we are so grateful to you for making the journey. You don't know the pleasure it has given to all of us, especially to Mummy.'

'We have been honoured,' Edward said, 'and we know it.'

'I know what you've all done for me,' Mrs Roberts said, 'and I don't forget it. Don't you think I do.' Her eyes were upon Maisie.

As Toby started the car, he saw the girl with her hand upraised as in salute. Yes, he would be jealous when she got married, which he presumed she would, one day; he realised that he had hardly on this occasion given Claire a thought. But he would think of her again.

'I don't think much of that Peter,' Mrs Roberts said, as they drove off, 'he seems like a pansy to me.'

'Right first time, as he'd be the first to admit. But he's clever, and rather nice.'

'Queer sort of set-up,' she said. She had assimilated certain modern idioms, which she used with a kind of pride. 'All those games. I liked the music, though. That pianist, I mean.'

'He's probably going to be a great one. Does that thrill you?'

'Anyone who is going to be great thrills me,' said Mrs Roberts, though as if it were unlikely that she could ever be thrilled. She had delighted, however, in her own reception. 'They seemed to be making a fuss of me. Too much. I liked the Scotch girl.'

'Come, Mummy, you're not absolutely immune to flattery.'

'Nor are you, I suppose.'

'I shouldn't be, if any of it came my way. But I don't see why it should.'

'That Amanda's a type. I've never seen anything like her.'

'And you won't again.'

Behind the veil of rain the sun had sprung up, lurid, yellow and orange. Before long they saw a vast rainbow, sharp in its colours, and Mrs Roberts exclaimed, 'I must paint one of those, that is, if I can.'

'Oh, you can.'

'I used to say that I'd give seven and sixpence every time I saw a rainbow.'

'And I'd give ten bob.'

They drove for a way in silence. She was brooding, and he knew it.

At last she said, 'I can't understand you throwing Maisie over for that great girl. It beats me.'

Toby replied judiciously, 'Can we ever account for these things? Maisie and I finally didn't hit it off.' Again the bite of regret. 'It was nobody's fault.' (Liar, he thought. Being at Amanda's always made him honest with himself.)

'I think it was yours.'

He glanced at her. She was biting her lips together hard, as she often did when she felt very sure of her ground, and was determined to keep to it.

'Look, Mummy, we'd better drop the subject.'

'Are you going to marry that Claire?' The 'that' showed the extent of her hostility.

'For God's sake, how can I afford to marry anybody? Claire and I get on well and, as I told you, her people may be useful to me.'

Mrs Roberts said this sounded cold-blooded. 'You don't want to marry into that sort of family. You'd be a fish out of water.'

'You've no idea how many waters I can swim in nowadays,' he said, with the touch of impudence that sometimes pleased her but this time did not.

Again they drove in silence. The rainbow had faded and the rain had ceased.

Then came a surprise. 'I've had an invitation to go to America. They're giving me a small show there.'

'Good God,' said Toby, 'and congratulations. Will you go?'

'What do you think I am? Of course I shan't. Traipse all that way, and probably for nothing.'

'I think you should make the effort.'

'You don't realise,' said Mrs Roberts, 'what making efforts, as you call it, costs me. I hate it. I sometimes even hate going to the shops, because it means going out. Cooking I don't mind – that's restful – but it took me all I had to get to that house today.'

'You enjoyed it.'

'Some of it. I must say I wouldn't pay sixpence for those little eggs. That's all they are, little eggs.'

'You enjoyed the music, and the fuss they made of you.'

'I hope I haven't entirely lost my humanity,' said Mrs Roberts, with sudden grandeur.

He thought how fond he was of her. He was fond of his father, too, but in quite a different way. The reverential atmosphere which had surrounded her that day had had its effect upon him; which meant, that he was less impatient of her probing than he might otherwise have been. He knew that, in her heart, she envied him the education she had been able to give him. Eremitic, class-conscious, she would never change; but she would have liked to be able to change. Haddesdon faded behind them as they covered the miles: but not Maisie. Yet it was Claire whom he would see next week, happy Claire, with no problems, joyous in her own iron will which, he supposed, would eventually become his will too. Did he love her? Yes, he supposed he did, in a way; perhaps in so far as it was possible for him to love entirely. She would jockey him into some sort of success; she would see that he fitted his life to her own. But the ghost of Maisie's infinite delicacy would not leave him that day.

26

In the following month Toby took up the introduction. Within a week of telling Llangain that he would like to do so, he received a letter from Clive Baumann, making an appointment for Friday at half-past eleven. A civilised hour.

Toby went to the City in a state of considerable curiosity. He had never imagined what a merchant bank could be like. He came to a handsome building built, he imagined, in the middle eighties, with window boxes of blue hydrangeas storm-coloured against the pale stone. He was shown into a waiting-room. It was small, handsomely panelled, and with some good prints on the walls. It contained a table and four leather armchairs. He expected to be summoned to Baumann's presence, but instead Baumann came to him, introduced himself, and took the chair opposite to Toby's. He was a small, huge-eyed, sorrowful-looking man who resembled, Toby thought, a picture he had seen of the young Proust. But he did not seem sorrowful at all. He was singularly insouciant.

One of the first questions he asked was, 'Any relation of Edgar Roberts?'

'Not so far as I know,' Toby replied, a little put out.

'He was at Cambridge with me. Oh, well. But that's years ago, in the dark ages.' Since Baumann could be no more than thirty-three or four, they did not seem so very dark. 'Nice chap. Thought at one time that he might join us here, but he found it would fence him in, for the moment, at any rate. He's always travelling.'

He offered Toby a cigarette, took one himself. He went on: 'Of course I've heard of you from Lord Llangain. He's a nice chap, too. I know that you've got a good First in History—' Toby wondered how he knew it was a good one; he himself had always felt that by a miracle he had just scraped through.

'—and that you're doing post-graduate stuff now. Why do you want a change? Don't you fancy history much?'

'I don't think,' said Toby, 'that I'm cut out for the academic life.

Surprisingly few people are, when you come to think of it. I'd like to know a bit more about the real world.'

'Well, if you came to us, you'd learn a bit about one other world, certainly. Do you know anything already about what we do?'

'Honestly,' said Toby, sufficiently in awe to use this word which commonly denotes the intention to be dishonest but in this case was a just one, 'I have no idea at all. I'd have to be taught from scratch.'

'Scratch,' said Baumann, 'is not a bad thing to be taught from. At least, I didn't find it so. I don't suppose you've given any thought to whether you'd be interested in investment, company finance, or banking?'

'I should have to find out what all those things meant.'

'Well, I suggest that, in a bit, you should look in on our Staff Manager. He could tell you all the laborious part. Quite sure you're not related to Edgar? You've got a look of him.'

Toby was quite sure.

'I have the pleasure of owning one of your mother's paintings. She's astonishing, isn't she?'

'I think so.'

'And she started from scratch? As I said, scratch is no bad thing.'

'She did, but she's learned a lot since. All by herself.'

'I admire her very much. I do collect, but in a small way. By the way, I've no idea where you live.'

Toby gave him the address and saw that, by doing so, he had quenched the last hope in Baumann's mind of his relationship with Edgar Roberts, whoever he might be.

'Pleasant part of London,' said Baumann, who could not have known it at all.

'There are better ones. But my mother is set in her ways. I'd like her to move and so would my father, but it's no go.'

'I must say I rather admire that, as I admire her work. Stick to what you want. I sometimes think there's an eternal policeman behind us all,' said Baumann imaginatively, 'who says to us, "Move along now." But I don't see why we should if we don't want to, do you?'

'I suppose if there really were a policeman, we'd have to.'

Toby had seen that Baumann liked politeness and a degree of fun, but did not demand exaggerated respect.

'Would you care to see around the place a bit? Then we can go up to the Staff Manager.'

Toby said he would like that. Toby made a tour of the building, much of which had been built out and modernised for office convenience. His impression was that everyone whom he saw looked friendly and at ease, especially when Baumann made some random introductions. He wondered, as he usually did, what it would be like on a wet day; it was pleasing on a bright one. He also wondered what, if they accepted him, they would be likely to offer him in the way of salary. More than he was getting from his grants, he supposed, though he did not allow his hopes to become too vaulting.

'Well,' Baumann said at last, 'it's been good to meet you. I hope you'll think us over. It may strike you as all very strange, but it's surprising how one gets into the way of things, don't you find? I always do.'

He left Toby in the hands of the Staff Manager, who was not insouciant, but a businesslike grey man who was more terrifying. However, having no cards but his First to play with, he acquitted himself fairly well. The Manager gave him a history and a survey of the firm since its beginnings, its world connections, its present needs. This took quite a long time, and it must be said that at the end of it all Toby was not much the wiser.

'Company finance,' the Manager said thoughtfully, 'might suit your book better than most things. We'll have to think it over. Of course, we'll have to think everything over. How are your Maths?'

Toby, deciding not to bluff – much – said that though they were not his strongest point, he thought he could get along.

'Anyway,' said the Manager, 'you can read a balance sheet.'

Toby's silence gave consent, though it occurred to him that he had never seen a balance sheet in his life.

The other then took him briskly through his career, such as it was. Then he said, 'What particularly interests you about this kind of work?'

'It seems to lead to wider horizons, wider, anyhow, than those I've already got.'

This brought the interview to an end. 'We'll be getting in touch with you,' the Manager said, 'to find out whether you've had any second thoughts' – and Toby was out again in the hurrying streets, making his way towards the Bank tube station.

Pondering on his way home, it occurred to him that he had not done too badly. With Baumann, anyhow, a certain informality seemed to be the order of the day. He doubted whether, if they took him on, he would ever see much of him again. What on the earth would he do if they did? But he knew that his I.Q. was pretty high, and that what he was taught, he could learn. What he would not learn was what he did not want to be taught, by Tiller now, or by anyone else in the academic field.

That night he went home, and took his hopes to his mother and father. Never having heard of merchant banks, they were unexpectedly – to him – horrified.

'After the grand start you've made,' said Mrs Roberts, 'you want to be a bank clerk? We'd hoped for better things.'

'Well, it's really not quite like that. I don't know how to explain.'

'It seems to me that you've got some explaining to do,' said his father, his tone less mild than usual. 'I don't want to rub it in, but getting you through your education hasn't been all that easy.'

'Then don't rub it in,' Mrs Roberts said sharply, 'you know that's the least of it. But we all have our dreams, and mine was to see you settled in one of those colleges as a don, as you call it. I can't help dreaming. It does seem to me that this mania for change is something to do with that Claire.'

'It's not my dream,' said Toby, 'I can't help that. As for Claire, she plays a very small part in it. I wish you could see that she's a nice girl. You've always had something against her.'

'I've got Maisie against her,' Mrs Roberts said stubbornly.

'That's not quite fair, Dora.' Her husband had calmed down somewhat. 'We can't teach the young what to do with their hearts.'

'There's something fishy, all the same.'

'Look,' Toby said, 'if this came off – which it probably won't – I might make a good deal more money. I'd be able to help.' Though he knew she would not let him.

'Thank you, but I don't need help.' And she did not; through her painting she had been able to buy a few modest luxuries, and they were all she needed. 'A bank clerk,' she mused, 'behind bars, just like in the Zoo.'

She was not to be appeased that night. They had supper in relative silence, and she refused to show him her recent pictures. 'They're all more or less the same,' she said, 'you wouldn't be interested.'

Next day he met Claire in their usual pub and told her how things had gone.

'I should think you'd gone down like a house on fire, sweetie,' she said, 'just the right tone to take with Baumann, the little I know of him. You go in and win.'

A week later, a letter from the Staff Manager came. They were prepared to offer him a post, at a starting salary of nine hundred pounds a year. Nine hundred! To Toby this seemed a fortune. He could hardly believe it. The future lay bright in front of him as a cornfield in the sun. Corn in Egypt! He could not believe that the news of the money would not soften his mother. He was so excited that he wanted to tell somebody at once, Claire, of course, Bob, Adrian and – yes, he wanted to tell Maisie. There was no doubt that his hankering after her was growing, but he did not believe it would ever be more than a hankering. He simply wanted to see her; and, after he had written his letter of acceptance, it was she to whom he first wrote.

It was a brief note, simply asking her if she would care to have dinner with him shortly. It did not exactly say 'for old times' sake', but it implied it.

Next, he wrote to Tiller, who was in France, and received a brisk reply.

'Dear Roberts,

'You must, of course, do as you wish, and I hope you have good luck in your new career. I certainly never felt you had your heart in history, so perhaps it is all to the good. Best wishes.'

So that was that. He did not go home again at once, but wrote to his mother saying that he was to enter the bank in September. He gave her the financial details, and hoped that at least these would raise his stock with her. But he knew that, for a while, nothing could raise it, and he had a brief resentful feeling of being orphaned.

Maisie did not immediately reply.

Meanwhile, Claire was jubilant. She had done something for him, hadn't she? Or rather, Daddy had. A letter to Llangain was of course necessary.

Meanwhile, they enjoyed themselves in bed. She might look marmoreal, but she was also accomplished: and he liked it when sex filled her with hilarity. She was the most *healthy* girl he had ever known – he could not imagine her sick for a day, not even with the common cold. When they had had their mutual pleasure, they would sit up in bed, smoke, and drink a bottle of wine together. At these times she was most chatty. She had seen Alec, she said, but oh dear, his chin *was* too small, and anyway, he was just off to Italy. 'You must meet him,' she said. 'He's not much to look at, but he's by no means a dope. Don't boast about your First, because he's got one too, though one wouldn't believe it. And I really must go down to Haddesdon, because there hasn't actually been a breach, has there? Anyway, we've known them for ages. Amanda loves Mummy, and lets her soak to her heart's content—'

This seemed to Toby's domestic soul like disloyalty.

'—though I've never seen her, Mummy, I mean, miss a step or heard her blur a word. She's wonderful in her own way, though not too bright. Daddy adores her, though you might not think so.'

He felt her breast through the silk dressing-gown.

'No,' said Claire, 'certainly not again. What a glutton you are! I want my dinner. Where shall we go?'

He loved her, he believed, for her ease with him and for her pleasure in sexuality: though for him, this had never come with any difficulty. He did take her once more, as she laughed and protested, but this time plainly felt the satisfaction was all on his side. Nevertheless, her spirits were not dashed. She dressed at ease, and then they went out to a small restaurant where they had been before. They had yet another bottle of wine, and it struck Toby that she had something of her mother's head for liquor.

Yes, he thought, he would ask her to marry him, though there was still time, plenty of time. He had weighed up in his mind the advantages of this social connection: he had never much cared – consciously – about such things before. But he knew the Llangains liked him, and that Hairy did too. He would, of course, have a little more now to offer her, but not much. Still, Hairy had said that didn't matter in these days, and Toby was almost disposed to believe it. What would Claire look like in twenty years from now? He did consider these things. Rather like Moira Llangain, he supposed, and that wouldn't be too bad. He did hope she would not take to vodka. He doubted it; it would not be in tune with her general overpowering air of well-being. The truth was that she made Toby feel well too, though he was not often accustomed to feeling otherwise. She was a kind of ozone.

But he could not help but be haunted by Maisie. Maisie at Cambridge, Maisie in Paris, Maisie at Haddesdon. The thought of her nagged from time to time (when he was not in bed with Claire) at his spirit. He thought of her damp-looking fair hair curling against the pillow, of her slender, almost bony, arms, of the dews of night on her forehead. The trouble is, he thought, that I have got myself into a bit of a mess, but there is no doubt that I shall get out of it.

The bright cornfield stretched ahead, rising to the horizon in the glorious sunshine. Claire would not be marrying a nobody, since he would make himself someone. He would climb the ladder which offered itself. He made up his mind to get hold of a balance sheet somewhere, and to study it.

And still Maisie did not write to him. Nearly ten days later, her note came. 'I don't think it would be any use. That's all over. Someday, somewhere – perhaps. I don't know. But not now. Love, Maisie.'

He studied the word 'love' and supposed it was simply a courtesy. But he was dashed. It was absurd of her to think that they couldn't just go on being friends; indeed, the old intimacy between Glemsford and Haddesdon was likely in the end to enforce it, so they had better begin at once. All the same, he felt more discouraged than he liked to think he did.

At Glemsford he was received with greater enthusiasm.

'Well, I'm glad it went well,' said Llangain. 'I take it that Clive took to you; he doesn't take to people all that often. You'll enjoy it, I expect.'

'Toby,' said Moira, hugging her glass, 'you'll be a tycoon some day.'

'Of course he will,' said Claire, 'he'll be epic.'

The shabby, careless comfort of the house enfolded him.

After dinner, when Claire was washing up and Llangain had gone for an evening stroll, Moira told him something of herself, first looking round nervously as if afraid of hidden ears.

'We're having our silver wedding next week, did you know that? Now don't go sending bits of silver, because we've got enough, only most of it's in store. We never shut doors here, and it's an open invitation to burglars.'

It was not true that she never slurred a word: she was slightly slurring them now.

'Oh, we've got on as well as most people do. Idris isn't the soul of excitement but neither, I suppose, am I. I don't care to go out and about any longer, I just like to mess around here. Never expect excitement to last, Toby, because it doesn't. How long was I excited? About five years. That's all. That's damn all. Idris is too good for me, I know that. But we've our lives to live out. Claire's such a live wire that she makes me feel tired. I've only got to look at her to want another drink.'

She suited the action to the words.

'You're not exactly a live wire, are you? Composed, is what I should say. Well, that may be good for Claire. She needs quietening down.'

And Toby listened.

'There was this business about Alec, you know. He's all right, but he's not a live wire either. Still, we shouldn't have minded. I often think neither Idris nor I should have minded anything. Perhaps that's part of a good marriage. But what is good? Sometimes I feel I've missed something. I love it here, but I keep on thinking that there's something else I might be doing. But what? What is there to do at my age? I feel there are bright lights somewhere, and that I might enjoy them. I know Claire does, but then, she's young. I tell you, Toby, it's no fun getting elderly, which I am now and have to admit it. You can't look pretty any more – not that I ever did, really – and you can't take a real interest in your clothes, or anything like that. It's all pretty grey – help me to another, Toby, I'm too tired to get up – and it's going to get greyer. Not that Idris isn't a wonderful man in his own way. A wonderful, wonderful man.'

Toby listened.

27

Musing on Moira Llangain's revelations did not put Toby off his marital intentions. Five years for excitement seemed to him quite a long time; not that he ever was very excited, and he supposed that after that period comfortable adjustments might be made. Meanwhile, he decided to write to Bob, from whom he had not heard for a long time. He wanted to see what was happening to another marriage.

Bob replied by postcard. Could Toby call for him on Friday at the lab, about 11.30? They might walk on the Backs, if the weather was passable. He had a good bit to tell him.

So Toby went to Cambridge, and did as directed. Bob came away with him at once. 'We can walk for an hour, and then have a bit to eat. Suit you? You're looking chipper. What news of you?'

But he did not want to tell Bob his news as yet. He was surprised when Bob walked at his side for a while in silence. Bob, he thought, was looking far from chipper: he had a boiled look about the eyes. But he didn't seem downcast.

'I like Cambridge out of term,' Toby said, 'so serene.'

'It's never out of term for me. Nor for most of the scientists.'

'Aren't you slogging away a bit too hard?'

But to this Bob did not reply. Instead, he remarked as if casually, 'Reet's left me.'

'She hasn't!' Toby thought for a second how lame one's instinctive responses always were.

'I tell you she has. She upped and went – it must have been three weeks ago. She's got a chap, and the queer thing is, I don't think she likes him all that much. But he's someone different from me, and I suppose that's all that counts. Her mum and dad are hopping mad.'

Toby made a sympathetic comment.

'Oh, you needn't worry yourself about me. We never did get on. And one night I found out that she was pestering that poor bugger Adrian with letters, and we had a flaming row. That tore it. So

201

then this other cove turned up, and she was off like a shot. She's living in London somewhere, I don't know where exactly. Makes one feel a fool, doesn't it?'

The trees were just perceptibly beginning to bronze under the sun of late summer. The river was quiet and full of light, only an occasional punt slipping under the bridges.

'I don't see why,' said Toby. 'You've nothing to reproach yourself with.'

'Forgetting things, aren't you? Don't you know that I'm a wife-beater?'

'You've got to forget about all that. Everyone else has.'

'Except Reet. Before she cleared off, she was very strong about it.' Then Bob gave an unexpected gleam. 'But I tell you what: she's left Estella with me.'

Toby exclaimed.

'She never cared for the kid, you know, not as I did. Not a quarter as much. She handed her over as if she was some bloody old suitcase that she didn't want any more.'

'Then how are you managing?'

'I'm still keeping on at Lensfield Road. I've found a woman to come and look after her during the day, and I'm usually in time to put her to bed. She loves that, Estella, I mean. She's bright, I tell you. She likes being told stories – though I'm not so hot on that – but she likes mucking around with her fingers even more. Do you know, she can't only take a pocket torch to pieces, she can put it back again?' Bob's face shone with pride. He was all father, and Toby guessed that he now had few regrets. 'I tell you what, if that kid isn't going to be a scientist, I'll eat my hat. I'm teaching her her numbers too, and she picks them up a wonder. She's starting nursery school next month, but only half days, at first. I'm still going to need Mrs Maddox to give her her dinner and look after her things.' He paused. Then he said, with a wondering look into the trees, through which the sun was filtering in golden sovereigns, 'Do you know, if anyone had told me, say, even seven years ago (because of course I knew it the moment she was born) that I could hang my whole life on a kid like that, like you hang up a coat on a peg, I'd never have believed it.'

Toby asked how the work was going.

'Oh, that's fine. I'm doing pretty nicely, on the whole. And I like life in the college. Of course, I'm a very junior Fellow and I have to keep my trap shut most of the time, but some of those old boys aren't half bad. They teach you a thing or two. And I like all that silver shining, especially when there's a Feast on, and all the wine. So don't moon about me, will you? I've been lucky in most ways. As for Reet – do you know, there just seems nothing about her to remember, except the rows? That's what puzzles me. Nothing at all, I tell you.'

They turned back into the town, and had lunch at the café to which Toby had usually taken Maisie. This did give him a pang. He remembered the suit just a little too bulky, the Frieda Lawrence tam o' shanter. Heaven only knew where she had bought that. The hum of the refrigerator revived his memories further, and he tried stringently to repress them.

Bob's misadventures did not seem to have put him off his food, and Toby began to suspect more and more that he was a happy man. Of course he would marry again eventually; that was certain: choosing less an attractive wife than an ideal stepmother.

'Now about you, Tobe,' Bob said, through a mouthful of baked beans.

So Toby told him about his job, and found Bob a great deal less ignorant of its nature than he was. 'Christ, you're going it, aren't you? That's one of the bleeding posh banks. They've got houses all over the world. I'll say you've a knack of falling on your feet. Well, good luck to you. A banker, by God!'

'My mother insists that I'm going to be a bank clerk and sit behind a grille all day. She's pretty mad with me, but she'll get over it in time.'

Bob asked what the money was like: he was never diffident in enquiring about these things.

Toby told him.

'Nice,' Bob said. 'And more to come, as you make your marble good.' This was an Australianism of which he was proud. 'How did you get a look in there?'

The story of Lord Llangain came out; Toby was talking more than usual.

'Phew. You do get around with the nobs.' But Bob was quite without envy. 'Nothing like a nob to give you a shove in the right direction.'

'And I may be going to get married.'

At this Bob laid down his knife and fork, and he stared. 'Who to?'

'A girl called Claire Falls. You don't know her. She's Llangain's daughter.'

'I can see which way the wind blows. Or can't I?'

'Not really. It's not because of that. You'd like Claire.'

'Debby type? I don't think I'd go down with them.'

'No. Tall and lively, makes friends with everyone. She used to be keen on horses, but that seems to be fading away. Mind you, nothing's certain yet.'

'Congratulations, anyway.' Bob looked at him with clear eyes, from which the boiled look had momentarily departed. 'See anything of Maisie these days?'

'That's been over a long time.'

'I liked Maisie.'

'So did I,' Toby said, 'but it wouldn't have worked.'

'Even Reet liked her, you know. She somehow made our wedding work. It wasn't exactly St Margaret's, Westminster, was it?'

Toby smiled, but said nothing.

'I liked Maisie,' Bob repeated.

'And I told you, so did I.' This seemed to bring the conversation on the subject to a halt.

'Like to come back home and see Estella?' Bob asked.

But Toby had a train to catch. He left behind him a man who was at any rate three-quarters happy, and who would one day be wholly so: a man whose career was not in doubt, who was living the life he had desired, and who had kept the custody of his beloved child.

So Bob saw him to the station. 'One thing I didn't tell you,' he said. 'If Reet ever wants a divorce, which I suppose she will, and I hope so, she says she'll let me divorce her, and that she won't ask for Estella back. I tell you, there's some good in Reet.'

It was satisfactory to Toby that Bob should think so.

In the following week, Toby set about looking for new lodgings. He was lucky enough to find two rooms, kitchenette and bath off the Fulham Road; they were just within his means. He would permit his mother to decorate them until she was blue in the face; it might almost certainly mollify her. Claire came to inspect them, and approved.

'Not half bad, sweetie,' she said. 'I think you've fallen on your feet. But then, you always do, don't you? It'll be nice for you to have a proper bedroom to yourself again. I never thought a bed-sitter was really attractive, not with all that smoke and the smell of food.'

She embraced him. He was taller by two and a half inches than she, but somehow she always seemed to engulf him. Junoesque, that was the word for Claire.

'Hairy's coming home on short leave. You must give a house-warming, just for him and me. I'll cook. I promise you, I've improved. Mummy's been dredging up tips for me out of her buried memories. Do you like garlic?'

Toby did not, and he said so.

'Then you shan't have any. All you want you shall have, and what you don't want, you shan't. I do make rather a nice Spanish stew, though,' she added – wistfully, for her.

That afternoon they were to have tea with Mrs Roberts. Toby had obliged his mother to invite Claire several times, though he knew she was unwilling to do so and that it was never a success. High tea was, as usual, remorselessly laid in the kitchen and, as usual, surveyed by Claire with a formal squeal of delight. But Mr Roberts, who liked her better than his wife did, was there that day for the meal.

'What's all this about Toby joining a bank?' he asked, not with hostility but with real interest. His son, since the initial rebuff, had not been forthcoming.

'Well,' said Claire, 'it's not exactly a real bank, I mean, not the kind you're probably thinking about. It's a sort of private bank. Ooh, Scotch eggs! I adore them. Do you make them yourself, Mrs Roberts?'

'I make everything myself. I don't know, it seems a funny job for Toby, after all we'd hoped.'

'You might care more about my hopes,' he said, 'you know I didn't fancy the academic life.'

'But to live in that beautiful place!'

'Cambridge? It would certainly have been somewhere else.'

'"Don't Fence Me In",' Mr Roberts sang good-humouredly.

'Precisely.'

'It's odd,' Claire said, 'but you seem to like being fenced in, don't you, Mrs Roberts? Toby doesn't seem to take after you.' She spoke with a degree of deferential cheek.

'I keep myself to myself. I always have.'

'And I need wider horizons,' said Toby, 'so let's leave it at that, shall we?'

The talk turned to his new flat – he could call it that now.

'I shall want you to make it nice, Mummy,' he said, trying to conciliate her.

'I wish you'd let me help,' said Claire to his mother, 'I adore buying curtains and things.'

'I'm easier doing things on my own.'

'Oh, come, Dora, it only means ups and downs for you.'

'I can make my ups and downs when I choose to do so.'

'You've got lovely taste,' Claire said, 'I only wish mine were half as good.'

Mrs Roberts did not offer to show any of her pictures, not even the one of the smile in the meadow. She did chat a little, though not with any great interest, about the American show.

'I wish I could get over to see it. I do hope it goes marvellously.' Claire, too, was conciliatory.

'Run over to New York,' said Mr Roberts bluffly, 'you could if you wanted to, I bet.'

'But I don't like flying and I don't like the sea.'

'What, a girl like you? I should have thought you'd take to anything.' He pushed his cigarettes at her. 'Riding horses, and all that.'

'Ah, but I'm not horse-sick.' She looked up at him beneath her sandy lashes, almost flirting.

'Cowardy custard,' he said. This was an odd thing to call Claire, of all people.

'Why don't you go over yourself, if Mrs Roberts won't?' she asked, and Toby thought how little she knew them both. He guessed that, when they married, she would not become deeply attached to his family.

He replied, as he always did, that he couldn't leave the shop.

'Maisie,' Mrs Roberts said suddenly, 'told me that if she kept a newsagent's, she'd read all the papers and smoke all the cigarettes and eat all the sweets.'

Claire was undisturbed by the name. 'I expect I should, too. It must be a temptation.'

'Sweets don't tempt me,' said Mr Roberts, 'except for Mars bars. I like a Mars bar now and again.'

Claire and Toby left rather early.

'No go, sweetie,' she said to him, as she drove him back to her house, 'I shall never go down big with your mamma.'

'She's rather odd,' Toby replied, 'she never says all she feels.'

'I think,' and this time the comment was rather tart, 'that she's managed to say a good deal. Pity, because I like her, and your pa too. I think he may have a soft spot for me, though it's no bigger than the head of a pin.'

'Much bigger than that.'

Toby was to move into the flat in September, and Hairy would be home in the second week. They spent a good deal of the rest of the day discussing how they should feast him.

Mrs Roberts was as good as her word. She did go to and fro, hanging curtains, laying carpets, washing everything in sight. She repainted the wall of the sitting-room cream, with a peach-coloured underglow. She gave Toby two of her paintings to display. During these decorative visits she seemed to have warmed to him somewhat at last; perhaps she was beginning to understand what the nature of his job would be. But disappointment lay beneath it all, disappointment that he was not to become a don and not to have Maisie. He tried not to show that he noticed this. He would have done much for her except to allow her to direct his life; she had never before tried to do so, and he took it hard that she was just a little wretched because now she could not have her own way. He hoped she would come to like lively, good-natured Claire in time, but he doubted it. He knew her stubbornness, the stubbornness that made her cling to the small house in the shabby street. She was, as Claire had once said, 'an original', but now he was beginning to believe that a little unoriginality would not have come amiss. And he also believed that his father, too, had his regrets.

28

'*Gesundheit!*' said Hairy, downing half a glass of beer in a single swallow. He looked with approbation around Toby's living-room. 'This is just the stuff. I let my mother do up a room for me in college, but it made me look like a poufter. Pink, believe it or not.'

'Well, this is nearly pink,' said Claire.

'It's a manly sort of pink if it is, then, but it looks like white to me.' Hairy sat down and stretched his extensive legs. 'I'm glad you're joining the old firm.'

'I've joined,' Toby said.

'How are you liking it?'

'Very much. There's a lot to learn, but I think I'm learning it.'

'Baumann's a good chap. A bit flip, but that's a sort of soothing thing to be. Or so I find.'

Toby said everyone was very friendly.

'Yes, they are. Sometimes I'm quite sorry I didn't opt for it myself.'

'I'm grateful to your father.'

'Oh, he loves to get everyone fixed up. No loose ends.' Hairy asked after the clerical friend Toby had talked about: as it happened, he had heard from Adrian that day.

'Well, for one thing his mother's died—'

'So sorry.'

'And the old priest is sicker than ever, but won't go into hospital. God knows how Adrian copes, but he says he gets a lot of help from the daughter of the local doctor.'

'What about the old girl who wanted to be exorcised?'

'Well, the bishop sent down an experienced canon, who performed what I believe's called "the laying on of hands". It wasn't quite what she expected – I gather she wanted bell, book and candle – but she seems to be pacified for the moment. No, the trouble seems to be with the other woman, who takes him all her marital difficulties.'

'She's got an eye for him, of course,' said Claire. 'Such a nuisance, being as pretty as he is.'

She rose to get the meal. When it appeared, it was what Toby considered a rather nasty stew. He decided that when they were married she would have to confine herself to breakfasts: he would lunch in the City, and in the evenings they could usually go out to meals. There ought to be plenty of money about for that. He made up his mind that he would soon let her understand the extreme simplicity of his tastes, inculcated in him by his mother, the like of whose cooking he would in all probability never encounter again.

'Any news?' Hairy said to her.

'What should there be? Mummy's still torpid, Daddy plays golf more and more. It's come to be a religion with him.'

'Ever go over to Haddesdon?'

'Not much. Amanda seems less inclined than she was for the big fiestas.'

'See anything of Alec?'

'Sometimes. Dear old Alec,' said Claire with a grin, 'he won't exactly set the Thames on fire, or make a name for himself. But then, he's got one already. He's puddling around Fleet Street a bit, hoping someone will take him on. He's politics-mad, Alec is. He really knows about them. I wish I did.'

'You get on pretty well without,' Hairy teased her, 'you let the world go by.'

'But I ought to know more about the Far East, or something of that order, and keep myself awake at night over Berlin.'

'Oh, I don't know. I knew a woman who had a raging good time all through the thirties, and was absolutely astonished when the war started. Did you know that Mummy actually *demonstrated*?'

'With a banner? What about?'

'Spain.'

'Oh, Spain,' said Claire. 'Mummy's Red period, I suppose, like Picasso's blue. It seems a bit far away now.'

Hairy said he could quite well understand it. He looked troubled for a moment, as he often did, but the look soon passed away.

'I suppose,' she said, 'that we don't know much about the other half.'

'I do,' Toby put in. 'Or rather, I know what the petit bourgeoisie's

209

like. I'm petty-bourgeois myself.' He felt the time for pretending was long past.

'Now you're going in for inverse snobbery,' said Claire. 'You can't think with what an air of pride you came out with that.'

'Nothing to be proud about, or not to be proud about.'

'It looks rather cosy to me, though I admit I can't see myself as a miner's wife in the heart of Wales. Alec has a terrific social conscience – or rather, he's developed one recently. I wish I had. "I'm a worthless cheque, a total wreck, a flop—"' she quoted – 'but I rather like it that way. We've only one life to live, so we may as well enjoy it. Alec has so much on his mind that he seems to enjoy it less and less. He can't order an avocado pear without thinking of Indian peasants.'

Toby felt they had heard quite enough about Alec. He said to Hairy, 'How's your social conscience?'

'I hardly know. I just carry out orders. I suppose what social conscience I have, I shall exploit in the House some day. Daddy still goes occasionally, but it bores him stiff nowadays. He seems to spend most of his time in the bar. I mean to turn up with fair regularity. But that's all in the dim, distant future. By the bye' – he turned to his sister – 'I've met rather a nice girl. If I think more about her in time to come, Daddy will tear his hair and so will Mummy. She's German, of course.'

'Forgive and forget,' said Claire, 'I suppose one must. But you're right, the parents will be fit to be tied.'

Hairy, whose palate did not seem a highly developed one, had a second helping of stew. 'Her name's Anneliese,' he said, 'and her record is pretty impeccable. Her parents were anti-Nazis, and skipped the country in 1937, bringing her here with them. No – they aren't Jewish.'

'Nobody cares about that any more,' said Claire.

'But as soon as the war was over, she went back. They didn't. She's got a social conscience, if ever anybody had one.'

'Hairy, I believe you're serious!'

'I don't know. I could be.'

'What does she look like?'

'Not like a blonde *Maedchen*. She's got dark hair, and one might take her for French or Italian. She plays the piano. You like music, Toby?'

Toby thought of Maisie and said that, while it was not a primary passion with him, he liked it quite a lot.

'You must get a record-player,' said Claire, 'everyone's got one now. I'll deal with your uninstructed taste.'

Though he knew that her own taste was far from instructed, and that she would not care if she never went to a concert again in her life, he was delighted by these hints that she gave him as to a future.

'Bananas *flambé*, next,' she announced, 'my *chef d'œuvre*.' But they had ceased to flame before she had time to get them to the table. 'What's the matter with us both?' she said to her brother, 'we haven't so much as drunk to Toby. Come on, now. To Toby, his palatial surroundings, and his future.'

'*Gesundheit*,' Hairy said, for a second time.

Toby was delighted with their company. He felt that Claire was now his for the asking, and that Hairy was prepared to regard him in the light of a brother. He could think of very much worse brothers that he could have. But underlying all his pleasure was the fret of something lost. Then he thought, were not most things in early youth likely to be lost? How long were any of them often retained on the way upstairs? For to him, time consisted of stairs, not of a smooth upward ramp. It was necessary to proceed by jolts from one to the other, he supposed. He had just made a jolt, and he was not going to look back over his shoulder, where he might see Maisie's curving smile.

'Now you're going into a coma,' said Claire, 'you sometimes do. You think too much.'

'I think a bit, too,' said Hairy, 'though it may surprise you to know it. Let Toby reflect on whatever he's reflecting about.'

'I'm sorry,' Toby said. 'I suppose I haven't much time to think all day, except about the job in hand.'

'He's a conscientious beast, isn't he?' Claire said.

Hairy grinned.

The wine, which was good since he had bought it himself – he had been able to take some tips from Bob – had gone a little to Toby's head. 'I'm not going to let your father down, anyway.'

She raised her eyebrows. 'Hear the good little boy! But of course you're not. And I don't suppose you have to be an Einstein, not even in that business.'

'I am not going to let him down.'

Hairy yawned. 'He'd be glad to hear that, I suppose. But when he gets something done for anyone, it's done, and I've never heard him ask questions afterwards.'

'Perhaps I sounded dramatic,' Toby said defensively, 'but that's how I feel, anyway.'

'Then feel a bit less and think a bit less,' said Claire, 'or we shan't have fun. And fun I must have. I suggest that when I've done the washing-up—'

'I'll do that,' said Toby.

'No, you won't, not tonight – that we all go round to the pub.'

She was neat-handed in her way; she had cleared and washed the dishes within fifteen minutes.

'Now,' she said, 'let's go. I feel like a lot of noise and juke-box music, and people pushing and shoving.'

Toby became less and less sober as the evening wore on. He decided not to go home with Claire – as a matter of fact, he couldn't, because Hairy was staying in the house with her – but that he would certainly propose to her within the next fortnight. There was no hurry, no hurry at all.

In the pub he told them the story of Bob and Rita. Claire had heard it before, but Hairy was interested, as he seemed to be in most things. 'Poor devil,' he said, 'to be caught at that tender age. But he seems to have come out of it all right.'

'Bob will be OK,' Toby said, seeing everything in a preternaturally clear light, 'he'll be a great man one of these days. You'll see. He'll be in the Royal before many years have passed.'

'What's the Royal?' Claire asked, but did not stay for an answer.

She and Hairy left a quarter of an hour before closing-time. It was getting stuffy in there, she said, adding that Hairy had to be up at the crack of dawn to catch a train.

Toby, alone, measured the distance from his chair to the bar. He did not think his legs would betray him, but he could not be quite sure. He tested the matter, and found he was walking steadily. Elated by this, he ordered a final pint of beer. He knew that he was pretty drunk by now – but why? It was not usual with him, and he did not think he had been in any state of tension. They had both been friendly, had drawn him into themselves. Had he been just a thought subservient to Llangain? 'I'm not going to let your father down.' He must have said that, in some form or another, twice. But it seemed to him merely an expression of ordinary gratitude. The trouble was that he did not really know how either of them was likely to take anything, and for a fleeting moment they seemed to him like exotic golden birds, as hard to understand as birds. Yet why should this be? They were simple enough. He was not, he believed, at all beglamoured by them.

Yes, it was stuffy; but he didn't mind. His mouth already dried with smoke, he lit another cigarette. Golden birds in the golden cornfield. Very nice birds, too.

'Get your legs out of the way, mate,' said somebody, and he smiled in the direction of the voice.

The barmaid began to shout, and Toby hastily swallowed the rest of his beer, hoping that it might not at once take effect. He rose, and this time he was glad he had not far to walk home. He came out into the street crisscrossed by flashing lights from the headlamps of cars, satined by a recent fall of rain. But the sky had cleared and there was now a full moon, which for him had not yet lost its mystery.

He was joyfully drunk, but controlledly so, although he kept near to the walls as he went along, lightly touching a railing with his finger-tips when it presented itself. Yes, it had been a wonderful evening, and it had somehow been a source of happiness to celebrate the end of it all by himself. 'Maisie,' he said aloud, to test the feel of it, and saw the surprised face of a stranger staring at his own. A wonderful evening, and a wonderful swimming world. He saw with great clarity a tabby cat sitting on a low wall and, bending to pat it, nearly fell over. Whoa! Better be careful. 'Better be careful,' he added, again loud, and was charmed by the precision of his voice. Felicity. It was a moment pure and supreme; perhaps he would never know anything comparable again, so he tried to hold it.

He made his way rather slowly up the stairs to his flat, and when he got indoors opened a window. It was surprising that Claire, such an outdoor girl, never seemed to open one if she could help it. The room slowly cleared of smoke, and became chilly. Well, there was something he could do about that, something to prolong the celebration. He took a bottle of whisky from a cupboard and poured two fingers of it into the nearest thing that offered itself, which was a coffee cup. Water from the tap. He sat down, and in solitude rejoiced. Tomorrow was Saturday, so there was no rush to get to bed. Who wanted to get to bed? He didn't. Noticing that one of his mother's pictures was hanging crookedly, he got up to straighten it; but this was not easy, and in a few minutes he gave up the struggle. Let it wait till the morning. He found beside him on the sofa a purple silk scarf: Claire's. She had left it behind. Touched by unwonted sentiment, he laid it to his cheek. It smelled of her scent, which she always used a little too lavishly. He must buy her something soon. Eventually he would have to buy her an engagement ring, and hoped she would settle for something semi-precious. She would have to, he thought, for a second as angry with her as if she had just refused to do any such thing. The cat on the wall. He wished he had a cat, for he liked them, but it occurred to him that it might be unhappy when he was out all day. A Siamese, maybe, or an Abyssinian, suitable for Claire. Something with a pedigree. As he touched the scarf, it seemed to him that he touched breathing fur.

To his amazement, he suddenly felt sick. He staggered to the bathroom, glad of its proximity (in his old lodgings, it had been a full flight downstairs) and threw up some of the delights of the night. Easy. Even pleasant, though the terminal retching made his throat a little sore.

He went back to the sofa. He still felt giddy. And it was cold in here, beastly cold. He was obliged to rise and shut the window.

He had barely undressed and got himself to bed, when he had to go and be sick again. This time it completely sobered him, but not to any thoughts of woe. Contented, he lay back recovering on two pillows (he did not fancy lying flat yet) and thought of Hairy's moustache golden in the light of Maisie's lamp. He thought also of the beautiful line of Claire's back and shoulders as she went with the dirty plates towards the kitchen. He thought of her on horseback, as he had never seen her. Did she ever think about Maisie? Did it worry her to have that lamp about? Perhaps he had better stow it away somewhere. But not yet.

29

He had sent a letter of condolence to Adrian, and had given him his new address and telephone number. He was surprised when Adrian telephoned him, said he was coming up to London next day and would like a chat. They had, he added, sent him a supply priest to hold the fort while the old man was so ill. Unfortunately the former, too, was old, and 'you would scarcely believe it, lame', so he wasn't getting much relief. However, it was possible now to take a few hours off.

When Adrian came, Toby was shocked by his appearance. He looked thin, tired and – yes, old. Nothing could mar his handsomeness, but he had acquired something like a prison pallor.

'This is nice,' Adrian said, 'yes, I'd like a drink. Anything you've got.'

'I was so sorry about your mother.'

'I was badly cut up. But she hadn't much to live for, except the London Library.' He hesitated. 'I don't really want to bore you with my affairs, but it's a relief to talk to somebody.'

'You won't bore me. What's the news now?'

'Well,' Adrian replied, with some diffidence, 'Mrs Allen settled down after her so-called exorcism. What the canon said to her, I don't know; but I fancy it may have been tart. Anyway, she's been fairly subdued ever since, and doesn't torment her husband when he comes home by back-dives into the dresser. I made her throw away that awful book of hers, anyway. It was my sole triumph.'

'And the woman who badgers you about her marital problems?'

But here Adrian's face clouded. 'She's still at it. I've had to cut down my visits, it's far too embarrassing.'

'She has taken a fancy to you, of course,' Toby said.

Adrian made no pretences; he was too despondent. 'I suppose so. These women have a pretty dreary life, and anything will do for a change. I have to say that it makes them come to church, and since we've scarcely a congregation beating down the doors, I suppose that's something to be cheered up about. No, I haven't told you the worst. There's another of them doing the same thing now. None of this is under seal of the Confessional, or I shouldn't be telling it to you. They'd shout it out to the whole village, I believe, if they could. This one's even younger and prettier, and she's only been married for two years. She's pregnant, and she claims that since she started the baby her husband refuses to sleep with her. I told her it would all come right in time – perhaps he was scared of harming the child, some men are – and I gave her a homily. But it didn't seem to cut much ice. She smoked all the time and yawned. Then she asked me to kiss her. Of course I wouldn't. Then she said something like "You lot, you're just a lot of harumphrodites." '

'Sounds a nice girl,' said Toby, 'and knows big words, if a trifle imperfectly.'

For the first time Adrian laughed. 'It's good to hear someone thinking of the funny side of things. I get awfully solemn, and perhaps I need somebody not to be. My mother would have laughed; that's something I miss.'

On Toby's prodding, he gave him an account of his daily life in the three parishes. 'It wears me out, but I tell myself I've got a good deal of wear in me. The trouble is that I only know three people who I could really say to be devout, and they're all old. Why do people have to wait so long before it dawns on them to be?'

'I suppose when you're young, you never feel the need. You know I don't, though I'd like to, just to please you.'

'Somehow I wonder if I'll ever be a success at this game.' It was not like Adrian to speak flippantly, but he did so now. 'I haven't the skill, I haven't the patience, and I have to force the stamina. But let's get away from the subject of me, shall we? Tell me all about the new job. You seem to be prospering.'

After a while Toby said, 'There's a decent snack bar a hundred yards down the road. But if you're too fagged to go out, I could make a sandwich here. There's some ham and liver sausage, and I could open a tin of sardines.'

'Would it be a terrible bother? I feel I don't want to stir, just for the moment.'

Toby said that it would not. He guessed that Adrian still had something to say, and that it was not to be said in snack-bars.

Meanwhile, they talked of Bob and Rita. A tragedy, Adrian said, which could so easily have been avoided. Toby informed him that it was very little of a tragedy to Bob, who had his work and his daughter.

'One should try a bit harder at marriage than that,' Adrian said rather stuffily. He could not countenance divorce, and this he made plain.

'Don't you think you're a bit too young to be so certain?'

'It seems to me that I'm a bit too young for everything. But one has to have a place to stand.' He ate up the sandwiches as though he had eaten nothing for three days. 'I think one must try to keep one's promises.'

'It doesn't seem to me that Bob and Rita promised much. It was done in a registry office in what I calculated was eleven minutes flat. May not have been so much.'

Adrian disapproved, but his mind was plainly on other things. At last he came out with them. 'There's one promise I'm not sure I can keep.'

'What's that?'

'I promised to stay unmarried, and give God what tatty piece there was of me. Now I'm not so sure.'

'Do you mind if I say hooray to that?'

'I don't mind what you say. But you'll forgive me if I can't.'

Toby asked who the girl was.

She was, of course, the doctor's daughter whom Adrian had once mentioned in a letter. Her name was Ruth. He did not know what he would have done in these last months without her. She took all the work off his hands that was within her capacity. She ran errands for him. She made visits to his convalescents; they knew she had done a bit of nursing, and they were pleased by that. She had been, said Adrian, who did not despise clichés, a prop and stay. 'If I threw everything overboard and married her, I'd be able to get on all right. We wouldn't be exactly poor, since I've now got a bit of money of my own. And I'm getting steadily fonder of her every day.'

'It would get those other females off your back,' Toby suggested.

'Probably it would. But you don't know how it is, when you've dedicated yourself to a purpose, and then find you're weakening.'

'I think the good Lord would understand you perfectly,' said Toby, 'if he knew what you had to put up with.'

'I don't know. With a part of me, I'd always feel that I'd let Him down.'

'You were a coot to take any decision so young, in the first place.'

'As Rita used to tell me, *ad nauseam*,' said Adrian with the faintest glimmer. 'By the bye, I now understand why she's stopped writing. Poor girl, I didn't even like her. My charity always broke down where Rita was concerned, but then, it does seem to break down all too easily.'

Soon after that he left, and it was a long time before Toby saw him or heard from him again. In one sense, he knew, Adrian had been guilty of concealment. He was certainly in love with the girl, despite his dry description of her usefulness to him. Toby could about understand his scruples intellectually, but emotionally not at all.

He did think, regretfully, that of all his friends, he could bear to see the back of Adrian the most easily. He was good, fervent and kind, but nothing in his mind matched Toby's. He did not believe that he himself was a particularly good man, but then, neither did he believe that he was a bad one. To his friends he had always been ready to lend a receptive ear; they had all appreciated that, and he thought he might on occasion have given them some comfort. A ready ear was one easily extended but not, he thought, by everyone. He had kept his own secrets as long as he could – though by now, mainly through the exploits of his mother, most of them were out of the bag – and he fancied it had made it easier for them to confide theirs. So he had at least been good for something.

As for Adrian, he went on hoping for an announcement in *The Times*.

He did not propose to Claire during the next fortnight. Hairy had left for Germany, they were having too good a time together for disturbances of any kind, no matter how agreeable. He had bought for her a large greenish turquoise in a silver setting, and had put it away in a drawer until the time was ripe. It was a very pretty thing in a modest way, and he hoped she would be pleased with it.

Meanwhile, his mother had had her show in New York. Nothing happened at first; the slenderest of press notices, few customers. Then there had arrived an elderly rich woman from Vermont, who had taken an enormous fancy to the paintings and had bought seven of them. Even Mrs Roberts showed signs of excitement. In anticipation of the money coming in, she bought Toby a handsome briefcase, which he was rather ashamed to take to the bank, especially as he usually had so little to bring home in it.

'You like it, don't you, dear?' she said a little anxiously. 'It makes you look a real business man.' It would appear that she had more or less forgiven him.

'All you want is a bowler hat,' Mr Roberts jested, 'and an umbrella.'

'Yes, you ought to have an umbrella,' she said to Toby without humour, 'you're bound to get wet sometimes.'

'I have never had an umbrella in my life, Mummy, and I'm not having one now.'

'Oh, tough, are you?'

'Moderately. Old habits die hard.'

Yet it was not true that he had never sheltered under an umbrella. True, when he was at the grammar school, he had been content to walk there and back with the water trickling over his hair and down his neck. But when he was five or six, they had all lived in a small villa on the borders of Epping Forest, where there was a garden. Not a big patch and pretty unkempt, since Mrs Roberts had never had a passion for horticulture. To a child, however, big enough. There was a mass of golden rod in late summer, where the small golden spiders spun their miraculous webs giddily between the spires: and there were clumps of daisies, ragged, purple and pink. Here Toby had loved to walk every day, and especially on rainy ones, toting his father's huge and heavy umbrella. He had loved to see the webs diamonded with dew. Unlike many infant memories, his comprised bad weather too: all on account of the umbrella.

What had Mr Roberts done then? What had precipitated his move into the shop in town, the purchase of the house? Toby never knew, he had never asked.

It struck him that, though he loved his parents, he had been singularly incurious about their past. He had not asked questions before, and he was unlikely to do so now. It was possible that the future might divide him from them even more than he was now divided: let the future take care of itself. They would never diminish in his affections. It would be their business if they even attempted so to diminish.

He believed that they had drifted from him, as he had from them:

this thought brought comfort with it, his conscience was clear. His mother had now her own life to live, and his father a life to live which was agreeable to hers. He supposed all sons, all parents, did drift, and he knew a degree of sadness for the autumn garden, where he had been happy to be alone in the rain, but joyful when his mother came out to take him by the hand and hold the big umbrella aloft over him. But life was a staircase, as he had reflected before, not a ramp, and he believed that as he grew older it would seem so more and more. Jolt, jolt.

Whatever Claire might plan for their future, he knew that his mother would stubbornly refuse to be a part of it. If real fame came to her, and she had had a minimal taste of it, she would still be the same. She was like Antaeus, only secure when her foot was on the soil of her own earth: and would resist anyone who came to haul her up. Happy people, in a way, or partly happy: his mother and Bob Cuthbertson. Well, not many people, so far as he had observed them, were happy even in part. If he had ever permitted himself to have anything recognised as a temperament, it might have had its depressive side: he was aware of that, as a danger at the back of his mind. But he was determined that it was never going to come to the forefront.

He thought, I am going to keep my head. And Claire will see to it that I do.

30

It was an unseasonably warm October night. They had been making love in the Chelsea house as usual, he with his customary happy confidence, she bucking and arching beneath him, and giving her own peculiar love-cry, which made Toby think of a View Halloo, though he had never heard one. Now they were sitting up against the padded head-board of the bed, the wine on the bedside table, and both were sweating pleasurably. She pulled on a new dressing-gown of light paisley silk, which Toby admired very much.

'I'm so glad you don't turn straight over and go to sleep,' Claire said, 'it's so uncompanionable.' Her thick hair was loose on her shoulders, and she looked handsome.

He poured the wine, chiefly to give himself courage, but did not light a cigarette.

'What times we do have!' she added, with a long sigh. 'Such nice times.'

Then he put his arm round her. 'We'll get married soon, shall we?'

She did not for a moment reply. Then she turned upon him her blue, affectionate, amused gaze. 'Oh, sweetie, I don't think that would do at all. Do you?'

Taken by utter surprise, he could only blurt out, 'But you said yourself—'

Claire was quick. 'You mean that piece of nonsense at Glemsford, that day. You shouldn't have taken it seriously. Look, let's just go on as we've been doing. We have fun, don't we? Then why want more?'

He tried to sort out the feelings that were stirring in his head. In part, he knew the sense of rejection, and knew also that it was final. Also, a dream of brightness was fading. He said, 'I don't understand.'

Claire said, more gravely than was usual with her, 'Let me be straight with you, if I can. I admit that I did think it might be an idea once, but you're such an old slow-coach, aren't you?'

'You mean, I should have asked you before. But I hadn't much to offer you, had I?'

'Oh, that wouldn't have mattered. But you did let the time go by, and as Hairy would tell you, I never get that sort of idea in my head for long. I have much too much of a high old time.'

She lit a cigarette now, and so did he. He poured himself another glass of wine, and he gulped it.

'Greedy guts. What about me?'

He supplied her need in silence.

'Why on earth,' she said, and there was just a hint of a plea in her voice, 'can't we go on as we are doing? Honestly, I don't want to marry anyone yet.'

The sweat was chilling on him now, and he pushed the bed-clothes back. 'Hairy would have liked it. He as much as told me so.'

'Oh, sweetie, Hairy makes plans for me if I so much as say good morning to someone.

'But I am me,' she went on, 'I am not Hairy, nor my parents. Hairy has taken a shine to you, yes, and I can quite understand it. So have the other two, but believe you me, if ever I decided to marry Alec, which is quite unlikely, they'd like that just a bit better. They're snobs at heart, though they'd run ten miles not to seem so. Does that surprise you so much?'

Toby was by now too numb to feel the emotion of surprise. He did not reply.

'You see,' she went on, 'this – bed, I mean – is the only thing we really have in common, but that's lovely, isn't it? I'm not as clever as you are, and you'd pretty soon get bored with me. I can never see why people persist in making things permanent, anyway, till they're a good deal older than we are. No, you forget about all that, and let's go on as we have been doing. It's such rapture!'

He studied the pattern on her dressing-gown, blue, pink and purple. He thought he would remember it all his life.

Still he was silent.

' "What, sweeting, all a-mort?" ' She had had another of her rare literary memories.

'What do you expect me to be?'

'To stop being silly. Count your blessings. You've got a very nice job, and you've got me, if you'll take me on my own terms.'

'I appreciate all your father has done for me.'

'Stuffy!' she cried. 'You've no idea what you looked like when you said that.'

Another emotion was stirring in him: humiliation. 'I don't understand you,' he said. 'I was pretty sure you felt the same way about me.'

'But darling, I feel all sorts of wonderful things about you!'

He could not stop himself. 'You made a good deal of the running at first,' he heard himself say.

She replied slowly, 'Sweetie, aren't you being a teeny, teeny bit vulgar?'

'I suppose you think that's what I am. That's always been the trouble.'

Her response was a patient one. 'I suppose it was partly my fault. I *do* like to make all the running at first, and it's what I always do, though you weren't to know that. All right, I take back what I said. No, it's not a class thing, not for me, and you mustn't think it. It's just that you kept me waiting beyond the time when I might just have said yes. I think I probably shouldn't have, but no matter. Now, just when I thought we were having a whale of a time, you have to bring it up.'

He lay down, staring at the ceiling.

'Toby, are you listening?'

As if he were not always doing so.

'Look, I want you to wipe all this out of your silly old head, and we'll begin again where we left off.'

He said, 'We won't,' and got out of bed. He began to dress himself. He had brought the ring with him, and was only glad that he had not produced it. Claire watched him in apparent wonderment.

'Sulking, I don't believe it! What are you going to do now, plunge off into the night?'

'Yes.'

'Come back to bed,' she coaxed.

'No. I'm finished.'

'You'll feel differently about all that tomorrow,' she said comfortably, as she lit another cigarette.

'No.'

'Never?'

'It's over.'

'Pooh to that. You know as well as I do that we've had gorgeous fun together, and that we can go on doing so.'

'I'm not a stallion,' Toby said.

Now she became, for her, rather angry. 'That's a bit rude, isn't it?'

'Perhaps. I'm not in the mood to pick my words.'

'You don't hit on very nice ones.'

As he completed his dressing, he thought bitterly how something of his background had come out that night, a rawness he believed he had conquered for many years past. 'I'm sorry. But that's how it seems to me.'

No more Claire, no more Glemsford, no more Hairy, whom he had liked so much.

'Take those silly things off, and come and be nice and friendly.'

But he was obdurate. He had told her that he would not come back, and he meant it. He had never meant anything more positively in his life. He could not have meant it perhaps, he thought with a flash of insight, if she had really broken his heart, but she had certainly damaged it, and had wrecked his pride.

'Dear me,' Claire said, 'these tragic farewells! Ring me next week, when you've soothed yourself down a little. Now come and give me a lovely kiss.'

He would not kiss her. She lit another cigarette, poured another glass of wine for herself, stared at him round-eyed.

He went out of the room, and out of the house.

When he reached home his thoughts were in such a turmoil that he could hardly sort out one from the other. He sat down on the sofa, and almost at once felt something hard sticking into his buttocks. He swore. It was the ring, of course, in its satin-lined box, the box which had promised more than its contents. He put it on the table, and let it lie there.

You were not, he said at last to himself, and the inner voice was quite clear, in love with Claire. But you wanted her, and what she stood for. He knew she would wait confidently for his return; she had always had exactly what she wanted. But she could wait for ever, so far as he was concerned.

All his life before he had been indecisive. This time he was not so. He was bruised and angry. He would have nothing more to do with this big, rich girl, so buoyant in her independence. Perhaps she would marry Alec in time, and he wished him joy of her. In himself, joy had been destroyed.

She wrote to him flippantly next day. He was not to be a coot. They could have all the fun of the fair, for as long as he liked. Men just mustn't behave like this; in fact, in her experience, they usually didn't, for more than a fortnight. 'Perhaps three weeks in your case,' she added, 'because you're as stubborn as a mule. We'll go to the Connaught and stuff ourselves. I shall yearn for you.'

To this he did not reply, and when she telephoned, he spoke as to an importunate stranger.

He thought he had better get things over and done with. At the week-end he went home, and got his mother to himself.

'It's all over between Claire and me,' he said, 'I thought you'd like to know.'

Two emotions chased each other across her face: one of pure relief, one of anger that any girl should dare to reject her son. But she said, 'I'm sorry.'

'You're not, you know.'

'Well, I never did think much of her. But I'm saying nothing that's going to make it worse for you.'

'You can't, really. I shall get over it.'

She gave him the only consolation she knew, which was to ply him with food. He did not refuse it.

When his father came in, he repeated his announcement.

'Hard cheese, old man,' said Mr Roberts, not knowing what else to say. 'But there are other girls in the world.'

'Yes, there are,' said Toby, 'or I shall soon begin to believe again that there are. Anyway, I'm not going into mourning.'

'I liked her more than your mother did, you know.'

'I can't be a hypocrite,' said Mrs Roberts. She was still wearing her apron at the table: it was a habit she could not, or did not choose to discard. 'Still, I must say she was a good-looker. Not so much as Maisie, of course,' she could not resist adding.

Toby found it odd that they should all be talking of Claire in the past tense, but remembered that it was he himself who had put her there.

The contrast between his home and the house at Glemsford could not but fail to strike him painfully: yet had he ever cared very much for outward trappings? Perhaps. He was not quite sure. Certainly

he had cared much more for the trappings of Haddesdon. Lady Llangain's domestic carelessness had always seemed to him odd when he
thought about the perfect neatness with which his own mother had
surrounded herself. Already his disappointment was beginning to
fade, more quickly than he liked to admit to himself. Oddly
enough, it was usually Hairy he thought about, the big man, with
his golden moustache catching sparks from the lamplight.

'Well,' said Mr Roberts, 'let's have our usual dram, shall we?
And better luck next time.'

'I thought we'd take coffee in the sitting-room, for a change,' Mrs
Roberts said, injecting an element of surprise into Toby's evening.
The coffee was surprising in itself, and so was the change of *venue*.

'I'll take the whisky there,' said her husband, 'coffee keeps me
awake.'

She had bought certain luxuries for the little parlour: a new sofa,
handsomely upholstered, three new armchairs, a console table like
the one Bob had bought when he was first married to Rita. All were
in excellent taste, and Toby admired them.

'The trouble is,' Mrs Roberts said fretfully, serving coffee with
some state (a new coffee service) though still wearing her apron,
'that when you get new stuff you have to tip the dustmen up to the
eyebrows to get them to take the old stuff away.'

'Won't the second-hand shops take it?'

'Yes, and give you fourpence ha'penny. It isn't worth the bother.'

Both his parents seemed to know, though they had been alarmed
at first, that his heart was not broken: and that if his pride had been
wounded, it would soon mend itself again. He was consoled by
them, appeased for the first time since he had walked out of Claire's
life, and had meant it, too. Toby felt an uprush of affection for them
both. He had not been a particularly attentive son during these past
years, yet he did not think he had been a bad one. Suddenly he felt,
as most children do at some time or other, shut out from them. They
had made their own lives in their own pattern, and despite the
successes which had come to his mother, they would never change.
The small house seemed to him as changeless as Westminster Abbey.
It would always be there to come home to, turpentine and all.

Next week he wrote to Maisie again. It was not a careful letter, as
the last one had been: it was written in haste and with energy. It
was absurd that they should not see each other now and then. They

could simply be friends, couldn't they? He had missed her. He had not, he admitted, behaved so well before, but now he was prepared to behave precisely how she pleased.

He thought that when they met he would be able to convey to her that he loved her: for he did love her: he had never really loved anyone else. But this he did not say.

He concluded by sending his love to Amanda.

No answer came. He told himself that she would most likely be on one of her mother's winter tours. As he was aware, letters were unlikely to be forwarded: all Mrs Ferrars' friends knew that.

He went on steadily with his job, and when he was not doing so, he thought of her. He had put the turquoise ring away in a drawer behind his socks and handkerchiefs. He never knew when he might have a use for it again. And his spirits rose.

31

Edward wrote to him. It was just a note, brief, but perfectly cordial. They hadn't met for some time. Would he like to come one evening for a drink? There was a good deal to talk about. He suggested two dates, both for 6 p.m., Hertford Street.

Now Toby believed that Edward could have got his new address only through Maisie, and his hopes leaped. Could he be her emissary? Of course, if that was the case, he, Toby, would have to be prepared for a pi-jaw (he clung to some of the usages of his childhood), but there were worse things than that. Or it might be about the new play; *The Hostess* was closing after a long run, and he had read in the press that the prolific Edward was ready with another. However, the grape-vine between Haddesdon and Glemsford, though somewhat withered by now, must still operate, and he imagined that Edward had heard all about the break with Claire. So he gladly accepted, by postcard. Edward was ex-directory, and Toby had mislaid his number.

He went cheerfully to Hertford Street, and was as cheerfully received. The handsome, shabby room seemed not so very unlike the hall at Glemsford, though the Llangains had no pictures that were at all remarkable.

'You're soaked,' said Edward, 'is it wet out? An idiotic question, of course it must be. I haven't left the flat all day. I think you'd better have a towel and dry your head.'

Toby thought he had better, too. He accepted the towel and a drink.

'What are you doing with yourself these days?' Edward asked. So he had not heard about the bank.

Toby told him, with no small pride, and Edward seemed to marvel. Was Edward just a little stouter? But he had lost the grey look, and his cheeks had colour in them. He was a nice man, Toby thought, and modest, though he was still eminent and the dreaded tide, though creeping up, had not yet turned against him.

'Are you finding it interesting? I should think there were opportunities for you there. Pity about *Saint-Just*, though. I was rather looking forward to that.'

The gentle lights, the cushions, the sagging springs.

Edward said nothing more for the moment. Then – 'I am going to marry Maisie.'

It entered Toby like a shock-wave. He heard himself say, and the words were out of his control, 'You can't.'

Edward paused before replying. At last – 'Toby, for you, that is perhaps a little crude. Yes, I know. I am old enough to be her father. But I think I can give her at least fifteen good years, and I don't suppose many of us can look forward to as much as that.'

Toby lay back. The room was swimming about him, the lamps were glazed like gibbous moons. 'I don't know what to say.'

'Suppose you leave the talking to me? I know you pretty well, Toby. I always have done. I know how Maisie felt about you once, but now, I assure you, there's no going back. Though I gather that you've been trying to see her. Listen to me. I have loved Maisie for years. Why else did you suppose I was always at Haddesdon? Not for Amanda's circus, though I'm fond of her for her own sake. That kind of thing never appealed to me. No, it was always Maisie. Now I want to look after her, and I think she wants it too.'

'Does she love you?' The nightmare was persisting.

'She says she does, and I'm too fond of her to disbelieve her. In fact, I daren't. But yes, she wants to marry me, and she wants it very much. It will be in December, and then we shall spend the winter abroad.'

An old, stout, grey-haired man, Toby thought, seeing Edward through the disproportions of his own youth.

'I don't want to make things harder, but you have nothing to blame me for but my years. And they're not so great as all that. You know how she felt about you – and I believe you were more than a little in love with her; but the temptations Claire offered proved a bit too great, didn't they?'

'Did Maisie ask you to say all this?'

'No. But she asked me to tell you about herself and me.'

For want of something to do, Toby picked up the damp towel from beside him and rubbed at his hair again. Edward refilled his glass.

Toby felt he could not bear to be any longer in the same room with him, but had not the strength to move.

'Don't imagine that I don't know,' Edward went on, 'that this has been a blow to you. I admit I rather hoped it wouldn't be so bad a one. If it's any satisfaction to you, you make me feel just a little degraded, which is an emotion I don't feel very often. But you'll recover. You're born to recover. Llangain will never withdraw his patronage – he never does – and you'll make your way up the ladder. When I first met you at Haddesdon I knew instinctively that you'd do that, though of course I didn't know how.'

Oh, shut up, shut up, shut up, Toby thought savagely.

'I like you quite a bit, and I hope you may reciprocate the feeling as the years go by. Anyway, Maisie will hope it. Your trouble is that you never allow people to get in your way, and believe me, sometimes you should. It's not only politic, it makes for the fullness of life.'

Maisie was going to marry Edward.

'I think I'd better go,' said Toby.

'If you must. But I'd rather you didn't. Believe me, I know how you feel, or rather, you've made it pretty self-evident now. But you've been so little hit by anything in your life, that I didn't think you'd be much more than disapproving of this. Yes,' Edward mused, with a certain amiability, 'you do make me more conscious of my years than I like to be.'

Toby said, 'I want to see her.'

'My dear chap, I'm sorry to say it, but she won't see you.'

'Perhaps because she's afraid to.'

'No,' Edward said, 'there aren't many things that Maisie's afraid of, except, perhaps, wasps. But a certain soreness does remain, and it wouldn't make her happy to be reminded of it.'

'I still want to see her.'

'It's not in my power to make her. Do come to terms, Toby. Perhaps I was stupid to think that you might come to them much more easily. It's partly your own fault. You charm people, but you've always liked to give a lightweight impression. I believe you if you say you love Maisie now.'

'Is she happy?'

'Very, I should say. It may seem odd to you.'

Now Toby did try to pull himself together. He was getting sick of this analysis of himself, so he swallowed the rest of the whisky and sat up.

'Do you mind chucking that towel over?' said Edward, 'it's making the sofa damp.'

Toby chucked it and the other caught it neatly, as if they were playing some peculiar game.

'Thanks. Refresh your glass?'

Toby refused. However, he did light a cigarette. Because he felt that at last he had done enough listening, he began to talk. Yes, he had once treated Maisie badly. He had felt that her feelings were always too deep to be comfortable, so had been led off on the wild-goose chase for Claire because she seemed to have no deep feelings at all. But that had come to an end. She had turned him down, and he had found, after his first chagrin, that he didn't particularly care. But all the time he had been thinking of Maisie, longing for her, until he had known that he did in fact love her, and always had.

'Now, I like feelings to be deep,' said Edward, 'but of course, one doesn't always like them to be so when one's young. Life then seems too good to be troubled by the sensibilities of other people. Maisie does feel deeply, which is something her mother never did. It suits me down to the ground.'

'If I can't have her, I don't know how I shall bear it.' Toby had never spoken like this to anyone in his life before.

'And I can say precisely the same thing to you. You've all your life before you, and you'll be in love many times again. For me, this is the last thing,' Edward said ruthlessly, 'and I've no intention of letting it go.'

He got up. After a fraction of hesitation, Toby heaved himself to his feet. 'I'd better clear out.'

'Yes, I suppose you had,' Edward said almost sadly, 'I've hurt you far more than I thought I should, and I've talked at you intolerably. Don't lose touch with me entirely, however much you may feel like it now, because, as I say, I like you and I'm interested in you.'

He looked out of the window, adding conversationally, 'It's still raining cats and dogs. Can I lend you an umbrella?'

Toby walked the teeming streets in a state of misery which he had thought he could never know. He raged first at what he thought would be the horrible conjunction of the flesh. Hideous images rose, almost hallucinatory, to the forefront of his mind. Maisie, delicate, golden, slender, so seemingly frail. And that man! He was loathing Edward with his whole heart. Fifteen good years! Toby could have given her forty. Even now, he could hardly believe that what he had been told was final.

Rage was succeeded by a kind of numb sorrow. Where he walked he did not know, nor for how long. He did not want food. Just to walk and walk. His mackintosh itself was sodden through and the rain was streaming down his face, so that he had to dash it free from his eyes. The whisky had worked in him not at all, for good or for evil, only the utter insobriety of grief and disappointment was present. Also, he was bitterly humiliated. Of course, everyone would have to know. His mother and father. His friends. That old man! (Edward was fifty-three.) He almost hated Maisie because she could contemplate such self-desecration. Love Edward? It was impossible, it was beyond imagination.

He had an impression that the streets were flying by him, brilliant with the doubled lamps. Where he was, he didn't know. He was hard put to it to keep himself from crying; he had not cried since he was ten years of age. But why the bloody hell shouldn't he cry, if he wanted to? There was nobody to see, and tears and the ravages of rain would look much the same. A whore spoke to him tenderly, but he brushed past her, and was sworn at. Maisie, kissed by Edward, not as a friend but deeply, as a lover. Edward unclothed – a beautiful sight! Christ, it would be a beautiful sight! Ugly images arose from literature. *Othello*. *Lear*. Shakespeare had never meant much to him before, but he did so now.

Stop, said Toby to himself.

And stop he did. Where was he? He walked further, till he saw the name of the road where he was. Lisson Grove. How had he got there?

He realised that his feet were sore, and that he was very tired. He looked at his watch. He must have left Edward's flat about seven: it was now ten to ten. He had been walking for nearly three hours. He hailed a taxi and was driven home. There, he drank a glass of milk, ate some cheese and a biscuit. A piece of chocolate. Then he sat down and wrote a long letter to Maisie. His words had never been wild and whirling, but they gave the impression now. He reproached her, he pleaded with her, he reminded her of Cambridge,

Haddesdon, Paris. He begged her to see him, if only for the last time.

But he never addressed an envelope. He read it through, and realised how foolish, how futile, it all was. Beside all that, it was demeaning to himself; and even now, Toby could not quite bear to feel that. So he tore it into small pieces and flushed it down the lavatory.

Then he unplugged the lamp she had given him and thrust it into the back of his wardrobe. It should shine on nobody again, not upon himself, not on herself, not on Claire, not on Hairy.

Realising that his right foot was very sore indeed, he removed his shoe and sock and found a pearly blister as large as a two-shilling piece. He routed for a needle, carefully sterilised it in the flame of a match, and pricked the thing till the disagreeable water ran out and it subsided. Had he got any sticking-plaster? No. So he wrapped a handkerchief round his heel, hoping the improvised bandage would stay on during the night. Performing these actions had, for the moment, put his miseries out of mind. When he had achieved them he felt steadier, more like himself. Still he was not ready for bed. He found an old detective story and tried to read it, but however steady he might be, the print was not. Rage and grief were becoming superseded by a more manageable sorrow; still acute, but paler in tone. He thought what a fool he would have made of himself had he not destroyed that hysterical letter to Maisie. She would not have laughed at it, but she would have left it unanswered. Perhaps she would have shown it to Edward, seeking his advice: yet he did not think so. She was not like that. They would never, he said to himself, have been even in a moment's collusion against him. Maisie was without flaw, he told himself; he would never find anybody without flaw again.

He had a bath and got into bed; it was by now almost two o'clock. Then he appreciated the random comforts that life sometimes bestows when one needs them most. The pillow was soft to his head, the sheets and blankets embracing. He felt like an iron weight, sinking through such a depth of down that it could never reach the bottom. He was still miserable, still wakeful, but he knew the relief of physical consolation. Only his foot was still sore, and the bandage had slipped.

32

Soon he went to tell his mother the news. He tried to conceal his own bitter disappointment, and thought for a while that he would be successful: but he guessed that with her sharp eyes, she was unlikely to be deluded for long. And he was not sure whether he desired, or did not desire, pity from somebody.

Her immediate reaction was one of shock, this purely because of the difference in age between Maisie and Edward. After she had expressed this forcibly, she suddenly calmed down. It was a great occasion, so she automatically took off her apron. 'Well, I suppose they know their own business best. And of course, the fifties don't seem to me so old as they must do to you. I liked Mr Crane, he was a nice man. These things often do work out, you know. Of course I hope so. I hope for anything that will make Maisie happy.'

Then those sharp eyes went to work.

'You don't mind too much, do you? I know it was all over and done with between you two long ago, and sorry I was for it. But you do look a bit down in the mouth.'

It had never been Toby's habit to take his parents too far into his confidence. Now, however, he did need someone to comfort him, as he had done when a child. 'I was a bit in love with her, Mummy. That never stopped.'

'While you were carrying on with that Claire? Oh, get along with you.' But despite the asperity of her tone, he knew that the comfort, if he should desire it, was not so far away.

'I'm only telling you how it was.'

'And you don't need me to tell you how I wanted it to be. But then we all have our wants, and we don't always get them. Come on, dear, we must accept things as they come. I always have. I shall send them a wedding present, of course.'

'What will you send them?' said Toby, roused out of his torpor to a degree of curiosity.

'I've got that picture of a girl sitting in a field. I thought she'd like that.'

And you know perfectly well, he said to himself, that she will recognise it at once. His mother, an artist in one thing, could not but help to be something of an artist in many others. It would be her way of saying good-bye to Maisie as to someone she could have loved.

'I expect she would,' he said.

Mrs Roberts was bustling about the kitchen, arranging flowers – which she now bought freely as almost her sole extravagance – dodging in and out of the scullery. When she had achieved some degree of repose, she came to sit at his side.

'I don't peep and pry, you know that.'

'I know it.'

'But you're taking this hard, aren't you?'

'I like Edward too,' Toby said evasively, 'but it does seem to me an awful mistake.'

'I want great things for you. Or rather, I want you to be happy. And you will be. You mustn't mope about Maisie.' Then she added, having a severe side to her nature, 'Anyway, so far as I can see, it was your fault. You never appreciated her.'

'I never did, till now.'

'You can't be a dog in the manger. Youth to youth the whole world over, is my motto, and I can't pretend to like all this. But if I know Mr Crane, it's already done. You used to like him, I like them both. They'll settle down and make some sort of a go of it. You can make up your mind to that.'

He felt that he had never been so close to his mother as now.

'I've been a bleeding fool,' he said.

'There, there, you know I don't like that sort of language in this house.'

'Shaw was using the word before you were born, or the equivalent.'

'Certainly not before I was born,' said Mrs Roberts firmly. 'But swearing won't help you.' She gave him a peck on the cheek, and he did not draw away from her. 'Laugh and the world laughs with you. Weep . . .' She did not continue.

'I'm not exactly crying my eyes out, Mummy, am I?'

'No. You're tough. All the Robertses are tough. But you're not laughing your head off, either.'

She put her arm around his shoulders, and still he did not resist.

'More fish in the sea, darling, more fish in the sea. But of course you can't feel that's much of a comfort yet.'

'Not much of a one, no.'

'You were never a boy to weep or wail.'

'I'm not doing either, Mummy.'

He went back shortly to his flat. He had endured all the familial emotion he could take, and he was not waiting for his father's return from the shop. His mother could tell him all there was to tell.

As he drove home, he felt ashamed of himself. He had revealed himself to his mother as he had not done since manhood had been upon him. But if he were ever again to reveal anything to any living soul (as to Edward, another disgrace) it would be to her.

Before Christmas, the pictures appeared in the evening papers. Mr Edward Crane, the playwright, to Miss Maisie Ferrars, daughter of Mrs Amanda Ferrars, the well-known hostess to the Arts. Maisie looking radiant, as a bride was supposed to be, in a wide-brimmed hat, outside Caxton Hall. Edward looking down at her, gravely smiling.

Toby had heard from her. He had sent her the green turquoise ring, without any instruction upon which finger she should wear it. He had a very pleasant letter in reply. How pretty it was! How kind of him! He must come and see Edward and herself when they had settled down.

Strangely enough, her letter to Mrs Roberts was never shown to him at all. He was not to cease to ponder over the possible contents.

But with that marriage over and done with, his spirits tended to revive: he hadn't thought they could. He had perhaps entertained up to the last moment, despite himself, the hope that something might still go wrong: and of course hope was always a great mainstay. Now it was gone, and he had to start building his life again.

At the bank all was well. He knew that he could rise there. Baumann, on the rare occasions when Toby saw him, was encouraging. On the equally rare occasions when Llangain came in to the building, he would seek Toby out and give him an avuncular pat on the shoulder. Obviously he thought he had not sold a rotten orange to his friends. He had said, 'Come down to Glemsford soon, you haven't been for some time. Moira's beginning to wonder what she's done.'

Toby was learning a great deal about the job, and about money.

He found the latter subject a great deal more interesting than he thought it would be. He was fascinated by the extent of the bank's empire, which was far greater than anything he could have imagined. Tiller and *Saint-Just* seemed things of the past.

He was, nevertheless, lonely. Though he knew he was reasonably attractive to girls, he did not seek them out, and his physical life suffered somewhat. But things were always 'somewhat' with Toby. He even began to think that he would survive.

On New Year's Eve he took it into his head to drive to the highest point of Hampstead. It was a clear night, and starry, though too cold to walk about much. So he sat in the car, looking down at the vast smoke and glitter below.

What had Adrian said that day on the Backs, in a time long past? 'I wonder where we'll all be five years from now.'

Well, Maisie was married (he was simply making a list, so he would not allow himself to feel pain), Claire still single, though he thought she would marry Alec in the end. Adrian in his wretched parish, wearing himself to the bone, still wrestling with doubts about his embracement of celibacy. If Toby knew him, he would probably go on doubting for some time. Bob, his marriage broken, yet pretty content: his future lay bright before him. And himself? He fancied that his own future, too, could be bright. Out of the whole thing he had got a job, and he was not going to be distracted from it. He had enough money in his pocket for his creature comforts, and he believed that he would eventually earn a good deal more than that.

But the sense of wasted time was, just for a moment, heavy upon him, the sense of summers that would never come again.

You must snap out of it, he said to himself, and he got out of the car. Things had usually gone his way, and they would do so again.

He turned up the collar of his coat against the cold.

There was all London lying below him, and it seemed to him that it was there for the taking.

He did not say, as Rastignac did when surveying Paris from the heights, 'It's between the two of us from now on', since Toby had never read a word of Balzac.

But the challenge was there, and he did think something precious like it.